Quest For Eden

Book One:

The Mission

Quest For Eden

∴

Book One:
The Mission

By
Jeanne Desautel Foster

Sycamore Books
Pelham, Alabama

Dedication

Quest for Eden: The Mission is dedicated to my oldest grandson Cameron, who loves to read, and to all my writing students over the years who helped me hone my own writing skills while I was teaching them.

Acknowledgements

I want to thank my family and the members of my writing group for their encouragement, advice, and help. Writing is lonely work, and it helps to have people support and believe in what you are doing.

The cover photograph is courtesy of Matthew Bullard, a fine photographer.

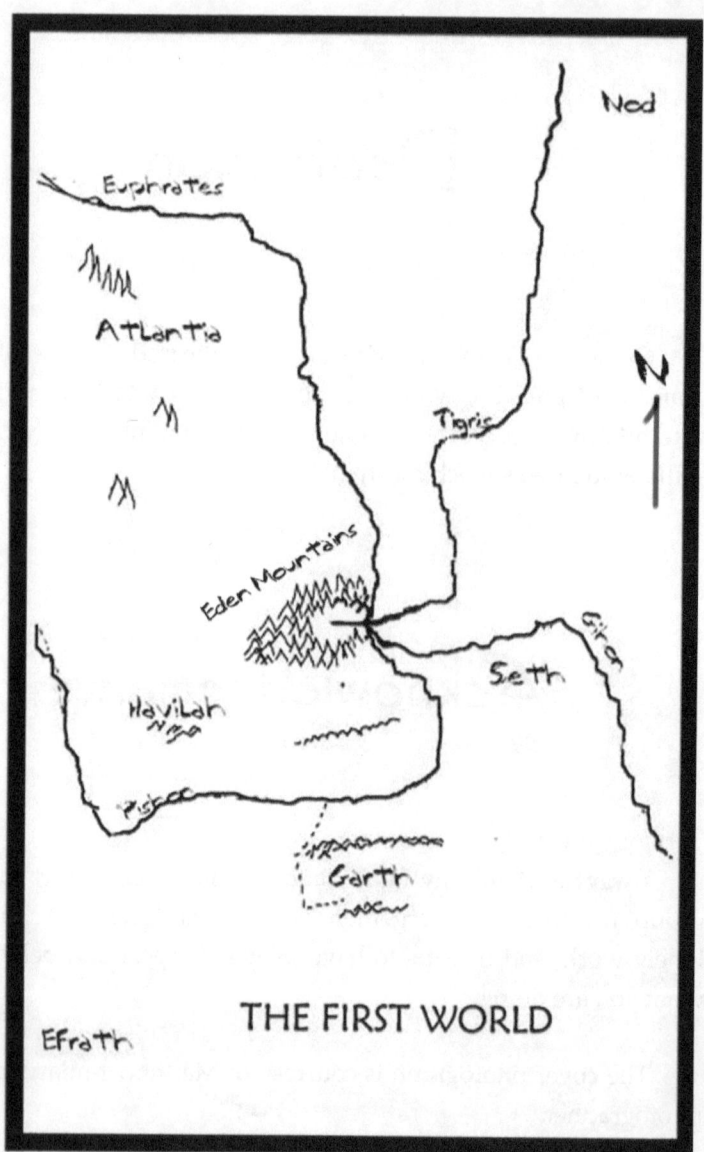

THE FIRST WORLD

Introduction

IT WAS ONCE UPON A TIME, AND IT WAS LONG, LONG AGO, BUT IT was a real world, the world before the great flood that wiped off the earth all humanity except four men and four women, who started the human race over.

Before the flood the descendants of Seth spread one way and the descendants of Cain spread another way. Then a third type of human came into being—the work of fallen angels, called Dark Watchers by Enoch, the man who walked with Elohim.

These new beings were fathered by Dark Watchers, but their mothers were human; these creatures were the giants called nephilim mentioned in Genesis.

Although we do not know what that old world looked like, we do know there were lands called Nod, Havilah—and Eden. There were also four rivers that flowed from the river bisecting the Garden Elohim planted in the eastern part of Eden.

We know this Garden was a home for the first man and woman, and we know they lost this home through dis-obedience.

My story is a fantasy based on what might have been—but surely was not. It is fiction. It is a tale of people like you and me, struggling through life and battling evil every day.

The reader should imagine this book is a translation from an original, now unknown, language. Many words are of obviously modern origin, but this is unavoidable in the telling of the story.

The theology and characters are biblically based whenever possible, but even these people are imaginary. None of us can know the truth of their lives until we meet them face to face.

Jeanne D. Foster
March 2010

Contents

◁ Prologue ▷

H ARTAGGA PUSHED HIS SHAGGY BLACK BODY THROUGH THE centuries-old forest of Garth. When no way could be found through the closely growing trees, he used his weight to ruthlessly smash a path, ripping up roots with sharp teeth and the crushing grip of his powerful jaws.

For months the tenacious creature had scouted Earth for a certain smell, the scent from the cradle cloth of an infant. Only Hartagga, bred of a she-bear and a fallen being—a Dark Watcher—could sense an odor seventeen years old. No man or animal used by the nephilim could match him.

1

After years of searching for this dangerous child, Kron, king of the nephilim, had called on his most faithful tracker, Hartagga, the monster he kept chained in his dungeon.

When he reared up on his hind legs, Hartagga was almost as tall as a mastodon, his fangs sharper than the razor-toothed behemoth, and his claws two rows of knives. His head, even though the mouth stretched as wide as a man's forearm, was small for his body. But a crooked hump at the top of his shoulders made him hunker hungrily forward. Even the nephilim trembled when Kron brought the misshapen and misbegotten beast to his throne room.

From his master's domain north of the Eden Mountains, east to Nod, south to Cush, and west to Havilah, Hartagga had relentlessly searched for the one human who would match the smell his black snout had scented and remembered.

Sensing only the odor of common animals in this forest, Hartagga reached up with a back leg to scratch at his golden collar.

He had enjoyed human meat often during his search, but none of them had been the one. If the human was not found in this last place, he would return to his master's abode where he would eat food tossed him by denizens of the fortress or chew on the leftover bones of Kron's enemies. Only this last hidden area to be scouted—a place only he had found in the king's almost two decades of searching—and he would be done.

Back up on his paws, the black-furred creature continued moving through the trees. Over his head a great bird—a haraani—lighted in the upper branches. Hearing its sound Hartagga shot up on his hind legs and swept one arm into the tree limbs above, hoping to catch a meal.

But just as quickly, he stopped and drew back his arm. *It is only Keoaw. Has he brought me something?*

Hartagga growled upward and was rewarded to see a strip of fur drop from the treetops down to his feet. He sniffed the object, a belt made from the skin of a long-toothed cat. He sniffed at the belt, which still smelled of the tiger, and found overlaying the original odor the scent he had sought so long. It reeked of that smell.

Hartagga picked up the belt and motioned with his snout toward Keoaw. The great bird lifted from the trees and began to fly toward an open space in the thick forest. It circled the area once before returning to settle in the surrounding treetops.

Carrying the belt in his mouth, Hartagga had followed the haraani as it directed him toward the clearing, an area strongly suggesting the work of man.

He began sniffing and circling, always staying in the cover of the trees. And then he saw, standing in the center of the clearing, a small human who stopped his work and turned to watch him. As he had done hundreds of times since leaving the fortress, Hartagga lifted his snout into the air and sniffed the current moving past the human.

3

The combination of odors entering his flaring nostrils slowly sorted themselves out. Freshly-turned earth, sheep dung, some green plant humans ate, a faint whiff of wood smoke, and . . . what was this? Human—the human in the field, but there was something else.

The aroma raced through Hartagga's memory back to the cloth Kron had held to his nose so many months ago. The same odor from the belt. This was the one!

The orders Kron had given him floated to the surface: "Find him and then lead us to him."

He stalked out into the clearing, his slow gait showing no sign that he was about to complete his mission. When the vulnerable human, holding only some type of stick for defense, stared back at him with infuriating audacity, Hartagga lifted his upper lip to show sharp fangs. Along his backbone a shiny black line of fur lifted.

"Don't kill him!" Kron had ordered.

Remembering, Hartagga roared out a protest, stretching out his wide jaws toward the human. The recalled savor of human blood started the saliva dripping from his tongue. His unsatisfied stomach rumbled. In an instant instinct overcame training, and he forgot his command.

Hartagga began to run toward his prey, dropping the belt from his open mouth as he ran. All thoughts of Kron and his orders had been forgotten.

He had one thought—kill!

◁1▷

A Threatening Menace

THE YOUNG MAN KICKED AT THE UNDULATING MASS OF VINES snarled about his sandals and then lifted his face to grimace at the water vapor churning above the green hills of Garth, hills covered with a mixture of tangled undergrowth and tall trees.

The water vapor that softened the sun's harshest rays came down to the earth as a mist, soaked the soil abundantly, and then breathed back from the ground each night. It rose to treetop level before drifting back to feed the lush plant life of Earth.

"If only these weeds would stop growing!" the young man groaned.

Hod ran one hand through his tousled red hair and grumbled over the task set for him by his father Elim, son of Jared, great-grandson of Seth, son of Adam. He always thought of his father that way, the way the old man so proudly intoned his ancestry whenever anyone would listen.

And Hod listened, but since he had left childhood, he was no longer as excited by the tales of long ago that did not affect his own dull life. He longed to be part of the family story, not just a listener.

Every day in Garth began the same. The entire family of almost two hundred men, women, and children arose before dawn, quietly put on simple woolen or linen garments, ate a breakfast of cooked barley kernels mixed with goat's milk, and trudged out to the fields to begin their various duties. Some planted, others pruned or harvested as was needed, and some tended the goats and sheep that provided the milk and wool for the large family.

But an eerie quiet brooded over the field this day. Hod's mattock froze in mid-stroke. He wiped the greasy sweat from his brow and lifted his head, ear cocked to hear.

A few minutes earlier he had seen a haraani, a giant eagle, lift from the trees at the northern perimeter of the clearing, fly toward him, and then swoop into the bean row farther down from where Hod was working. When it flew back off, his tiger-skin belt hung from its talons.

Hod had watched the bird fly back into the northern woods and settle into the treetops. *I must have lost my belt a few minutes ago and not noticed, but what is a haraani going to do with it? I hate to lose the belt made from the skin of that tiger that killed our sheep.*

Once more Hod stiffened and looked around. What was it? Silence—but a silence filled with apprehension. He listened for the sounds that should form the background of his work day. How could there be no sound? Hod's ears strained to penetrate the silence, and he smiled when he heard the distant splash of a rivulet and the closer chirping of a cricket.

"All is as it ever is. How could anything be different?" Hod said as he lifted his heavy two-edged mattock and let it fall on the green weeds.

But still there was something—a prickling of his spine, a sense that something was watching him.

He concentrated on the dense woods where the bird had disappeared. What was in there? What was watching him? Was it only the haraani?

And then his keen eyes caught a glimpse of something large and dark moving behind the trees. He watched as the black form circled the field.

"It's probably a bear," he said softly, and then whistled in amazement when the animal left the woods and came out walking on all four legs. It stared at him as if it knew him. Hod instinctively knew this animal hated him. Before it could take another step, Hod turned, dropped his mattock, and ran down the bean row toward a distant terebinth tree.

He did not look back. He did not need to. While the creature roared its rage and began noisily ripping through the field, the sounds behind him drew nearer.

When he reached the tree, Hod vaulted to the lowest branch and then pulled his legs up and out of the grasp of the creature that by this time had almost caught up with him. His first close look at his pursuer showed Hod an animal half as large as the tree he had climbed.

Hod scurried higher up the tree, up to the highest limbs. Balanced on two branches and in danger of falling at any moment, he was barely out of reach of the enraged, blood-shot eyes and stretching paws intent on tearing him apart.

He kicked at the claws that scratched the bark below him, and then he waited. There was nothing else he could do. Eventually the monster dropped back to four legs. While Hod watched, it ambled back across the field, rooted around in the dirt a while, and then came back a few steps toward Hod's tree.

The beast, which Hod noted wore a gold collar, now held in his mouth the belt the haraani had carried off. Then the haraani flew back over the field, circled the shaggy creature twice, and landed at its feet. Knowing the bird could easily pluck him from his tree, Hod moved down into the lower branches.

"What are they doing?" Hod whispered.

The bearlike creature dropped the belt and nosed it toward the haraani, which took it in its talons and, with a noisy flapping of wings, took to the sky.

Wondering why it wanted the belt, Hod watched the haraani fly due north without a backward look. Meanwhile, the shaggy monster looked once at Hod's tree before heading back into the northern woods.

After waiting long enough to be sure the danger was over, the young man had just decided to climb down from his tree and go to the next field to warn his brother when he saw Chay walking toward him. Hod stuck his head through the leaves and waved.

"Get down from there," Chay called.

Hod did as his brother wanted and was soon standing beside Chay, who as usual looked irritated.

"What were you doing in the top of that tree?"

"I was chased there by the biggest monster you've ever seen! It looked sort of like a bear, but it was almost as big as a behemoth!"

Chay's frown surprised Hod. "Are you exaggerating? No bear is that big."

"Let me show you his tracks." Hod pointed out the paw prints around the tree and leading back out into the field. "What's more, a haraani landed by him and took my belt I had dropped and flew off with it. It was the craziest thing I ever saw! It looked like they were working together."

Chay scowled, grabbed Hod's elbow, and began pulling him in the direction of the compound. "A giant bear—and a haraani? Come on! Let's go tell Father and find out what he thinks."

"Are you afraid that beast will threaten the compound?" Hod asked.

9

"Haven't you noticed the fortifications around our home? Don't you know our parents are afraid of something terrible finding us?"

Hod hurried home behind Chay, feeling ashamed never to have noticed this fear his brother spoke of. When they got back to the compound, he looked at the heavy gate made of logs thirty handsbreadths high bound together with strong hemp ropes. The log fence formed a semicircle closing off the opening into the ring of hills containing their home caves. He had never thought of this fence as a protection, yet now he noticed how difficult it would be for an ordinary enemy to penetrate this fortress.

"Father," Chay called as soon as he saw Elim. "Hod has seen a strange creature, like a giant bear, and a haraani—together."

"Was the creature almost as large as a mammoth and did he wear a golden collar?" Elim, his brow furrowed with concern, asked Hod.

"Yes, I did notice a gold collar, and he was similar to a bear, but twisted and distorted."

Elim put one hand on his youngest child's shoulder. "Did you see anything else? Perhaps one of the long-necked behemoths with a rider?"

"No. But one strange thing was that the haraani found my tiger-skin belt I dropped in the field. He flew away with it, but later I saw the bear had it and he gave it to the haraani, who flew away with it again."

"Did you notice which way he flew?" Elim prodded. He seemed to understand this better than Hod did.

"Due north—without circling or wavering." Hod wondered why their father closed his eyes a moment before he finally spoke.

"Call a family meeting immediately, Chay. We might be in danger."

While Chay ran to do his bidding, Elim looked around the packed dirt area that made up the center of their home compound, an area ringed with protective hills—most of which held the caves they slept in. Several women were cooking vegetable stew in a pot over a fire in the center. Children ran about playing a hide and seek game, and his eldest son Jediah was building a shed of small logs over against one rocky hill. All the young men and some of the younger women were working in the fields.

He shook his head and sighed. "It will take a while for the enemy to get here, if they are coming, but we must make preparations."

The family had never seen such fear in his face.

"In the last few months, relatives from the home of Seth have brought rumors of a monstrous creature named Hartagga who roams the earth seeking something and devouring those in his way. He chased Hod, and I fear he used a haraani to send word to the nephilim. There may be no hurry, but we must take precautions.

"This means the nephilim now know where we are; therefore, we must plan our escape. Meanwhile, the women must cook many loaves of bread and gather fruits and vegetables. These will be bundled so each person has emergency rations."

11

Everyone looked around at the other family members. Finally, Jediah spoke. "What do we do right now?"

"Go back to the closer fields and harvest what you can. Keep careful watch out while you work. I will send some of the young men to see if any nephilim are near."

Hod stepped forward. "Do you want Chay and me to go back to the far field? We can keep watch for this Hartagga."

Elim nodded. "No, forget about those distant fields, but you and Chay can show the scouts where you saw the creature so they can make sure he is gone. Afterward, I want you both back here. Hod, from now on wear a rag over your hair."

"Why a rag?" Hod cried.

"Your red hair is too noticeable. Just do what I say!"

Soon the brothers were leading two of their older brothers and one nephew back to the field. While Hod and the other three climbed a tall pine just beyond the field, Chay, who had always feared heights, stayed on the ground.

"What do you see?" Chay called up.

"There are some long-necked behemoths far off beyond the River Pishon," one brother answered. "They are grazing on the tall grass. Nothing unusual."

As Hod and Chay walked back to the compound a little later, the younger brother told the older more of what they had seen and not seen. "There were only the usual animals. No sign of Hartagga. I often, when I climb that tree, see herds in the furze fields on the other side of the Pishon. We didn't see any nephilim."

Chay laughed scornfully at Hod's words. "You wouldn't know a nephil if you saw one!"

"Well, I know they're twice as big as we are—and ugly."

"Humph," Chay snorted. "You don't know much! In the meantime, the family will have to start over somewhere else. All because of you!"

Back in the compound, Hod told his sister Hela—his closest friend—all that had happened. Neither of them remembered any home before Garth, and both found it hard to believe their home was in danger.

"Maybe our father will explain this fear of the nephilim the elders have," Hod suggested.

Brother and sister together took the old man aside as soon as they could.

"Father," Hela said. "When you talk of the nephilim, I know you fear them, but I don't know why."

Elim looked long at his youngest daughter before clearing his throat. "At first, it was not too bad, even though we had lost paradise. Men tried their best to be good. Even when I was a child, the world was a better place. And then, back when my father was young, word spread of a giant child born to a Cainite woman. He was a curiosity, but he soon grew so powerful his family could not control him. His name is Kron, king of the nephilim, still a name to make men tremble."

Hod and Hela did not interrupt as they listened with wide eyes.

"Word came that more such boys had been born. Then we heard they were fathered by Dark Watchers who took the form of men. Eventually these children grew up into mighty warriors, and Kron gathered them into a tribe of his own—a dangerous clan that wants to take over the earth."

"Are we truly in danger? What do we have that they want?" Hod asked.

"Food," Elim answered, but avoided looking in his youngest son's eyes.

"It takes a great amount of food to feed them, and they do not plant for themselves. Also, they are meat-eaters, so they are clearing off all the animals they find. Some breeds are almost gone."

This was the first time Hod and his sister had ever heard of beings who ate more than vegetables. He blurted out his question. "If they take our animals, will they leave us alone?"

His father looked at Hod and shook his head. "No, they might want more than food from us."

When Elim was finished, Hod met Hela's eyes and made a motion with his head to signal her to follow him to their secret cave and through the low, flat opening.

"Hela, do you think there is more about the nephilim that scares them than father said?"

"I don't know. Father always tells the truth." His sister's big brown eyes stared at him in the dim light of the cave entrance. "Why do you think this?"

"Just some things Chay said. It is almost as if I am especially in danger."

Hela laughed and shook her head. Her long yellow hair fluttered around her shoulders. Hod marveled at how different she looked from him. No one would guess that he—with his red hair and green eyes—even belonged to Elim's family. "Why would the nephilim want you?"

He joined her laughter. "You're right. Who am I to catch the notice of these giants?"

ζ

EARLY THE NEXT MORNING, HOD AND CHAY ONCE MORE prepared to leave for the fields. Because the scouts had found no sign of nephilim or Hartagga, Elim decided to take another day to prepare to flee their home. The youngest sons would harvest a closer field today as part of that preparation.

Both pulled on the short woolen tunics that fell to their knees, secured them with woven hemp belts, and slipped on sandals made of wood and rope. Just as his father had told him to, Hod covered his hair with a gray cloth and tied at the base of his skull.

After eating their usual barley mush breakfast, they chose sharp, strong mattocks made from iron bought by the older brothers on trips to the land of the Cainites and set off to work. They had just reached the field they would harvest when a loud thumping split the early morning quiet. As one, the brothers stopped and strained their ears to identify the sound.

"What's that?" Chay whispered.

"I think it's coming from the compound!" Hod grabbed his brother's shirt. "We've got to go back!"

Before they had taken ten steps, a splintering crash boomed through the morning mist. The screaming of women and children and the bellowing of more than one beast followed the first thumping sound.

"It must be the nephilim Father feared!" Chay cried. "Nephilim at the gates of our home! What can we do?"

Hod's heart tightened. Nephilim—giants—attacking his home! And his mother, father, Hela, and the rest defenseless since most of the younger men of the family were already in the fields.

"We must go help our family!" Hod cried as he turned and began to run back toward the compound with Chay behind him for a while.

But when they neared the compound, the sound of his brother's running feet stopped. Hod paused to look back.

"Chay!" Hod yelled when he realized his brother seemed frozen in place behind a wide tree.

He ran back to Chay. "Come on! We must fight them!"

"Impossible! They're giants! We're infants beside them. They'll kill us!"

When Hod turned to go, Chay grabbed his younger brother's garment with a shaking hand. Held for the moment, Hod surveyed the scene in the clearing before the cave. He looked from Chay to the destruction before him. He saw the flattened shed Jediah had been building, and then he saw the body of his oldest brother lying in a dark red pool near the center of the compound.

No other family members could be seen dead or alive. Two behemoth with nephilim atop were smashing and destroying everything—their tails knocking down outbuildings and tearing up small trees.

The nephilim were twice as tall as the tallest of Hod's brothers. With wide shoulders and enormous chests covered with skins, they looked like ferocious animals. Shaggy hair and beards ran together on their jar-like heads.

Hod pulled himself from Chay's grasp. "We cannot let them steal our food. We must stop them."

"Don't throw your life away, little brother. Father would want you to stay here with me." Chay held out a hand toward Hod.

"There's only two. We can take them by surprise. This is our chance to use our strength for something other than farming. Show you are brave!"

"Go ahead, if you are determined to do this," Chay cried. "But I don't want to die!"

◁2▷

The Dark Watcher

THE YOUNG WOMAN WALKING THE DIRT PATH TO THE LITTLE stream had no idea how beautiful she was. For all her sixteen years, she had lived with her family in Havilah, far from the land east of the Garden where her ancestors still dwelt.

"Don't dawdle, Mehri." Her mother stepped out the front doorway of their hut and called after her daughter. "We need that water for supper."

18

Mehri quickened her pace at her mother's words. She paid no attention to the torn up earth on both sides of the path but kept her eyes on the distant stream, really a rivulet, where her family got its water.

Most days when she made this trip, she mourned the ugliness of the world around her. Deep in her soul, Mehri longed for some beauty in her life.

"Oh, a flower!" she suddenly cried and left the path to clamber over a pile of slag. Growing behind the heap of mine waste was a delicate rose bush with one pink bud just beginning to unfold.

Mehri knelt and gently brushed her forefinger down the bud. *I wish I could plant this bush by the doorway,* she thought. *I would care for it until it grew tall against the house and decorated the wall with pink blooms.*

Her mother often told her of the beautiful land where she and Father had grown up only a day's journey from Adam's Garden. Grass vividly green and thick, covering gently rolling plains where terebinth trees spread their wide shady leaves for children to play under—this was what her mother remembered. This was the land called Eden.

Mother had told her that Eden was the land in the center of Earth. In the middle of Eden were the Eden Mountains, and hidden in the eastern end of those mountains was Adam's Garden. Mother had seen the guarded gateway once when her family went to visit their ancient ancestor Adam, who had died a year before Mehri was born. She could picture the River Gihon sharing its pure waters with all the descendants of Seth.

Mehri stroked the rosebush once more and smiled her dreamy smile. *I will watch this bush until it has stopped blooming, and then I will dig it up and transplant it to our house. I must have beauty for my eyes to look upon every day.*

Of her own beauty, she was completely ignorant. She had no mirror to reflect back her large blue eyes rimmed with dark lashes, black hair falling to her waist, skin as delicate as the rosebud she had stroked, and slim figure, so out of place in the chaotic minefields of Havilah. Her father, mother, brothers, sisters, even nephews and nieces all seemed to know that praising her beauty would not help her soul become as lovely as her face, so no one had ever complimented her on her physical appearance.

This beautiful flower of a young woman had been born and reared far to the west of Eden. Set where the great mountains dwindled down to foothills, Havilah held great veins of gold and silver close to the surface. Once men saw and desired this metal, they had torn up the hills to get at the riches.

Mehri's family, which had also come to find their fortune, lived in ugly wood huts in an ugly land. Primeval forests and green hills had been destroyed in the quest for the minerals beneath the surface.

Maybe it was because of their depressing situation that they loved their beautiful daughter above the rest, yet even though she was cherished, it never occurred to her that she was different from her sisters and cousins.

She did her share to keep the home going, just as the other women did. She worked hard with her hands, baking, sewing, and bringing water from the stream five hundred cubits away. Each day she walked the path through the woods with a clay jug balanced on her head, a very heavy jug filled to near brim with the slightly muddy water of their local stream.

This trip was so much a part of Mehri's daily routine that she made it without thought or fear. She knew everyone who lived near them and, although her mother warned her not to be alone with a man not related to her, she had never been treated disrespectfully by any man.

She was close to home on her return from the stream when a tall, fair-haired stranger with crystal blue eyes and a charming smile stepped from behind a splintered tree. He stopped directly before her, forcing Mehri to stop too.

"Good morning, young lady. How is it that I have never seen you before?"

His words made Mehri think he must not really be a stranger in this part of the world. Caught off guard by his handsome face and flattered that such a fine man would speak to her, she forgot her mother was in a hurry for the water.

"I don't know, sir," she answered with downcast eyes. "I have lived here all my life—sixteen years."

She peeked up at him, and his smile made her heart jump. At this moment, more than anything, she wanted the man to keep talking to her.

"Ah, that is the reason. I haven't been here in twenty years. You see, I spend most of my time far away in the land of Nod. Have you ever been there?"

"No, I've never been anywhere. And Nod, isn't that Cainite country?"

"Yes, it is. Is that a problem?" The young man's smile seemed to say how foolish she was to judge others. Mehri's sensitive soul felt the guilt of her attitude toward Cainites.

"I'm Sethian. We don't associate with Cainites, except for one old man who works for us, but they say he is different from the others."

Mehri spoke softly, meeting his eyes and then looking away as the shyness natural to her interfered with her desire to get to know him.

"So you're Sethian. I did not know Sethian girls were so beautiful." The young man reached over and took her hand in his.

Mehri knew she should not let a stranger touch her but found she could not stop him. He had a power over her stronger than her conscience. His charismatic aura drew her to him as she had never been drawn to any of the young men of Havilah who tried to pay court to her.

When he took her full water jug and held it in his other hand as if it were weightless, Mehri caught her breath.

"Come, I will walk you home," he said, pulling her a little as he started walking without dropping her hand.

"Who are you? What is your name?"

Mehri blushed as she spoke because the warmth of his hand was awaking unfamiliar feelings.

"Call me Aza, if you would like. It is a nickname." He stopped and turned her to face him. "I said you were beautiful, but do you know you are the loveliest human woman on the face of the earth?"

Mehri's blush returned and she did not know what to say. It was a new idea to think of herself and her looks. She dropped her eyes to the ground, but he lifted her chin with one finger, forcing her to look deeply into his eyes.

"I don't think that could be true," she whispered. "There are thousands of women on earth."

"Tens of thousands. And I have seen most of them. You must believe me when I say that you are the most beautiful." Aza's voice held a golden fluidity that caressed her soul. Mehri longed to hear more compliments from this stranger.

"Thank you."

Mehri did not know what else to say. She still did not believe him, but it was incredibly flattering to have him say so. To be the most beautiful woman in the world—how wonderful that would be!

I would be admired and envied by everyone I met.

Mehri pondered the new feeling of pride swelling her heart, unsure what to do with it. She cast her eyes shyly away from him.

When she glanced at her surrounding, she did not truly see the ugly heaps of ruin her glance fell on. Her mind was a turmoil of conflicting emotions, the uppermost of which was a breathless admiration for the countenance of her companion. The warmth and possessiveness of his hand holding hers made her heart race. No man had ever made her feel this way.

"Such beauty as yours does not belong here in this ugly mining country. You belong in the lush, green fields of Nod. You must let me take you away," he crooned. "I will take you with me today to my home."

"Oh, no, no! My father will never allow it." Mehri shook her head and tried to pull her hand away.

"Look at me!" he demanded in a voice suddenly harsh. She did not want to do what he said, yet she was unable to disobey. "I take what I want. And I want you!"

Mehri's breath caught in her chest while her head spun dizzily. At this moment she desired nothing so much as to go with this man, yet she could not understand what was happening to her. How could this stranger suddenly come into her life and make her do what he wanted? She knew she had to resist.

"I can't! I don't want to go with you. Please leave me alone. Please go away!" Mehri began to cry as fear and confusion overwhelmed her.

She saw that Aza did not melt at her tears as her brothers and father always had. Instead, his eyes became hard, and he grinned cruelly as if he enjoyed her pain. Noticing this change come over him, Mehri was horrified to even look at the man she had thought so handsome. But his soothing voice returned and began to wear down her fears. He exuded trust and sincerity as he smiled down into her eyes and caressed the back of her hand.

"You will go with me, my dear; however, you must go willingly. I cannot take you unless you agree."

Suddenly he was sweet and charming, reaching out to catch the tears running down her cheeks.

"I will be back for you tonight at sundown. Your parents will not be able to refuse me if it is your wish. You will be my wife, my queen. All of mankind will worship your beauty, but you will belong to me."

Mehri was speechless, staring at him as he began to back away from her. She jerked her body away from his gaze and turned away from him, but then a sudden desire to see him one more time made her look over her shoulder.

He was gone, as suddenly as he came. Feeling empty and lonely, scared yet excited, Mehri picked up the water jug he had set on the path and hurried the rest of the way home, intent on finding her mother.

The bond between mother and daughter was unusually strong. Neva had already borne fourteen children before they moved to Havilah, and, when several years passed with no new babies, she thought her bearing years were over. After the move, she had been surprised when Mathu and then Mehri had come along. Both were special to her, yet the black-haired, blue-eyed little girl—her last—was a part of her heart. They shared all their thoughts and feelings.

"Mother! Mother! I must tell you what happened!" Mehri cried as she ran in to the house. Neva's heart tightened at her first look at Mehri's face. She recognized the look of first love, and it made her heart sink.

Mehri immediately told her mother what had happened on the path, leaving out no detail, even sharing her conflicting fear and desire. Neva said nothing at first, but her eyes grew wide as she listened to the terrifying story. She held her daughter's hand and pulled her behind her as she searched for her husband.

Dolian's eyes grew dark when he heard it all, but before acting or saying anything to his daughter, he called a family meeting. Once again, Mehri told her story to her family, stammering as she saw that her brothers were over-flowing with anger.

"I'll kill him!" Mathu cried and others joined his denunciations.

Some advised caution, but all believed the stranger must be confronted at least for the insult he had given her. When all had their say and nothing had been resolved, the old Cainite Juban—a family servant—stood to his feet. Knowing he rarely spoke and anticipating great wisdom, the entire family fell silent.

"This is not a man," he croaked, turning to look at the gathering but pointing his bony finger at Mehri. "I have seen him—or others like him—many times in Nod. They are beautiful to look at, when they want to be. Trust me, they are evil. This one was not a man."

"Then what is he?" Dolian, Mehri's father asked.

"A Dark Watcher—Azazel, no doubt."

26

The name hung like a sickness in the close air of the family's home. No one could speak, or hardly breathe, at the terror invoked by Juban's words. The old man paused and sighed, and then began his tale.

"He came for my youngest daughter too, and I could not stop him. She wanted to go. He cannot take the women if they are not willing. But he has a power that draws women to him. I begged her not to go—to no avail. She lived with him for three months before she came home, ruined and in shame."

Neva looked quickly at her daughter. "You do not want to go with him, do you?"

"No, oh, no," Mehri's words came out weakly. "That is, I don't think so, but it's true he has a power that draws me to him. I am afraid of him."

The old Cainite nodded. "You should be. My daughter was never the same. Her mind had been driven to the brink of insanity. And then we discovered she was with child."

The story she was hearing held Mehri in a spell of terror; it was as if she were the girl, the child of Juban. She intuitively knew that this would happen to her if she went with Aza. She jumped up and held out her arms in an appeal to her father and brothers.

"You all must help me! I'm afraid I will not be able to say no! You must save me from him!"

Her father looked at Juban, his eyes wild with desperation. "What can we do to protect her? Has your experience given you wisdom into ways to defeat a Dark Watcher?"

Juban stood up and looked around the room and behind them. "They fear only Elohim. We must call on Him immediately. Azazel may be watching now.

Immediately Dolian rose to his feet, raised his hands above him, and began to intone: "Creator. We are weak and in peril from the evil ones around us. We ask you to ring us in protection."

When Dolian finished, others added their voices in desperate supplication. Mehri felt peace begin to replace her fear, and she slumped against her mother.

"Now we can talk openly," Juban said. "I sense that the vision of the Dark Watcher has been blocked. I believe we are now ringed with pure Watchers. I will continue my story. My daughter carried her baby a full years, three months longer than natural.

"We were terrified because we knew other women had given birth to giants—nephilim. We knew not what type of child we would see. My daughter died giving birth, but we saw only an innocent child, weak and helpless."

"What did you do with it?" Mehri's brother Mathu asked.

Juban smiled, a sad smile full of old memories. "I brought him here. Do you remember that when I came here I had a child with me?"

"Kodi?" Mathu said. "I remember Kodi. We played together when we were little—before he grew up and went away. We never knew he was a nephil!"

"My grandson was only three when we came here, yet I let you people believe he was ten. By the time he was ten and looked eighteen, the nephilim discovered him and took him away to live with them."

Everyone looked with wonder at the old man who had fooled them all during the years since he had worked for them. He was shorter than they, his bald head showing only tufts of white hair, and he was more stooped than any of the Sethians his age would be. Hard work and a hard life had ravaged him physically, but his kind spirit had impressed the family.

"I thought I could keep the child away from them and teach him to worship Elohim. And I did until the nephilim expanded their territory into Havilah. I tried to hide him, but they saw him one day and knew immediately what he was."

Dolian shook his head and sighed, perhaps seeing the man who had always been an outsider in their world in a new light. "You told us he went to live with his other family. We never knew you had been so hurt."

The old man sighed at the memories that never went away. He turned his gaze slowly around the group, lingering a moment when his eyes came to any of the young men who had played with his grandson.

"I didn't want to cause fear. I stayed here in hopes Kodi would find his way back some day, that he would remember how I loved him."

"But he is a nephil!" Mathu blurted out. "He is one of those who persecute us."

"Yes, that is true; however, my hope is that he remembers what I taught him and that this will make him different from the rest."

Dolian walked over to Juban, put a hand on his shoulder, and motioned him to be seated. Then he took his daughter by the hand and stood with her in the midst of the group.

"I need a place of safety where I can hide Mehri from the Dark Watchers and their children, the nephilim. Does anyone here know of such a place? If she stays here, she will be in danger every day."

No one spoke. What did they know—living in their homes and working the mines of Havilah—of the world outside this place? Each looked to another in the circle, hoping someone would be able to help.

But it was useless. Who among them had ever been able to leave the mines and explore the world?

With no warning a white figure, elegant, almost translucent and like nothing any of them had ever seen, walked into the center of the group. They all gasped and fell on their faces, convinced this was the Creator.

"Stand up, you people. I am a created being like you. I am Remiel, Watcher of the Watchers, here to give you guidance in this time of peril.

"This young woman Mehri is chosen of Elohim for a special purpose. Her daughter will marry the son of the son of Enoch and become the mother of one who will save his people from the great catastrophe which will bring an end to the nephilim and cleanse the earth of their corruption."

Dolian was the only one with the courage to speak to the heavenly being. He stood and held out a supplicating hand.

"We welcome this word from Elohim, but we are in great fear. We need to know if there is a place of safety where my daughter can hide from the Dark Watcher. She is afraid he will take her away."

Remiel's smile held comfort and hope for the frantic family. He looked at Mehri with so much compassion that she burst into tears and buried her face in her hands.

"There is such a place high on the western slope of the Eden Mountains. Nestled between sharp rocks, at the base of a waterfall as beautiful as those in the Garden, is a grassy glade where trees bearing fruits and nuts flourish. This place is favored by the Watchers, who continually are around and about it. I will take this girl and her mother to live in this glade. They will be shielded by our power from the sight of the Dark Watchers and their minions."

Mehri, hearing the hopeful words, lifted her face from her hands and looked at Remiel. "Can we go right away? He said he is coming for me tonight."

"Gather your belongings," Remiel replied. "We will take you as soon as you are ready."

Neva took her daughter's hand and led her to the back of the house where they chose clothes and blankets and a few eating utensils.

"I hope this will be sufficient," Neva said. "I cannot even guess how we will live there, but I trust Elohim to provide. Now let's hurry back to Remiel."

Mehri put a hand on her mother's arm and gazed at her earnestly.

"I'm sorry I have caused all this trouble. I know we will be safe, and I'm glad you'll be with me."

"Oh, I would never let you go without me."

Taking a last look at the small windowless room she shared with her two nieces, Mehri turned her face toward the future and followed her mother back to the rest of the family.

Before they left, her brother Mathu took Mehri aside and hugged her warmly. "I will miss you, little sister, but I am so thankful you will be safe from this monster. If anything happened to you, I could not go on living."

"Mathu, don't worry about me."

"I'll try not to, but if I have to, I will give my life to save yours."

The whole family whispered as they said good-bye to Neva and Mehri. All sensed the evil drawing closer to their home, and all knew they must help her slip away before she was discovered.

Remiel had disappeared after his announcement, but when the mother and daughter were ready, he reappeared. Beside him were two handsome, pale young men who smiled at the family but said nothing.

"These Watchers will go with us," Remiel said, looking only at Mehri. "They will ensure that Azazel cannot see you."

With the family watching, Remiel took Mehri's and Neva's hands and stood between them. The other Watchers took each woman's free hand, and then the three heavenly beings led mother and daughter away from the hut.

They were walking very fast, faster than seemed humanly possible. Before long Mehri felt as if her feet were not touching the ground, as if she were floating on her tiptoes. The Watchers' hands were cool and comforting and nothing like the seductive warmth of Aza's hands.

The sun was setting and the sky darkening as Mehri and Neva rapidly covered many miles, always moving upward and away from the evil being who wanted her.

◁3▷

Birth of a Warrior

T HE YOUNGEST SON OF ELIM DASHED FROM TREE TO TREE, keeping his eyes always on the enemy. The nephilim had dismounted their beasts and were dragging stores of fruits and grains from the cave. Before acting, Hod listened to the nephilim gloating.

"That was too easy!" The taller one laughed as he slung a full sack on the ground.

"These Sethians are not warriors, Gradrach!" the other agreed. "I don't know why Kron makes us raid all these distant Sethian camps."

The one named Gradrach shrugged and gave a push to his behemoth, which was sniffing the sack. "It's not just for their food, Karlef. He's always looking for the fire-hair."

"Kron believes the story, but I think it's just another Sethian myth."

"It's not a myth. They say Kron has kept the fire-hair's stolen cradle cloth for years just so he could track his smell. Some time ago he sent Hartagga after the scent. It's possible he has found it at last."

"How did Kron get the cloth?"

"He had a spy in the Sethian camp, a Cainite who pretended to be a loyal servant. He stole the cloth at Kron's orders."

Karlef did not appear as interested in the story as in the food he was stuffing in his mouth. Gradrach, however, continued to inform his friend of what he knew.

"It's a good thing you and I were only a half-day's journey from here when Keoaw brought the fire-hair's belt to Kron's tower. We were close enough to get here quick."

"But it will take another day for the rest to make it."

Gradrach laughed. "We won't need them! He is here somewhere. We'll find him."

When he heard the nephil's story, Hod looked back at Chay and then touched the rag covering his red hair. He wanted to know how he fit in with their story and why they wanted his belt.

Neither giant looked around to see if anyone would challenge them. They were obviously confident of their superiority over such creatures as the Elimites. Hod had crept near enough to hear the insult, but knowing surprise was necessary to have any chance against their great size, he controlled his temper.

"How they ran," Karlef said. "But I saw only brown and yellow hair."

Karlef sat on a stump and began digging in another bag. He pulled out a huge handful of bread loaves, no doubt some of the food Hod's mother and sisters had been preparing for the escape.

"All ran except this old man who thought he could fight a behemoth."

"He was old," Karlef agreed. "These Sethians live long. He might have lived another four hundred years. How much bread is there?"

"Enough to feed this whole tribe for several days."

When the other nephil stopped to eat with the first one, Hod stepped from behind his tree and did his best to let out a blood-chilling cry. The two nephilim looked down in disbelief.

"Do you dare to attack the sons of Elim?"

The giants looked at each other and then at Hod, who behaved as if he were their equal. He swung his heavy mattock with its sharpened double blades with all the strength of his mighty left arm upward toward Karlef's chest. It spun end over end directly at the nephil and embedded so deeply in his chest that only half the handle showed.

The giant groaned and fell lifeless. His body shook the ground when it landed and blood sprayed both Hod and Gradrach, who screamed in rage and reached for the iron sword hanging from his belt.

Hod was surprised at how easy it had been to kill a nephil. Although he had never before taken the life of any creature, he pushed aside the sick feeling in his stomach, ran to Karlef's carcass, and pulled an iron dagger from a blood-soaked belt.

"Go after that one!" Hod yelled back at Chay and was relieved to see his brother step between him and the second giant.

Now full of confidence in his strength, Hod ripped off the head rag, which had fallen over one eye, and turned to the nephil Chay was facing.

Gradrach, his open mouth showing sharp and pointed fangs, bellowed in rage and seemed to hesitate a moment. Hod got a better grip on his stolen dagger—a weapon that was for him a large sword—and dashed in to help Chay. At that moment the giant was wielding his sword above his head, ready to cut the older brother in half.

When he saw the tiny human who had killed his friend, the giant growled, "The fire-hair!" Then he turned toward Hod.

To Hod's relief, Chay took advantage of the diversion to dash at Gradrach and chop at his legs with his mattock.

Hod then ran at the giant and stabbed him several times in his thighs with his new sword. The giant roared out his anger and, now limping badly, hurried to his behemoth.

"We know where you are!" he snarled at Hod as he mounted the beast. "You won't escape Kron. We'll be back for you!"

The other behemoth—minus its rider—followed the first out of the compound while Hod and Chay lowered their weapons to their sides. Once they were sure the giant was really gone, the brothers ran to Jediah's broken body, apparently crushed by the foot of a behemoth, and gently carried him to the mouth of the cave.

"I've never even seen a dead man." Hod struggled with grief and guilt. "And now, not only is Jediah dead, but I've killed a man myself."

Chay seemed to ponder his brother's words. "You have killed a nephil—not a man! I never thought you had it in you to be a fighter. Maybe the old story is true. Wouldn't that be a surprise?"

Before Hod could ask the meaning of the strange words, Chay left him and went to search for their family. Hod leaned against the outer wall of the cave, but his legs began to tremble and he slid down into a squat. He had much to consider, particularly Chay's enigmatic words.

What old stories could he be speaking of?

Stories were part of life in the Elim family, the stories of the creation of the world, stories of the great crime of the first father and the curse he had brought down upon them all, stories of the beautiful Garden where weeds did not grow and food was there to be picked.

Elim had never spoken about what had made him flee his old home closer to the Garden. The eldest children had been old enough to remember their former home and the journey that took them to the valley of Garth. Hod only knew that Elim, younger brother of Enoch the great man of Elohim, left the home of his father Jared to live in the safer, more distant Garth. Here they saw few relatives, few visitors, and—until today—no enemies. But they were safe, his father always said.

Little by little, the family returned from their hiding places in the thick woods surrounding the encampment while those working in the fields also came in response to the noises they had heard.

Family members rejoiced to see each other safe, but when they saw the body of Jediah, they began to weep and mourn. Hoping to encourage his family, Hod left the women to take care of each other and led his brothers over to show them the body of the dead giant, pointing out how he had felled him with one stroke of his sharp mattock.

"A lucky blow, I am sure, little brother!" Ahuv, the second eldest brother, nudged the bloody body with his sandal. "Nephilim do not die so easy."

Barti, a nephew who was twenty years older than Hod, held up a hand as if calling for attention. "It wasn't chance. It was foretold. Remember the story."

"The story?" Hod said and his question was echoed by several of the youngest.

But the rest fell silent at a frown from Ahuv. Only Hod pursued the answer. "That is the second time someone has mentioned an old story. Won't someone tell me what it's about?"

The hesitant, questioning glances that flew between his brothers did not escape Hod. He knew there was something they all knew, all except him, that is. Even the giants had talked about him—had called him "fire-hair."

But what could the story be? If it had to do with him, why was he the only one who didn't know?

"It would mean that you have ruined our lives for the second time," Chay snapped out before turning and stalking away.

Before he could insist they answer, all were distracted by the sight of their father emerging from the woods leaning on Hela's shoulders. Ahuv, Chay, and the rest of the brothers hardly glanced at Hod as they ran toward their father.

When others had taken Elim from his daughter's support, Hod put his arms around Hela. "I'm thankful you aren't hurt!"

"When I heard the first noise, I saw Father out in the open, almost as if stunned, so I grabbed his arm and pulled him after me."

"I'm proud of you for acting so quickly. Look at him. What would the family do without him?"

Hod and Hela watched their father scan the scene of carnage, the smashed outbuildings, and the dead nephil without a word, only a sad shaking of his head and the most mournful look Hod had ever seen in his eyes. But when he saw his eldest son's body, Elim lost all strength and fell to his knees.

"No need to tell me anything. I know it all without asking. I am sorry it was Jediah who had to give his life. It should have been me. I have had a long life—three hundred years and fifty. He was not yet two hundred. Still many years ahead of him."

Elim, suddenly looking older than his years, slowly took in the large family standing around him. "Tonight we leave," the old man announced.

Hod's jaw fell open. "Why not stay and fight?"

The stern look his father turned on him reminded Hod of the need to respect his father. "I'm sorry, Father, but why should we leave? I killed this nephil, and, even though the one that ran off said they would be back, I think we can defeat them."

"No time for talking, son. We must go to save your life." Elim put a hand on Hod's shoulder and pushed him before him toward the cave. "Come with me as we pack what we need, and I will explain."

The women scurried around filling rough sacks with food while Hod and his father put clay pots, platters, and other vessels in a wooden box to be carried out to the cart. Some men were harvesting what food was ready to eat, others were rounding up the family animals, and others were preparing sacks to carry their goods. Hod stayed close, waiting for his father to talk.

They were deep in the cave with no one else near when Elim turned to his son. By the light of his torch, the aged father gazed deeply into the eyes of his youngest son, and then looked away before finally beginning.

"Until you were born, we lived near Eden, within a three-day visiting distance of the houses of my father, grandfather, and great-grandfather. We were happy— your mother and I."

"But you had to work hard to grow food?"

"Oh, yes. That is the curse we all must bear. Yet we were happy. We lived in a world of loving family with only an occasional trouble or sorrow."

Elim fell silent. Hod wanted to urge him on, but thought it better to wait. The silence grew until Hod's ears began to hum. He coughed softly.

"Where was I?" The old man shook himself. "Yes, we didn't know how happy we were. But things were gradually changing. We knew that. The Dark Watchers kept appearing as men, trying to fool us into doing their bidding."

Hod still did not know what he himself had to do with the situation or what old story had been told about him. "What did the Dark Watchers do?"

"I told you they bred with willing human women— all daughters of Cain, of course."

"Yes, and gave birth to nephilim! But what does that have to do with me?"

Elim nodded and looked solemnly into his youngest son's eyes. "Even as a newborn, you were different from anyone ever born into our family. You had a full head of red hair—and those green eyes. One of our old women was visited with a spirit of prophecy when you were born. She said you would prepare the way for the destruction of the nephilim."

"How?"

Elim shook his head. "She did not say."

"And the nephilim know of it?"

"Oh, yes. One of their spies, a servant in our family, told them—and stole your cradle cloth. They have been looking for you for seventeen years. And now they have found you. The giant saw your hair and feared you would kill him too, so he ran to tell the rest, who are no doubt nearby. When you killed that one out there, you revealed yourself."

Hod asked no more questions as he worked beside his father, but his mind did not stop trying to solve this problem facing his family.

That night the family of Elim held a long conference in the large cave. After the old man had spoken, each man was allowed to voice his ideas for the escape. When the elders had fallen silent, Hod cleared his throat. As the youngest son, little weight was ever given to his opinions, but his exploits of this day raised him in the esteem of his father and the rest of the family.

"You have words to add, my son?"

Hod thought he knew what should be done to save his family, but he felt they needed guidance, needed to know that any decision holding life or death in its shadow, had the approval of their God. Carefully, he touched upon his thoughts.

"I feel we should ask the blessing of Elohim in this decision."

Elim frowned at Hod. "When we left the family, we left His protection and His land. I have never believed I had the authority to offer a sacrifice. Sometimes I think He does not concern Himself with us here."

A gasp and the crash of a dropped pot drew the eyes of all the men to the women who cleaned dishes in a corner of the cave. The wife of Elim stared wide-eyed at her husband, sons, and grandsons. The rest of the women turned their eyes away in fear of drawing Elim's wrath. Only the oldest woman seemed unafraid.

"Well, woman, do you also desire to have a word to speak tonight? It seems like today has become an upside-down day. Everyone has his, or her, say."

She stepped forward, her hands outstretched in a plea. "Hod is right to desire a blessing. Elohim has not forgotten us. We are still people of Seth."

The old man was silent, staring at his wife as if he had never truly known her. All watched his habitual worried frown ease into a look of resignation. He shrugged and exhaled a long sigh.

"Yes, we will do that, wife. Perhaps I have become an old fool who must learn wisdom from children and women. You are right. We cannot do this in our own strength."

A lamb was brought from the flock, an altar of uncut stones was built, and the sacrifice to Elohim was made, the first sacrifice Hod had ever witnessed. Elim led in the prayer asking their God to protect them in this perilous time. Toward the end of the prayer, his lips moved yet the words were nearly inaudible.

Afterward, Elim began to lay out the plan of escape.

"The children are sleeping now and that is good. We will travel fast. Now I want you women to go to sleep for three hours, so you will be strong for the trek."

Again Hod cleared his throat to signal his desire to speak. When Elim nodded, Hod paused a moment, then spoke. "I have another idea."

Undeterred by his father's thunderous face, Hod continued. "There is a small cave in a nearby hill where Hela and I used to play. We could move food and necessary belongings there and then make this place look abandoned. Some of the men could feign signs of a rapid departure and leave a trail into the thickest forest where the vines are so tangled that they will never be able to easily follow."

All the men regarded Elim intently after Hod stopped talking. When he nodded, all breathed a sigh of relief. "What if they stay around and the women and children cannot get food or water?"

"There is running water in the cave, and we have sufficient stores to leave them."

Elim regarded his family thoughtfully. "I like this plan. It is safer for the weak ones. We will take the women, children, and older men to the cave with enough provisions to live for a week. We will seal the entrance and disguise it. All the other men will lead the nephilim away. Those who survive must come back to open the cave."

Once the plan was set, no time was lost in moving the women, children, oldest men, and the stores of food into the cave. Families hugged and cried as they bid what could be a last good-bye to fathers and sons. Before the entrance was sealed, Ahuv insisted their father join those inside.

"You are our patriarch," he said. "We cannot lose you or we cease to be a family."

Elim sighed and moved wordlessly into the cave. It hurt Hod's heart to see his strong father so beaten down by the day's distresses. Before his father left, Hod called out to him.

"Father, may I ask you something before we part?"

The rest of the men went back to the main cave, leaving the patriarch with his youngest son. "What is bothering you, Hod?'

"I killed today. I've never even killed an animal. Am I as sinful as Cain? Will Elohim forgive me?"

"He knows you were protecting your family. When I killed the lamb tonight and offered him to Elohim, I asked Him to take away any blood guilt from you."

Hod squeezed his green eyes closed. "I did not hear that. At the end your lips were moving, but no sound came out."

"Yes." Elim put both arms around his son. "That was when I spoke for you. Your sin is covered by the blood of the lamb."

◁4▷

The Diversion

SHORTLY BEFORE NIGHTFALL, WITH THE WEAKER FAMILY MEMBERS safely hidden, the men returned to the home cave to gather what they needed for their flight. Hod, at the back of the group, stopped and allowed the others to go ahead of him.

For one brief moment, he turned back to study the hidden entrance, wanting to assure himself there was no sign a cave existed there or that people had been gathered around it. This cave at the far end of the compound had such a small opening that it had never been discovered by the older family members. Content with what he saw, he continued after his brothers. Not even to someone familiar with this area would the cave be detectable.

They will be safe, he told himself with confidence, but he took the precaution of rubbing a branch behind him to obliterate the last tracks.

If they are patient, they should be able to emerge safely. I must trust Father to make the right decision. Our mission is now to draw the enemy away from them, so they never suspect we have left anyone behind.

Only one torch burned against the large assembly room wall when Hod entered the largest cave, the home of at least a third of the family. Usually the room glowed with the warm light of many torches, but these lights were now in the hands of the men who had serious work to do in a short time. Hod thought the single torch looked like a lonely spark in the darkness of the new world he was facing.

He took what might be his last look around the only home he had ever known. The largest room in the extensive cave could hold the entire huge clan when they gathered for a feast. The ceiling, only a few cubits higher than the tallest of their men, was a soft gray-brown that absorbed any light cast toward it. The floor had been worn smooth by many sandaled feet, and several doorways opened into the side caves where different family members slept. It was a dry cave, so it had been a comfortable home.

I hope I will come back here. I hope our family has many years to live in Garth. I think maybe dull and boring is not such a bad thing.

Under Ahuv's leadership and after spending some time making the compound look hastily abandoned, the men who would try to lead the enemy away from their home began to separate into squads of four. The plan was for them to leave the cave one group at a time at spaced intervals, taking the broad path that led from the compound through the thick jungle and on to the River Pishon, a half day north. They would drag bags of rocks to make the enemy think a large group of people had left with all their possessions.

The path stretched west an hour's walk before bending around a heap of craggy rocks and turning north. The rocks marked the beginning of a long, low ridge that paralleled the River Pishon and extended for many leagues to the west.

When they reached those rocks, the men planned to work their way into the dense forest to their left, moving always farther away from the camp. They would scatter in all directions, making an easy trail to follow at first but eventually erasing all tracks so that they could then meet again at a waterfall on the Pishon.

"Hod, you will go with the first group," his brother Ahuv said after explaining the plan to all the men. "Chay, Gedi and Hagot will be with you."

"Is it safe for Hod to be in the first group going out?" Chay asked, his voice showing disdain for his younger brother. "We may meet nephilim heading this way. I thought our baby brother had to be protected from a fight."

Hod moved uneasily in the half dark. Why was Chay blaming him for this trouble? Although he was used to his brother's complaining, pessimistic attitude toward life, he had never been so much the target of Chay's acid tongue as in the last days. They had always vied for attention, which he had thought natural as the two youngest sons, but now Chay seemed resentful of him.

"You won't go out the front door or down the road," Ahuv replied. "There is an escape hole at the back of the cave known only to a few of us. The back opening is at the base of a hill in the thickest part of the underbrush north of the compound. You will be east of the road. After we leave the path, we will be west of the road, leading any enemy away from you."

Ahuv lit a new pine knot torch to the one burning on the wall and motioned for Hod's group to follow him. On the way he explained his reasoning.

"Above all, we must keep you safe. That is why we are doing this. We are waiting until the moon sets, so it will be completely dark, but you all know these woods well. It should be easy for you to head straight for the waterfall. You must hide in the cave behind the falling water until we get there."

Hod considered this change in what he thought had been settled. Understanding why they wanted to protect him, he said nothing as Ahuv continued.

"Chay, your work is to protect Hod. If you should see nephilim this time, hide rather than fight."

When he heard Chay's contemptuous snort, Hod jerked back from Ahuv. "It's not right. I am the only one here who has killed a nephil! I don't need protection, and I want to help when you meet the enemy! After all, I am taking the giant's dagger with me."

"Your time will come, little brother." Ahuv gave Hod a rough but fond shake, and then hugged him to his strong chest before letting him go. "We all know the prophecy. Your time will come, and when it does, I expect you to fight bravely—for all of us."

The lump in Hod's throat made it hard to swallow. "When will we be able to join the rest of you?"

"Wait for us at the waterfall. Go directly there through the thicket, staying out of sight," Ahuv repeated. "I don't know how long we'll be. If we never make it there, wait a few days and then come back to help our father and the women and children."

When they were far, far back into the depths of the cave, Ahuv pointed out the exit. So small an opening would probably be overlooked by their enemies when they searched the cave, Hod supposed. He looked up at the jagged, oblong hole in the roof of the deepest depths of the family cave and immediately knew why Ahuv had chosen the three men to accompany him. Only a slim, wiry man could wiggle through there, and his companions—like him—were among the smallest in the tall family of Elim.

Hod smiled as he realized the wisdom of Ahuv's choice. Unlike many of their broad-shouldered, wide-chested brethren, these men would not only fit through the exit, they would be able to work through the tangled vines. Hod and Chay were not as small as the other two yet would be able to make it through the hole.

When word was passed to them that the moon had set, Chay went out the hole first, boosted on the others' shoulders, then Gedi, and Hod. Hagot, the smallest, would have only Ahuv to boost him to the opening, but his light weight would make this easy.

"But I—," Hod began before forcing himself to stifle his protest. He wanted to be first out so he could watch for enemies, yet he knew they were determined to protect him. His time would come, Ahuv had said, and he must wait for that time.

Once he had wiggled out into the cool night air, Hod began to understand the reason for going out this way. Immediately upon emerging he was immersed in a world of vines, underbrush, and low, twisted branches of cedar trees.

Among the four, Gedi was the eldest by fifty years, so the others tacitly agreed to follow his leadership; however, Hod was surprised when Gedi chose Hagot to go first and find a way through the tangled underbrush. He had never seen the small man show much initiative, and he would never have selected him for such an important position if it had been his choice.

But again Hod soon saw the wisdom of this decision. Hagot's small body found tight openings in the underbrush, which were widened as he moved through, making it easier for the rest to follow.

Occasionally they routed a raccoon busy looking for supper or caused an owl to hoot out a warning overhead, but for the most part, they traveled quietly enough along the trail Hagot was breaking for them.

An hour before dawn the nightly mist began to rise from the ground. It began as diaphanous tendrils snaking upward like ghosts of fallen vines but soon had become a solid bank of moisture rolling through the forest until it became a wall of water that thoroughly soaked the four brothers. The poor visibility forced them to go slowly. Between darkness and mist, it was difficult to be sure of their direction.

"Hagot! Gedi!" Hod hissed as loudly as he dared and was rewarded by Chay looking back with an irritated frown.

"What is it?"

"Tell Hagot to stop so we can find out where we are."

Chay snorted and rolled his eyes but did turn and call out to the leaders. "Hey, wait a minute."

When the first two paused and he caught up to them, Hod repeated his concern. "Do you know where we are?"

Gedi looked thoughtful as he silently pondered this. "I was sure we were headed due north before the mist rose. I've never tried to travel this time of night, though, and I could be off. It's near dawn. Let's wait for the sun to lighten the mist before we continue."

The brothers agreed and huddled together, their shoulders hunched as they patiently endured the wet. Hod was amazed at how silent the last shreds of night seemed. Not an animal or insect stirred. It was as if the heavy mist shrouded all sound even as it fed the thirsty earth. He knew that at home the vines were growing unimpeded in the empty fields with no one to hack them back.

With dawn's light the mist had reached its peak daytime density. In a few hours, it would be completely gone. The men stood and stretched before looking a-round to get their bearings. It did not take long to realize they had drifted to the west and were probably closer to the path the rest of the men were taking than they intended to be.

"I think we're not too far from the ridge," Hod said. "A big rock hangs over the road right at the bend. If one of us climbed it, he might see what is happening. If there is no sign of nephilim, we should try to meet up with the others. Father may have been wrong. They may not even come back for us—or maybe not for many days."

Gedi paused, chewing at his lower lip as he consi-dered the possible problems.

"Perhaps, but even if we do go up on the rock, the mist might still be heavy enough to obscure the view. Besides, Ahuv told us to keep you safe. That is our primary order."

"Wait, wait," Chay broke in. "Hod might be right. It could be we *are* wasting our time and scaring the women and children for nothing. Who is to say there is really any danger? I for one would rather be home, even working in a field, than out here."

Hagot nodded and—though he rarely spoke his mind—agreed with the other two. "Let's discover what's happening first. We don't really know what is out there. It's so quiet. I too find it hard to believe there is danger anywhere near."

Without a word to his brothers, each man fell silent, straining with all his might to catch any distant noise, but no sound marred the silence. No thumping behemoth steps or battle cries penetrated the woods. Gedi finally spoke. "Hagot, you go ahead quickly and climb the ridge. We'll wait here until you return."

The remaining three found a dry spot under a spreading cedar and pulled out some bread to break the night's fast. Water from their waterskins supplied a slake to their thirst. Before long they heard Hagot softly calling for them.

Each one waited for the bad news that Hagot's dark features foretold. His words were slow and deliberate. "I could see what must be two of our groups moving together up the path, almost to the point where the first groups would have gone into the woods, that is if some of them made it to the woods."

Gedi nodded. "It's been hours since we left. By now most of them should be well into the forest. You must have seen the last groups that have caught up with each other. But I can see you are worried. What's wrong?"

"A large group of nephilim is coming directly at them," Hagot said. "It looks as if they have several behemoths and some smaller men with them. If our men are not warned, they will meet the giants at the bend in the road."

"Lamechites. I've heard the Lamechites are their minions." Gedi was looking more and more concerned.

He looked quickly from one face to the next. He may have been the eldest, but he seemed at a loss for how to handle this situation. The rest of them exchanged glances. None seemed sure of a course of action, yet each looked for help from the others.

Hod spoke first. "Two of us should go to warn them."

"Why two?" Gedi asked.

"Because one may not make it, and someone must get through. I want to volunteer, but . . . ." Hod looked at the ground and then up into the treetops.

"But you know we will not let you," Gedi finished for him. "Your idea is good. You and Chay stay here while Hagot and I go. It's not far."

All knew this was the best plan, so no more arguments were made. Chay clasped the right hands of the other two as each moved out. "What should Hod and I do? Wait here or go on to the waterfall?"

"Wait. We should not be long."

When the two older men were out of sight and sound, leaving only the youngest brothers, Chay moved away from Hod and then turned his back on him without saying a word. Hod looked with pained eyes at the brother he loved but could not seem to please. He considered leaving him alone; however, he knew this was not right. They were facing dangerous times, and either of them could die soon.

Hod stepped toward his brother and put a hand on his arm. "Why do you act this way toward me? What have I done?"

At first Chay would not answer or even look at his brother. He gave his customary dismissive snort and shrugged his shoulders. But Hod would not give up.

"Why are you angry?" His grip on Chay's arm tightened.

"You aren't worth my anger!" Chay shook off Hod's hand. "Who are you but a pampered, protected baby who has caused our family to run from our ancestral home and live as outcasts in this land of Garth?"

"I know the nephilim want to kill me, but how is that my fault?"

"You were born. That was enough!"

Hod felt tears in the corners of his eyes. He turned from his brother before Chay saw them and was confirmed in his belief that Hod was a baby.

"I didn't choose to be born."

"No, you didn't," Chay agreed. "So I don't hate you, but I *am* tired of worrying about you. I'm angry that I was once more given the task of watching over you."

"What do you mean, 'once more'?"

"I suppose it never crossed your mind that I always have to be in the field next to you or that you never go anywhere without someone near you? Usually me!"

Hod wondered if Chay really did hate him. He had always felt that there was something keeping them from being close, and now he was beginning to understand what it was.

The two older brothers had left quietly, had woven their way soundlessly through the underbrush with care not to attract the attention of any nephilim outliers who might possibly be near. Knowing they too must be careful not to alert the enemy to their presence, Hod and Chay fell silent after their brief exchange of words.

The sudden disruption of the silence—a crashing, limb-snapping chaos approaching through the woods—threw the brothers into instant action. Hod snatched the giant's dagger from his belt while Chay leapt behind a tree. But when Hagot burst through the last hedge of brush and fell on his face on the damp ground, they both rushed forward.

"What happened? What did you see?" Hod cried. Chay went down on one knee and lifted Hagot's head.

"We were too late. The nephilim were almost upon our brothers by the time we reached them. The last group was about to go into the woods when the enemy came around the bend in the road."

"But you did warn them?" Hod said.

Hagot looked guilty as he nodded. "Gedi made me hide while he tried to warn them, but he was only in time to join the fight."

"Did you leave him?" Chay demanded.

"On his orders. He wanted me to run back to let you know what had happened. He made me promise."

Hod and Chay exchanged a look of agreement not to say more of this. Hagot had done what he was told.

"But what happened to our family?" Chay said.

"They must have heard the nephilim coming just as Gedi shouted his warning. There were less than ten of them facing at least six nephilim and several Lamechites. Our men turned and faced them. Some of our family who had not gone far into the woods—earlier groups—came back to help but they had no chance."

Hod stood horrified, unable to comprehend this disaster that had befallen his peaceful family. "Were any captured?"

"I don't think so. Many were killed in the battle, and some took off into the woods opposite of where I was. They may have escaped."

"And Gedi?" Hod asked.

"He was one of the first to die."

Hod knew Chay was looking at him and knew there was more accusation in his eye. Was he, indeed, responsible for the ruin of their family? Was he to blame for the deaths of so many brave brothers and nephews?

"I should give myself up to the nephilim. If they kill me, they will leave the family alone."

Chay said nothing, but Hagot was quick to respond. "Father would never forgive us. The prophecy said you would bring about the ruin of the nephilim. You are more important than any of us."

Again Chay was silent, but his crossed arms and a deep frown showed he did not agree with this conclusion.

"Are you sure you weren't followed?" Chay asked. "We should get going before they find out we're here."

"I can't be sure. I ran without looking back but imagined—maybe it was imaginary—that I heard noises far behind me. I didn't dare stop to be sure."

Hod laid a hand on Hagot's mouth. "Quiet! Let me listen."

There was something. Still a way off, a rustling of branches but not the sound of large bodies crashing through, more someone small disturbing the brush.

"It's not nephilim," Chay said. "But something smaller is following you. Probably Lamechites. Let's quit dawdling. We need to move fast."

"Where do we go?" Hagot asked.

Hod could sense that Chay thought he should be the leader now. This was not the time to think about that. He joined Hagot in looking to Chay for a decision.

"We'll head for the waterfall. Anyone who made it will go there," Chay said.

As he turned to follow his two brothers, Hod's worry about the safety of his family overwhelmed all other thoughts. Frozen in place for a moment, he watched the older men disappear into the underbrush. The crashing noise behind him finally put him in motion, and he turned to follow.

They began ascending the steep ridge, which had less underbrush and fewer tangled vines to impede them. They pulled themselves upward by grabbing at tree trunks and exposed roots. Because they could hear their pursuers only a minute behind them, they did not pause when they reached the crest but immediately began running down the back side of the ridge.

It was while they were trying to keep their footing on a bed of old pine needles that the attack came. The three creatures who came screaming down the incline at them with upraised swords shaped like scythes were not giants but rather small, muscular men with hairy bodies and long, dirty black hair trailing down their shoulders.

At the sound of screaming, all three brothers drew their weapons and turned to face the enemy.

"Lamechites!" Hagot yelled. "Hod, run while Chay and I hold them off."

"No! There's three of them. You need me!"

Hagot, usually reserved and soft-spoken, turned on Hod and almost growled. "Don't be a fool, little brother! These are the worst of the sons of Cain. You above all of us must survive. Now run!"

When Hod still hesitated, Hagot screamed at him. "I'm ordering you! Get out of here!"

Hod knew Hagot was right, yet he saw that Chay gave him a last accusing look before turning to fight. With a sick heart but knowing he must do this, Hod left the last of his family he was sure were alive and dashed through the woods, down the last bit of slope and out of the wooded ridge to the level land beside the Pishon.

Behind him he heard screams and sounds of clashing iron. His brothers were giving the Lamechites a fight, but they had little hope of prevailing against three with superior weapons.

"I should have stayed!" he muttered.

Hod almost went back, no matter what his brother had said, but when he heard Hagot's scream followed by silence, he was sure Hagot and Chay were dead. He did not know whether the waterfall was to the right or left, yet he knew he was more likely to run into nephilim if he turned left. So he ran wildly the other way without knowing exactly where he was going.

"I am not worth any of them." Hod stumbled on a root and fell to his knees on the riverbank. "Elohim, help me! If I have a reason to survive my family, let me know it. Give me a purpose for going on."

 ◁**5**▷

Captured

A STIFLING STINK FORCED ITSELF INTO CHAY'S OTHERWISE oblivious mind. He began to wake up even though he could not move his body. *Where am I?* he asked himself as memories began to take shape in his foggy thoughts. *Am I dead?*

He remembered that one of the small black-haired Lamechites had knocked him down with the side of his curved sword and then kicked him again and again until all went black. He suspected those men were the source of the odor.

Chay's thoughts were coming awake, but his eyes seemed glued shut.

"This one's still alive," one of the men growled and kicked Chay's leg.

When Chay groaned, the other man laughed, grabbed him by the neck, and pulled him to his feet. "Ugh! Trying to make us believe he's dead. What do we do with him, Niute? Kill 'em too?"

"No, stupid. Didn't you hear Gradrach? Kron says bring one of the family back if we didn't find the fire-hair."

The one who had kicked Chay, a grown man by his face but a head shorter than Chay, looked up at the captive. Chay wondered why he had so much hate in his voice.

He noticed the filthiness of these beings whose faces looked as if they had never known washing and whose matted hair was filled with sticks, leaves, and caked mud. Their breath reeked like rotting carcass.

"I wasn't listening," the second one said. "Those nephilim—always telling us what to do. I get tired of them. What made us their slaves?"

"Shut up, you idiot, before one of 'em hears you. We Lamechites decided years ago to serve the nephilim—they're our gods. We're their willing servants."

"I know that! I was the one who suggested they let Boldar smell the belt the haraani brought back. He still has the best nose of any Lamechite."

Chay listened and learned. He decided the Lamechites were an evil breed. And he didn't know anyone on earth worshipped a god who was not Elohim. How could a god be killed as the one called Karlef had been by Hod? They were obviously fools. Still, they had captured him.

"On your feet, Sethian scum!" the leader of these Lamechites barked when Chay's knees began to buckle. "We'll take you to the nephilim. Then follow your brother. Where'd he go?"

Chay shook his head and shrugged, too dazed to utter a word and unwilling to send them after Hod. His brother had certainly brought ruin and death down on the family, just as Chay had expected, yet he didn't want him to fall into the hands of the nephilim. In fact, he hoped that Hod was safely under the waterfall by now.

"Never mind then. We'll follow his scent." The leader turned to the complaining Lamechite. "Buzza, take this Sethian back to the nephilim and bring back one of our brothers to help us hunt the fire-hair. Tell Gradrach that when we catch him we'll take him directly to Kron."

"All right. Come on, you." Buzza tied Chay's hands behind his back and looped a rope around his neck, and then began pulling the prisoner at a rapid pace up the ridge and back toward the nephilim.

Chay gradually lost his first fear of this man who had been called stupid by the other one. When the fellow slowed his pace eventually, Chay tried to speak. The choking rope on his neck made it difficult, but he was finally able to speak loudly enough for the man to hear.

"Where is Kron?" Chay voiced the question uppermost in his thoughts. He expected to be kicked for his question—and he was right.

"What? So you can talk after all. Ha! You should wonder about Kron. He's in his fortress, but you should be terrified by his very name!"

"He is the nephilim king?"

"He's the only king." Buzza sounded proud to be a part of what Chay was sure must be the army of evil.

Emboldened by the willingness of Buzza to answer him, Chay pushed for more knowledge that might help him in whatever trials he faced. "Where does Kron live?"

"The north side of the mountains of Eden, called Atlantia. Maybe Gradrach'll take you there." Buzza cackled, seeming to be getting great enjoyment from the picture of Chay as a captive of Kron.

Chay shivered as a foreboding chill struck his heart. If Kron was worse than the nephilim he and Hod had met, he would be terrible.

"Have you been there—to the fortress?"

"We Lamechites live among the nephilim. We're their friends."

"What do they do for you?" Chay remembered the words of the other Lamechite who had said they were willing slaves of the nephilim. "If they're your friends they should help you."

Buzza puzzled over this idea a moment before snorting and jerking on the rope so that Chay stumbled and almost fell.

"We do things for them—that's the way it works. Nephilim don't serve anyone."

"Great friends!"

"You shut up! You don't know who you're talking about." This time Buzza jerked the rope so hard that Chay fell to his knees. "Get up, and don't talk!"

Getting to his feet with his hands tied behind his back was difficult, but Chay managed to do it. He said nothing more to antagonize his captor since by now they were close enough to their destination to hear loud, surly voices. Within minutes they burst through the forest and directly into a group of nephilim and Lamechite warriors, the ones who had attacked his family, Chay assumed.

"You got him!" the nephil Gradrach, the one he and Hod had wounded the day before, shouted. "Wait! He doesn't have red hair! Kron doesn't want this one. Don't tell me you let the fire-hair get away!"

Buzza went down on his knees before the giant, still holding Chay's halter. "Forgive us, master. The fire-hair escaped, but Niute's following him, and I'm to bring another back to help trail him. We'll get him. Don't fear."

"Fear? I've never feared anyone in my life!"

As Chay watched the giant limp toward him, his heart thundered and his knees shook. He bent his head back and gaped upward at the monstrous man. The anger distorting the nephil's face convinced him that he would soon be dead. Gradrach grabbed the rope around Chay's neck and pulled him up until he was dangling and choking a foot off the ground.

"I know who you are," the giant boomed. "You're the human who cut my leg. What's your name?"

"Chay, son of Elim," he rasped out as his legs flailed.

"Are you a brother of the fire-hair? You were with him when he killed my brother. I saw you." The nephil lowered Chay to the ground.

"Do you know where he is? Tell us or I'll cut your heart out—brother for brother." Gradrach reinforced his threat by snatching up his dagger and pressing it against Chay's chest.

"Yes . . . I . . . I am his brother, but he was the one who killed your brother. And I don't know where he is. All I know is that he escaped and left me to fight for my life. I am not responsible for what he does. I disown him. I don't care what happens to him."

Chay wondered if this was a lie made in the hope of saving his life or if he meant what he said. He watched the nephil's face reflect a struggle to decide if Chay told the truth. Thunder and lightening played across his brow while his snarling mouth twisted like a deadly snake.

The giant bent over and peered more closely at his captive, as if analyzing his words. When Gradrach's scowl cleared, Chay slowly let out his breath.

"I should kill you, scum! But I'll take you to Kron. Buzza, hurry back to Niute. Catch the fire-hair—bring him quickly to Kron."

ξ

THE NEPHILIM WERE IN NO HURRY TO DEPART FROM GARTH. Leaving Chay tied up and guarded by a surly Lamechite, they spent the next three days tracking Chay's family through the woods. Hungry and uncomfortable, the young Sethian grumbled to himself.

This is what I get for trying to save my ungrateful brother. Now he is free and probably safe at the waterfall while I am here at the mercy of our enemies. And what did he care about the family? They could all be dead by now, and it would be his fault if they are.

Twice a day the Lamechite would untie Chay to feed him some nuts and let him take care of personal needs. Then he would bind him again and leave him to think his own miserable thoughts. When Chay finally saw the nephilim and their Lamechites returning from the woods with angry faces, he hoped it meant they had not found the men of the family. They brought no captives back with them, but this did not mean any-thing. They might have murdered them all in the forest.

"Stand up!" Gradrach kicked Chay's sandal. "Your family has disappeared. I can't waste more time looking for them."

Chay knew his surviving brothers and nephews had not gone that far into the forest, certainly not as far as Efrath. He was sure they would have doubled back, using the small stream that ran through their valley to hide their tracks. Even now they might be hiding in the thick woods near their compound waiting for the nephilim to leave so they could free Elim and the women.

The nephil leader grabbed Chay's arm and jerked him to his feet. "We're going through your compound one more time, and you're going with us. Maybe we can find someone hiding there who can tell us where your brother is."

Thoughts of all the weaker family members hidden in the cave haunted Chay as they untied him and pushed him ahead of them all the way to the destroyed gates. Once inside the compound yard, he took in the look of abandonment they had worked hard to create on the day the men had left, noticing that it looked the same as it had that day.

Pots, clothes, and tools were scattered across the ground and a few chickens wandered about. Chay stood in the yard while the nephilim searched the main cave and the two small caves across from them. Finding nothing, they went on to the back part of the compound very close to the cave where his father and the women were hidden.

What will I do if they find the opening to the cave? How can I stop them from killing my family?

"What's back there?" Gradrach asked.

"Nothing. We don't use that area."

"Humph!" The giant cast a glance around, not finding anything of interest. "It doesn't look like anyone has been around here lately."

Chay shrugged and acted resigned. "I guess they all got away—if you didn't kill them."

"We killed over twenty. How many of you were there?" Gradrach barked.

"Ah, less than fifty," Chay lied. "I guess the rest did go farther south. My father planned to set up a new home far away."

While he waited for the nephilim band to finish searching, Chay looked up as casually as he could at the tops of the hills surrounding their home. He scanned the thick foliage growing around the bottoms of the trees. Eventually he spotted an area that was darker than the rest of the greenery.

Chay slowly turned and looked around at his captors. At the moment they were not concerned about him. Even the Lamechites were searching the compound, more interested in scavenging and stealing than finding a Sethian. Chay nonchalantly turned back and gradually lifted his eyes toward the dark spot.

The greenery parted slightly and a gray-bearded face with dark eyes looked at him. While he watched, his elder brother Ahuv signaled first a thumbs-up and a circular motion, which Chay interpreted to mean many were with him. Then he pointed at Chay, shrugged, put his hands together as if praying, and looked heavenward. Chay knew this meant that they could not help him but would be praying for him. He nodded slightly and touched his hand to his heart before waving his brother to move back and out of sight.

Not long after Ahuv had disappeared from sight, Gradrach walked back toward Chay and signaled his troops. "There's nothing here. We might as well head back. Kron will want to talk to this Sethian, and it's a two-day trip."

An hour later Chay was seated behind a young nephil—one much shorter than Gradrach—atop a lumbering behemoth. The nephil, who seemed half grown, still had the amazing large, delineated muscles of the older ones. He had shoulder-length yellow hair and clear blue eyes. Chay thought his face lacked the dark, cruel ugliness he saw in the others.

The young nephil had been irritated when he was told he must carry the Sethian. He had scowled as he reached down and pulled Chay up on the long-necked beast, but the prisoner thought the nephil was trying too hard to look tough.

Chay looked the nephilim in the eye and gave him a half smile, but the young giant only glared at him with hard blue eyes and looked away. Feeling fortunate to be alive and wanting to make the best of his situation, Chay made no further attempts at friendliness.

On top of the behemoth, he was almost as high as the tall pine tree Hod liked to climb to spy out the land. At first Chay was overwhelmed with fear of being so high off the ground, but once he dared to look around, he could not help but catch his breath with amazement at the view.

Before they had gone far, he looked back at the clearing of the family compound and offered a silent prayer for his father and mother, as well as the rest. Now all he could do for them was to protect their whereabouts. *I will probably never see them again.*

Looking to the north, he could see as far as the Pishon and could spot the waterfall where Hod was to go. He wondered if his brother had made it or if the three Lamechites had caught him. The nephilim seemed to think he should know where Hod was going, yet all he had was a guess that his brother might have gone to the home of Seth near the Garden. However, it was only a guess.

As the caravan headed away from the compound, they did not travel through the thick woods and over the ridge, the quickest way to the river. Instead, they followed the road they had come on, probably because of the size of the ponderous animals. Eventually they reached the river, turned west, and followed the valley for many miles. They were moving away from the waterfall, much to Chay's relief.

When he looked over his right shoulder as they traveled into the setting sun, he could see spiky purple mountains on the horizon far to the north and thought they were the mountains where his father's brother Enoch was said to live. Wanting to make sure these were those mountains, he ventured to talk to the nephil he rode behind.

"Are those the mountains of Eden?"

The nephil, whom he had heard the others call Kodi, jerked his head around and stared at Chay a moment before answering his question.

"Yes, but we call them the mountains of Kron." The quavering tone in the nephil's voice convinced Chay he was even younger than Hod, possibly a young boy whose voice was still changing. He was only a teenager trying to be as cruel as the older nephilim.

It occurred to Chay that this might be someone he could use. If he could gain this creature's confidence and get him to let his guard down, he might find a way to escape.

Trying his best to make his voice friendly and non-threatening, Chay pushed the conversation. "But isn't Adam's Garden within those mountains? That's what I always heard."

Chay saw Kodi's shoulders stiffen and knew he had hit a nerve.

"That ridiculous Garden! Guarded by a horrible monster with many faces!"

A contrary mood made Chay lean close to the youth and whisper. "There is the Tree of Life."

Kodi's head and shoulders turned toward Chay, and he suddenly looked as fierce as his older brethren. Chay knew he had to be more careful.

He dropped his eyes as if afraid, looked off at the horizon, cleared his throat a little, and finally repeated his words.

"I mean, have you ever heard of the Tree of Life?"

Kodi had turned his back on Chay, yet his growled words were clearly audible. "We don't talk about that tree!"

With these words, all conversation ceased, at least until they stopped for the night. When the group had made camp on the banks of the river, Kodi came to sit near Chay. For a while he said nothing, but eventually he looked at the Sethian prisoner.

"You spoke of the Tree of Life. What do you know

of it? If you can tell him how to get to the tree, Kron will reward you for information." The nephil barked out his words.

Chay shrugged. This was the chance he had been looking for to win the confidence of his guard. "I know only the old stories my father told."

"Maybe some time you can tell me those stories." Kodi's voice became a little warmer. "Kron is always searching for a way into the Garden, but he does not allow us to talk about it to each other. The Lamechites won't talk about it either because they know it makes Kron angry."

"I can tell you what I know, but I don't want to get in trouble with Kron," Chay said.

The young nephil turned back toward Chay again and lowered his voice to a whisper. "I would get in more trouble than you. I can't understand why he won't allow talk about it since he is always trying to find people who can help him get in."

Chay debated within himself whether he should tell this fellow what he knew about the Garden. He studied his face a moment and then decided to take a chance. What harm could it do?

"All right, then. I'll tell you what I know but wait until tomorrow. We won't be overheard if we talk on top of the behemoth."

Kodi grunted and nodded his head. "Good idea. Now we need to eat."

A campfire had been made, a huge, over-sized bonfire that sent sparks to the heavens, and entire carcasses of several of Chay's family sheep were roasting on small tree trunks suspended above the fire. Although he had never tasted meat, Chay thought the smell was appealing. When Kodi offered him a slab of roasted meat on a stick, he took it but hesitated to eat the forbidden food.

"Do you have any fruit or vegetables?" he asked. "I would rather have that."

"No, we don't eat that stuff when we're traveling. At home we do eat some fruit, but it's too much trouble to take along."

Chay's stomach was rumbling with hunger. After three days of eating only almonds given him by his captors and nothing today, he craved any food. He sniffed the roasted meat he held, and then tentatively licked it. The taste was like nothing he had ever eaten. He nibbled a tiny corner of the slab, chewed it a while, savoring the new taste, and then swallowed it. He felt as if he had crossed a threshold. For good or ill, he was now a meat-eater.

After Chay had filled his stomach with meat, he weighed the pleasant satisfaction he felt against his guilty conscience. All his life none of his family had ever eaten an animal. It was not even considered a possibility. They knew the Cainites and the nephilim ate animals, but to them it was perverse and savage.

Now he realized that animal meat made good food. When he thought about it, he had never heard that Elohim had forbidden it. Chay decided that at least while a captive of the nephilim, he would eat what he was given.

The next day the caravan came to a wide, shallow, rock-strewn part of the river where they all, no matter the size, were able to ford. On the other side, they continued west, staying close to the water. To the north Chay saw a great expanse of deserted, rocky, flat land and knew why they had ridden so far away from the mountains.

By staying close to the river, they avoided crossing land that probably contained no food or water for the men or animals. Directly to the north of the Pishon, Chay saw small hills he assumed were the western end of the Eden Mountains.

Looking across at these hills in the approaching dusk, he noted signs of digging and piles of rubble interspersed with small huts.

"What is this torn up country?" he asked Kodi.

"That is just Havilah. They mine gold and tear up the land." The young nephil was not trying to show how tough he was this morning. Chay felt like the giant was warming up to him.

"Who lives there? Who are the miners?" Chay asked. He expected it would be Cainites or Lamechites.

But Kodi's answer surprised him. "Mostly Sethian immigrants. But they work for us now."

"It's an ugly land," Chay said. "What kind of people could like it here? Are they beast-like and slow-witted?"

"No . . . that is . . . I don't think so. I used to live with them when I was a child. Kron says they are only good as slaves, but I think they are decent. I don't remember them too well."

Gradually the river turned north and the desert was left behind them, so the caravan changed directions and began to travel directly east toward the mountains. By going around the desert and following the river, they now approached the northern face of the mountains, the opposite of the side he had seen when leaving home.

While they traveled, Chay told Kodi all the stories of the Garden of Eden he had learned as a child. When he had finished the familiar stories of his ancestors and their banishment from the Garden, Kodi laughed.

"There is something I can tell you. My friend Nork once overheard his father and mother talking about the Garden. His father was describing it and telling her why it was impossible to do Kron's will."

"You mean finding the tree?" Chay whispered.

"Yes, his father said the barrier and the monster at the gate will stop anyone from getting through. Nork said the Eden Mountains are shaped like a gourd with an immense open area in the middle. At the eastern end is the gate to the Garden, the only way in, and it—as you know—is guarded."

Chay, impatient to learn secrets he did not know, only grunted.

"I know that. What is it like in the middle of the mountains?"

"All around the clear area where the Garden is are steep cliffs so high no one—not even a nephil—could scale them. The river that divides into four great rivers starts as a mammoth spring that wells up in the mountains, comes out halfway up the cliff, becomes a majestic waterfall, and then flows through the valley where it waters the trees and flowers."

"How do the nephilim know that? No one has seen the Garden since Adam and Eve." Chay was beginning to think Kodi was filling his ear with an invented story.

Kodi turned to look at Chay, and then leaned in to whisper in his ear as if being alone on top of a behemoth was not enough to ensure they were not overheard.

"Nork said when Kron was a boy, he climbed the Eden Mountains and found the den of the serpent who convinced the first woman to eat the forbidden fruit."

"He's still alive?" Chay whispered back.

"Yes, although very old and very large. Kron learned many things from him but not how to enter the Garden."

"What did he say about the monsters at the gate—what we call cherubim?"

Kodi shivered and dropped his voice lower as if he feared to even talk about this being.

"They have four faces—a lion, an ox, an eagle, and a man. They have a man's body and hands but the feet of a calf. Also, they have four wings. You see what I mean? They must be monstrosities."

"They do sound scary," Chay agreed. "And I heard they are very big."

"My friend's father saw one. He said it is twice as tall as a nephil."

"How about the flaming sword?"

"Like lightening that never stops!" Kodi said much too loudly.

The two young men fell silent when Gradrach's behemoth slowed down until they had caught up and their mount walked beside his. The nephil scowled at them, drying up their desire to talk.

"We're traveling all night. We need to make up time," the leader said. "Less talking!"

Some hours after sunset, Chay leaned his head against the back of his companion and went to sleep. When he awoke at sunrise, he saw they had reached the beginnings of the astonishingly huge mountain range that lay before them. Tall and rocky and devoid of vegetation, the mountains were forbidding and ominous, reaching up and up into the gray sky.

The morning sun had not yet passed the peaks, but its diffused rays could be seen like an aurora around the mountains far above the low-lying fog. Chay was surprised that this far from home the morning mist was still evident. Heavy and wet, it rose only as far as the shoulders of the behemoths, making the caravan look strangely like nephilim and behemoth heads bobbing through clouds.

"Look up there, Chay. That is the fortress of Kron," Kodi cried with pride.

Chay saw that the mountain was the fortress—a tall, steep peak carved into a magnificent and ominous tower. Stairs, windows, and doorways could be seen in the face of the steep, nearly black mountain face. Not a shred of green relieved the gray-brown severity of this peak. No shoot of nature found root or sustenance in this barren ground.

At the foot of the mountain were many small dwellings made of the same stone as the mountain and seeming to be continuations of it. Beyond them was a large, spreading lake filled with blackish water that reflected the gray clouds. Many dead or half-dead trees surrounded the lake and some of these looked as if they were in the process of slowly falling into the water.

He saw work being done here and there, but there was no sign of farming and no flocks of sheep or goats. Chay shivered as the gloom of this country called Atlantia settled over his soul.

How will I ever escape this place? I won't. I'll die here and my family will never know. There is no hope any normal man can prevail against these nephilim. I hope Hod and that prophecy are worth it.

◁**6**▷

A Pure Watcher

HOD STOPPED RUNNING AT A SPOT WHERE THE RIVER PISHON rushed loudly through a narrow gorge formed by steep granite walls.

Only a slim stretch of pebble-covered ground separated the trees from the edge of the gorge. The young man, who had never been so far upstream, walked to the rim of the precipice and looked down in awe at the foamy roar of the fast-moving water one hundred cubits below the bank.

He knew the waterfall was back to the west, the direction he had come from. After taking a moment to

study the land formations surrounding him, Hod decided he needed to follow the stream west even though it
might lead him toward the enemy. A glance in that
direction assured him the Lamechites were not in sight,
yet Hod could not shake off an uneasy fear that the hairy
sons of Cain would soon follow him out of the woods.

Since nothing moved in the trees, he turned his attention back to the water. If he could find a way to climb
down to the river, it would be impossible to cross the
rushing waves. Hod decided it would be safer to climb
down and make his way along the boulders piled near
the river's edge until he found a way to cross or came to
the waterfall. At least he would be hidden from any
approaching enemy.

He drew a deep breath, slid over the edge, and
began to work his way down the wall, face to the cliff
and fingers grasping at protruding rocks. One at a time,
his legs reached for toeholds and occasionally slipped
off damp rocks. His fingertips ached, rubbed raw by the
rough stone, yet he dared not relax his grip as he worked his way to the bottom.

"If the prophecy is from Elohim, then he surely will
protect me," Hod muttered after he had recovered from
a near slip.

Hod clung to the rock wall for a moment, catching
his breath and waiting for his heart to slow. Eventually
he began to again descend the rock face. One foot after
the other, he found secure footholds. One hand after the
other, he moved downward. By the time he reached the
bottom, Hod put aside his concern over approaching

enemies and rested on a large boulder at the water's edge.

Taking a moment to catch his breath, Hod looked up and down the steep, narrow gorge with its rushing flood. Not an animal or human was in sight. Feeling like Adam on the day of his creation, Hod was overwhelmed at the enormity of his aloneness.

Back home he had always been surrounded by family. Everyone he knew was related to him and knew him well. They worked, ate, played, and slept in close proximity—in fact, family closeness was all he had ever known. Chay had shared his bed, a bed of rushes stuffed in a woolen sack and tucked away in a nook of the cave, since childhood. *And now Chay is probably dead. He'll never laugh or argue with me again.*

A snuffling and shuffling high above Hod, up on the bank, brought him to his feet. Something was up there noisily sniffing the ground as if it were tracking a prey—or looking for food. Hod's first thought was of the small dark men who had followed them in the woods, but this sounded like only one creature, with a much heavier body.

He had a spine-prickling feeling that a large animal of some kind had found his scent. He pulled the nephil dagger—now his sword—from his belt and stepped onto a boulder, a good pace out from the bank.

Watching and waiting, his breath suspended and his eyes wide, Hod prepared himself for anything. And then a black shaggy head appeared above him and bent its sharp-toothed, wide-open jaws his direction. Saliva dripped from its tongue and splashed in heavy drops on the boulder where Hod had been sitting.

It was Hartagga, the monster that had chased him in the field. When the creature met his eyes with bloodshot malevolence, Hod knew beyond a doubt that Hartagga had never left the area of their home but had only waited to make sure Hod did not escape before the nephilim found him.

Hod, holding his sword ready to defend himself if the animal came down to the river, balanced on the balls of his feet. Hartagga would not be able to climb down the steep bank as Hod had, and if he jumped, he would probably end up in the rapid current of the river. Hod hoped this would keep the shaggy beast up on the bank.

But Hod would not be deterred. He turned his stomach to the ground, slipped hind legs over the bank, and slid down to the boulders below where there was scarcely enough room for the monster to stand.

When he turned, Hartagga was only a body's length from Hod's rock. He reared onto his back legs, threw back his head to bellow, and then swung long arms and sharp claws toward the human.

"I'm not afraid of you! Elohim is with me!"

The holy name made the animal roar towards the heavens in a vain attempt to challenge the Creator's authority. Hod was suddenly without fear as he raised his sword to deal a deathblow to the great creature just as he had to Karlof the nephil.

When Hartagga fell heavily back down on all fours and started to lunge for Hod, the nephil dagger seemed useless against the claws aimed his way. And then a flash of light shot from behind Hod exploded in the creature's face. Hartagga swiped at his eyes, shook his huge body in rage, and moved blindly toward his quarry.

The frantic movement threw the animal off balance so that he fell backwards into the river, splashing a wave of cold water over Hod, and was swept away by the swift current. Hod saw his head bobbing above the water and knew Hartagga was still alive but temporarily blinded and unable to fight the water.

"What happened?" Hod cried and turned to look behind him.

As if in answer to his question, a misty, white figure rose before him and seemed to stand on the water, unfazed by the waves beneath it. Hod, speechless and unable to catch his breath, watched as this being dressed in white garments came nearer.

"The animal will not bother you for a while."

"Who are you?" Hod's quavering voice croaked out these words before it failed him.

He watched as the figure drew closer. It was a man with long white hair, no beard, and a beautiful face. His eyes were blue as a spring, and his skin was almost clear in its whiteness. His appearance was unlike anything Hod had ever seen.

"I am Remiel, a Watcher of Elohim." The being ignored Hod's first question. "I have been sent to tell you that the prophecy at your birth is a true one. You were chosen before your birth to destroy the nephilim."

Amazed at what he was both seeing and hearing, Hod was unable to speak and could only nod his head. The figure looked at him with a sympathetic eye. "You are wondering how you will do this."

Hod nodded again, thankful Remiel understood him.

"Your brother Ahuv will meet you at the waterfall today. You are to tell him he must wait three days before returning home, but you are not to return with him. You must leave your family and travel to the high peaks of Eden where your uncle Enoch dwells. He will tell you what task you must accomplish."

His confidence and courage returning slowly, Hod ventured to ask a question. "How do I find him— Enoch?"

"You must go through the land of the large beasts and cross the barren wilderness until you reach the mountains. You will overcome them."

"I cannot do this alone!"

Remiel smiled. "You will not be alone. The work will be done by a strong hand, five fingers, making an iron fist. You are only the first."

Before Hod could ask another question, the Watcher moved across the water to the other bank and dissolved into the moist air. For several minutes Hod sat awed and puzzled and unable to think clearly.

It was almost like a dream, but he knew it had truly happened. A messenger, a Watcher of Elohim, had appeared to him, had told him his purpose, and now he knew what he was supposed to do with his life, yet at the same time he had no idea how to do it. Hod stood, shook off his bemused mood, and began to move down the rocky river wall.

Although at first he had thought there were no animals in sight, soon Hod spotted a river otter working its way through the shoals. Its dark brown fur shimmered with cascading water when it breached the surface. He looked for the other otters he expected to see playing with the creature but soon realized the otter was alone just as he was.

The sun had passed its midpoint—in fact, was half way to the horizon—by the time Hod reached the waterfall. As he had progressed down the river, the granite walls slowly shortened until they finally disappeared. By the time he reached the waterfall, Hod was able to walk on the grassy riverbank. He heard the roar of the falls long before he got there.

As he looked for any sign of Hartagga around the river or waterfall, Hod noticed a patch of black fur hanging from a stick in a knot of trees and roots wedged in some boulders on the very brink of the fall. Hod decided Hartagga must have been impaled on the stick and torn himself loose. No other sign of the creature could be seen on the banks or in the water.

Hod climbed down to a ledge halfway to the lower riverbed and then took time to admire the beauty of the steaming plumes of water and the distant landscape. It was as breath-taking as he remembered from the last time he had come here with his brothers. The falling water gave off steamy mist and frothy foam. The Pishon flowed for many thousands of cubits toward the western horizon where it turned to the north and disappeared from sight.

Hod glanced down the river and over at the woods and fields on each side to make sure he was not being watched. Once he was certain no eyes were spying out his activities, he plunging through the falling water. With one foot reaching for the ledge of the hidden cave, he leaped through the water and immediately was standing on the granite floor of the small cave behind the watery veil.

"Hod! You made it!" a voice cried out. "I've been waiting for an hour or more."

He turned toward the voice. "Ahuv! I knew you were here!"

"Yes, I told you I would meet you."

Before Hod had time to look around at the hollow beneath the jutting ledge of the waterfall, he was swallowed in a bear hug. The elder brother grabbed the younger and clasped him to his breast.

Hod pulled back to look questioningly into his brother's face. "I know the nephilim attacked you. How many of us are alive?"

"Forty of us were far enough into the forest not to be found by the enemy. Two groups of four closer to the road heard the fighting and ran back to help. Two of them escaped the battle and let us know what had happened. They are waiting for me in the woods. The nephilim have taken the bait and followed our many trails."

Hod caught his breath as he subtracted the living from those who had gone out from the cave.

"So we lost seventeen men?"

"Only fourteen by my count," Ahuv said and then looked intently at Hod. "Where are Gedi, Hagot, and Chay?"

"They—." Hod's voice broke. He feared tears would follow, but he fought to control his grief.

"They died protecting me from the sons of Cain who followed us."

"All dead? And did you say sons of Cain followed you. Those who returned reported seeing some of those short, hairy men, the Lamechites. Are you sure our brothers are dead?"

"I didn't see them die, but I heard their death cries. And later a Watcher told me I was to go by myself to find our uncle Enoch." As Hod began explaining the news he had received, his eyes were caught by the sparkling rocks lining the cave around him, and he was unable to complete his thought.

Ahuv shook his head vehemently. "Never! I will never let you go away by yourself. The rest of us are going back to the compound to see if the others are safe. You must come with us!"

Hod did not answer at once. He could not take his eyes off the jeweled cave. Never in the many times he had visited this hideaway had he ever noticed the dazzling rubies, sapphires, and emeralds decorating the walls. They glowed, lighted by a mysterious source he could not identify. The glow seemed to increase until it filled the entire cave, making the stones dance with fiery brilliance.

"Remiel," he breathed and suddenly the Watcher was there right beside Ahuv, who jumped aside before falling to his knees.

"Stand up," the Watcher said. "I am only a servant of Elohim. He has sent me to confirm what Hod has said. It is true he has a mission. You must let him go."

"My Lord, my Lord . . . ," Ahuv moaned, still on his face.

"Come, stand," Remiel repeated. Hod, mesmerized by the peaceful face of the Watcher, watched as his elder brother stood trembling before the heavenly being.

"Your brother will take a long journey. He will find help on the way, and because of his mission, mankind will survive and one day the world will be rid of nephilim forever. You must not hinder him."

Ahuv trembled as he answered. "I will let him go. He is in the hands of Elohim."

The light faded, the cave darkened, and the Watcher disappeared from their sight. Ahuv clasped Hod to him before pushing him away.

"Go on, Hod. I can't argue with a Watcher. We'll have to trust Elohim to take care of you when we can't. Don't worry about our father and mother. I will explain all."

Hod nodded. "I think I'll spend the night here and leave at dawn. That way I'll have a full day to travel. Earlier Remiel said to tell you to should wait three days before returning home. Can you stay until morning?"

"No, the rest are waiting for me. I must tell them what I've learned. We'll wait three days and then go back to the compound. Come outside the water and show me where you plan to go."

Ahuv stepped through the waterfall and onto the rocks outside. Hod followed. Both brothers quickly looked around and, assured they were still unwatched, turned their faces toward the northern side of the river.

"I will head north, but the Watcher told me you would direct me. Have you ever traveled that way?"

Ahuv smiled, a tight grimace really. "I decided to leave our home when I was fifty when the family lived three days journey southeast of the Garden. I went first to spend time with Seth, and then I explored the world. Because of this, I have the words to guide your steps."

"Did you go to the mountains?"

"Yes, and to the ocean, the jungles, and barren lands. I was the one who discovered the valley of Garth. When I was a young man, I traveled for three years before I found a wife from Sethians and came home. In my journey I found our uncle Enoch in the mountains."

Hod's heart beat quickly as he felt the excitement of this coming adventure rise within him. "What does he look like? What did he say to you? How do I find him?"

"Patience, I will tell all I know. Enoch is older than our father. I think he must be more than three hundred and sixty years old now. When I saw him, he was about two hundred, but his face had no wrinkles beyond the crinkling of his eyes when he smiled. His hair was thick and long, like a lion's mane, but white as a cloud.

"When he talks to you, you hear the echo of the Watchers with whom he converses daily. Never has there been a man so close to Elohim since the first ancestor walked in the Garden. I wanted to stay, but he told me to go home, for I had a part to play in the great plans for man."

"Tell me the way to him," the younger brother insisted. "How do I get there?"

"Travel always north, keeping the purple mountains of Eden as your guide. You will cross that low ridge you can see from here."

Ahuv pointed across the land on the other side of the river. "Many large animals live there—meat-eating behemoths roam it. Be careful where you walk."

Hod nodded. "I will."

"At the end of it, you must climb another ridge and on the other side cross a rocky desert plain barren of water before you reach the great mountains which form the center of the earth."

A great feeling of relief, along with an eagerness to start this adventure, engulfed Hod. If Ahuv could do it, so could he. "Where is Enoch?"

"High in the mountains. Look and you will find him."

After Ahuv left, Hod went out to the riverbank and studied the direction he would take the next morning. Across the water, the land stretched off flat and clear with low, dense bushes giving way to bigger trees. Hod was sure it would be difficult to make headway through the thick furze, the prickly ground cover. At the far edge of the horizon, the dark ridge Ahuv had indicated ran parallel to the river.

"Enough of this," he said to the wind. "First, I must sleep in the safety of the cave until morning."

ξ

HOD ROSE AT THE FIRST LIGHT OF DAWN SADDENED TO THINK that only two days ago he had been safe at home with his family. Now he had no idea how many of his brothers had been killed or whether his parents were safe.

"I can do nothing about it," Hod said to no one but himself. "I can only obey Remiel and seek Enoch."

As soon as the darkness of the cave behind the waterfall had lessened, he made himself a breakfast from the provisions Ahuv had left with him, washed his face in the fresh falling waters veiling the cave, and slipped out of the safety of this place into the morning mist.

He followed the rocks to the other side of the river where dark green furze grew to the very edge of the river. Hod grabbed fistfuls of the prickly stuff, pulled himself up over the rocky edge, and stood a moment in the greenery taking stock of his situation. Far ahead, perhaps a distance of six leagues, was the first ridge. Behind it, he could see the purple tips of distant mountains, the great Eden Mountains.

He turned back to make sure no one else had risen at dawn with plans to come after him and end his life. Perhaps Hartagga had found his way from the river and returned to stalk the prey he had lost. Hod's keen eyes roamed over the edge of the distant woods, down the rocky walled canyon of the river, and even over the field he now found himself in.

Seeing nothing to alarm him, Hod stood and began to work his way through the furze. But before he had taken ten steps, he stopped, wheeled back, and listened with the full power of his ears. Something had loosened a rock and sent it clattering down the walls of the river-bank. He listened as the rock bounced off boulders and splashed into the river.

A shiver of foreboding trembled his frame and convinced him that he must quickly put as much distance as possible between himself and the small men or Hartagga or whatever could be following him.

Knowing his sandals would slow his progress, Hod pulled them off, put them in his backpack, secured his sword in his sash, and ran as fast as the thick vegetation would allow him toward the tree-lined ridge. This was not difficult. Running was one of his gifts. He had been known to run great distances without stopping.

As he ran, Hod did not think to enjoy the cool, misty air sweeping past his cheek, for his mind was filled with concern. Even though the prickling along his backbone hinted at distant eyes watching him, he knew no one ran like he could, so he did not stop until he was sure he had left his unseen pursuers far behind.

Finally, he slowed his pace and looked over his shoulder. The mist had long since lifted, so he could see far into the distance. Stopping under the cool shade of a spreading oak, Hod unslung his waterskin from his shoulder and took a long drink of the water he had drawn from the Pishon that morning. He ate some of his food and then, noticing avocados growing in an untended orchard nearby, took a moment to supplement his bread with the fresh, oily fruit.

When he was full, Hod knew it was time to be moving. He scouted the landscape around him first and saw that, as he had been told, many animals lived in this fertile plain. He smiled at the sight of a herd of small shaggy ponies grazing peacefully in a grassy field not far away. The tall necks of giraffes could be seen even farther off, and he saw behemoth tracks—from the many breeds of the giant creatures—all around him.

Recognizing the ominous splayed footprint of a razor-toothed behemoth, Hod began once more to run toward the ridge. He ran until he reached the base of the ridge an hour before sunset. Because he needed to rest his legs yet was wary of man-eating animals, he climbed the tallest available tree and found a safe seat in the branches.

From this perch Hod was able to scan the distance he had just crossed. The low, scruffy furze had given way to higher bushes and eventually to widely spaced trees.

Suddenly a flash of yellow moved into the shade of his tree, stepping quietly—so quietly that its heavy body made no sound on the grassy ground.

"Ah, the long-toothed tiger," Hod whispered.

Not long ago one of these always hungry cats had found its way to Garth and killed several sheep before his brothers had trapped and destroyed it. The sharpness of the long, curved teeth had fascinated Hod, and he had been pleased when Hagot gave him some skin to make into the belt the haraani had carried off.

Knowing he was safe high in his tree as the cat was too heavy to climb it, Hod watched it stalk a lone pony grazing nearby. The tiger moved delicately, eyes and ears intent on its prey, moving nearer and nearer to the peaceful pony.

Hod was about to whistle a warning, as his sympathy was with the grass-eater, when he became aware of large teeth framed by leaves, even with his head and not far away.

As slowly as he could, he turned his face to his left and saw through the thick foliage around him the profile of a razor-tooth behemoth's head.

Unbelievably stealthier than the tiger, a razor-tooth was stalking the cat. Hod froze, and then faded slowly back against the trunk behind him. Unlike the long-necked behemoth, this creature had a huge head and many sharp teeth. It moved more quickly, and it was a meat-eater.

Good thing I didn't warn the pony. The behemoth would have come after me. It would have plucked me out of this tree like an apple.

He slowly looked back at the tiger. Its shoulder muscles were bunched for a lunge, but before it could move, the razor-jaw pounced and snatched the cat up in one bite. Hod saw the predator hold the tiger high and shake it until it was still. The pony's head jerked up at the tiger's scream, and in an instant, the little animal galloped out of sight.

Hod's eyes returned to the razor-tooth in time to see it walk off with the still carcass dripping blood on the grass. The puddle of blood below his tree made him realize the cruelty of the world the animals lived in. They never knew when they would be food for another beast.

Maybe my own blood will soon be shed by my enemies. I am now part of this world where everyone is stalked by another.

It was impossible to know if someone followed him in all this vegetation, but Hod trusted the sense of danger that kept him wary. Before long, unable to spot his pursuers, he left the tree and began moving up the ridge as quickly as possible. He scrambled up the steep ground, grabbing at low branches to pull himself higher and higher.

At the peak he stopped and drew in his breath in a mighty gasp. A huge orange sun was setting to the west of the purple mountains on the far horizon. He had never witnessed such a sunset in the hills of Garth.

Between the mountains and the ridge where Hod stood, was a deserted land seemingly made of sand and flat rock.

He saw no trees, no hills, no rivers, no people, no animals. The land was light brown, the color of a riverbank, and spotted with occasional patches of sparse plant life and piles of stones. The desert seemed to go on and on and on until it ran into the distant mountains, black and purple against the orange sky.

What do I do now? Hod asked himself. *How can I cross this land without being seen by my enemies? Can I survive in a land so empty? How can I find food and water in a place like this?*

He turned and looked behind him. In contrast to the desert, the vegetation he had left behind looked safe and inviting. He had found fruit and nuts and could find water if he needed it. A man could stay here a long time and perhaps survive, but what would he eat or drink in this deserted land before him?

For many minutes he squatted on his haunches and stared at the green land. Even with all the predatory animals, he was tempted to turn back. And then he turned and looked out at the desert land. His waterskin was less than half full. Would it be enough for land without water? Surely he would die if he undertook to cross this foreign place.

It is too late to start now, anyway. I will decide in the morning.

◁7▷

A New Friend

W ITH NO ENEMY IN SIGHT, HOD DECIDED TO FIND SOMEPLACE where he could eat and rest for the night. He chose the branches of a knotty olive tree on the very summit, made himself as comfortable as possible after eating from his provisions, and fell into a light sleep. The earliest streaks of dawn sent his eyelids wide and Hod into immediate wakefulness.

He looked back at the southern slope of the ridge, but, even though there was no morning mist, there was not enough light to see anyone approaching. After

slipping quietly out of the tree, Hod stretched and prepared to continue his journey.

Before leaving the summit, he took one last look
back down the southern side and then froze. Something
far down the green ridge was causing the foliage to bend
and twist. Something was snaking its way toward him
with evil intent. Was it the small men—or something
worse?

Hod scrambled as quickly as his strong legs would
take him down the steep, treeless back side of the ridge.
Slipping and sliding on the loose sand, Hod soon reached the bottom of the declivity, but he did not stop there.
His bare feet never slowed as he kept running out across
the flat, deserted landscape toward the purple peaks just
beginning to be painted with the morning sun.

There was nothing to hide behind in immediate
view, nowhere to shelter and search for the enemy behind him. He knew he must be beyond their reach and if
possible out of their sight before they came to the bottom of the ridge. Not daring to look back, Hod ran and
ran until he reached a scattering of huge buried rocks
that reminded him of over-sized hippos with their heads
submerged. The thought of water made him lick his lips
and feel for the diminishing waterskin at his side.

"I have drunk too much since I left the river," he
muttered. "I must pace myself—a few swallows to keep
me going."

Hod quickly ducked behind the tallest rock, careful
to bend low so as to be totally hidden. First, he took a
small gulp from his water, and then he peeked around

the rock to see if he were being followed. "Something is there. Back at the bottom of the ridge —something is moving."

Evidently, whoever was following him was in no hurry. To his keen eyes, it looked as if two or three small people were gathered together, no doubt deciding their next step. Further watching revealed that the men were mounting some type of animal Hod had never seen before, animals with long legs and humped backs.

And then he saw Hartagga sliding down the ridge. *Maybe he will eat them. He would be doing me a favor.*

But he soon realized that the beast was friendly with the followers and had joined the chase. Hartagga was pacing back and forth as if eager to begin.

After one quick glance back at his enemies, Hod left his sheltering rocks and began running in a slow and easy pace, keeping a tall double-pointed peak directly in front of him. It was not as purple as it had been at first, and the individual rocks were becoming clearer, but he still did not seem to be any nearer the mountains.

The heat burned Hod's skin—an unfamiliar sensation for a boy raised in the mistlands. Several times he was forced to take drinks from his waterskin, which was almost empty. By midday Hod knew he could not go on. He had to rest. He had to find somewhere to shield himself from this burning sun.

And he had to find more water. Judging that he still had a day's run to reach the mountains, he knew he would have to find a place to spend the night, or he would never last.

When he dared to look over his shoulder, Hod quailed at the sight of the long-legged creatures galloping his way, still far off but closing the distance quickly. Alongside them Hartagga loped as if the drylands were his natural home.

Looking back north, Hod saw some strange treelike growths off to his right. He veered that direction hoping for a place to hide and soon was in the middle of a stand of these large plants—fat, green, barrel-shaped growths covered with thorns.

"No cover, no protection!" he groaned.

Suddenly a round, flat rock directly in front of Hod moved aside with a sharp scraping sound. He jumped and then gasped when a shaggy head popped from a hole in the ground and grinned at him.

"That all depends on what you mean by protecttion," said the head, its black eyes sparkling with good humor.

As soon as Hod realized the head belonged to a body—a body now hopping out of a hole once covered by the flat stone—he lost his first wariness of the stranger and looked him over.

It was a boy shorter than he, with dusky skin and dusty brown hair.

"Take a look at those creatures chasing me, and you'll understand," Hod said, pointing over his right shoulder with his thumb.

"Oh, my!" the hole dweller cried. "Lamechites on camels! And Hartagga—Kron's pet. Are they after you?"

"I'm afraid so," Hod said with a rueful shrug.

The boy grinned and grabbed Hod's elbow. "Then you'd better get in here quick."

The thunder of the hooves on hard sand was close enough to make up his mind, so Hod—with no argument—dived feet first into the hole. His companion quickly turned to erase their footprints with a cedar branch he held in one hand.

I wonder where he got the cedar in this treeless land, Hod thought before forgetting to think about it in his hurry to escape his pursuers.

At the bottom of the hole, Hod found himself standing on a dirt floor about ten cubits from the surface. Unsure what to do next, he stood still and waited for his companion. In the bright shaft of sunlight coming through the opening, he could see the boy slip into the hole and pull the stone back over it with a long vine attached to the stone.

"Get down," the boy whispered in the pitch dark caused by the replacement of the stone. "I'm going to open a small door to a passage out of here. When I do, you'll see some light. Crawl through the hole as fast as you can, and I'll follow."

Hod obeyed immediately without a second thought or question. This fellow seemed to be his only hope to escape the Lamechites and Hartagga. When he saw the dim light showing the escape route, he scurried through.

On the other side, he found himself in a small cave —large enough for four or five people to move around— lighted by a torch. They both sat with their knees beneath their chins and listened to the sounds coming from the other side of the small opening they had just crawled through.

"Sssh! Listen. They're moving the stone off the well," the boy said. "Don't make a sound. If they don't hear us, they might not guess we're here."

Before long the stone scraped back over the well, and both young men took deep breaths. It seemed that the Lamechites had fallen for their ruse.

"That's a well?" Hod whispered. "Where's the water?"

"Oh, it dried up years ago. I use it for a back door—and an escape route—when I need to get away from enemies."

The boy peered at Hod in the dim light. "Who are you? And what are you doing in the desert? I've never seen you here before."

Hod studied this stranger a moment without answering. He had been taught to distrust anyone not from his family, particularly Cainites. This boy looked much like the men who had followed them through the woods and killed his brothers. Why should he trust him?

"I'm running from nephilim and Cainites who attacked my family a few days ago. I need to make it to the mountains." Hod decided to trust the boy for the time but be wary.

"And your name?" the boy asked.

"Hod."

The boy watched Hod in the half-light of the cave, his mouth a quizzical twist.

"I think there is more to this story, but that will do for now. My name is Pazel. Welcome to my home."

"This is your home?" Hod swept his hand around the narrow quarters.

"Part of it," Pazel began when a renewed sound of scraping stone interrupted him. "They're back! Do you have a weapon?"

Hod pointed at the dagger stuck in his belt. "I have this I took from a dead nephil. It makes me a good sword. Will we have to fight? Will they find us?"

"Sssh! Someone has dropped to the bottom of the well. I hear him sniffing. He is looking for your scent."

Before Hod had time to pull his knife from his belt, a small, black-haired man pushed back the stone blocking the opening and scuttled into the cave. As soon as he was in, the Lamechite began swinging his curved blade. Hod and Pazel pulled their stomachs back from the lethal arc. Hod's sword was in his hand, but Pazel's club was quickly knocked to the floor by the swinging blade.

"You will die, you traitor!" the Lamechite screamed at Pazel. "You dare to help this Sethian?"

When he saw the man taking aim at Pazel's neck, Hod dashed forward and stuck his sword in his back. The Lamechite turned on Hod with a growl, his weapon changing its target, but Hod kept stabbing the small man's chest and abdomen repeatedly until he fell dead on the ground.

"You saved me!" Pazel cried. "Thank you, friend! I owe you my life."

Hod shook his head. "I'm fairly new at fighting— and killing. Taking human life can't be right."

"They were trying to kill us. We must protect ourselves. Anyway we're safe now."

"Not so fast. There were three of them. The others will follow him."

Pazel looked thoughtful a moment and then stuck his head back through the opening into the well. After looking around, he pulled his head back in and turned to Hod.

"The stone is off, but no one else is in sight."

"But they'll come back for him."

"We'll leave him here in this cave. I'll pull the stone back in place over the well, and then I'll collapse this tunnel. They'll think he has gone elsewhere. First, I'll climb the well and make sure they're not around."

When Pazel returned, he assured Hod that the Lamechites were not close, although he had seen Hartagga snuffling around.

Hod finally began to feel that they might escape the enemy. "Is this your whole cave? Is there another way out?"

"My home goes underground all the way to the mountains. I was on the mountain and saw you running across the desert, so I came down here to help you."

"I'm glad you did. What do we do now?"

"Let me block up the opening first, and then we'll go. I'll take this man's sword just in case I need a weapon."

"Your cave will be fouled by the carcass of this Lamechite," Hod said. "You might never be able to use this again."

"I'll deal with that later. Now follow me."

With this, Pazel turned and squeezed through a minuscule opening on the other side of the cave. Hod tried to follow but had a little more difficulty negotiating the space as he was quite a bit larger than his companion.

When he was through, Pazel hammered at the rocks above the door until an avalanche of large stones fell from the roof and totally blocked the way.

"This should keep them out even if they do find the body," Pazel said.

He had extinguished the torch and left it in the cave, so they moved in total darkness through a cramped tunnel. Worried about losing his rescuer in this unfamiliar place, Hod stayed inches behind Pazel's sandals, which occasionally hit him in the head.

Eventually they emerged from the tunnel into a huge cave, far bigger than that which Hod's family had called home. He blinked at the sudden light that, after the darkness, almost blinded him.

"Where is the light coming from?" Hod cried as he covered his eyes. Even with many torches on the walls, none of their caves had ever been as bright as this.

"Holes up above. They work better than torches, at least during the day." Pazel pointed at the cave roof where several shafts of sunshine shot down like spears before exploding into blooms of light on the cave floor.

Hod turned amazed eyes at the wonders of this gigantic room and saw many pillars of stone that seemed to hold up the roof, brilliant yellows, blues, and red-oranges streaking the walls, and—wonder of wonders—a river of crystal water flowing down the middle of the cave.

"Water!" Hod ran for the stream.

He fell on his stomach and submerged his entire head in the pure, icy water. It tasted better than anything he had ever imbibed, better than the clean waters of the Pishon or the mossy waters of the stream that ran by his home.

He drank his fill, rubbed his face with the leavings that streamed down his cheeks, and then shook his hair until droplets spun around him.

"I've never been so thirsty in my life. Or had my thirst so wonderfully satisfied! Who would have ever expected such water out here in these drylands? Where does this river come from?"

Pazel stood directly under a shaft of light, laughing and giving Hod his first good look at him. He was a head shorter than Hod, had thick, shaggy black hair, crinkling brown eyes under bushy black brows, and a wide mouth, showing large white teeth as he grinned.

"Tell me about yourself," Hod said, putting aside his first question. "Where are the rest of your people?"

Still grinning, Pazel shrugged and sat down by the stream next to Hod.

"I don't know. I'm alone. All you see is my domain, mine alone. And this is not all—my complex of caves continues all the way to the mountains and ends in many openings in the rocks."

Hod studied the little fellow who had been so helpful and wondered what his story was. "How did you end up here by yourself?

"I'm a Cainite, if you didn't figure that out from what the Lamechite said. You're Sethian, so we're supposed to be enemies. That's why he called me a traitor — for helping you."

"How did you get here?"

"My mother died when I was young. After that my father and I were emigrating from Nod to Havilah to join my grandfather. I was eight and sickly, and we were crossing the drylands going east to west when we were attacked by a great lizard. My father put me down the dry well to protect me. He was killed by the creature, but I was safe in the well."

"I'm sorry you lost your father. You don't think of me as an enemy then?"

"No, I have met many friendly Sethians since living here. I hope you'll be my friend."

Hod tried to analyze the motives of his companion to decide if he could be trusted. "My family lived far away from the rest of the Sethians. My father did dislike Cainites, but I never had a reason to. I'm not fond of those Lamechites riding the camels."

Pazel nodded. "They are the worst of the Cainites."

"Why?"

"Lamech, their ancestor, held a terrible grudge for Cain's punishment," Pazel said. "He also murdered a man and afterward hated Elohim. He passed this hate on to one of his sons. All that man's descendants are assassins. Now they've got your scent, they won't be happy till you're dead."

Hod's head jerked up and his eyes widened. "But I thought we lost them by closing the cave!"

"They won't give up so easily. They know you were heading for the mountains, so they'll search for you there. Their sense of smell is strong, and they have Hartagga to help. His nose is even better." Pazel stood and turned to lead the way. "I hope you know the mountains."

"No, I've never been here before. This may sound strange, but I was sent here by a Watcher."

Pazel stopped and turned back to look at Hod.

"I saw a Watcher once."

Hod clutched his companion's arm. "When?"

"Years ago, when I was alone after my father died. I was crying in the dry well. I tried to climb out but could not. And then, suddenly he appeared beside me." Pazel leaned back on his elbows.

"What did he say to you?"

"He said not to worry, that Elohim had a purpose for my life. Then he pointed at the bottom of the well and the opening appeared. He told me about the stream of water down below. He said it was the water of life and had the power to heal the sick. And he was right. I never saw him again, but I've been perfectly healthy since that day."

"Amazing! Healing water! Did he tell you where it came from?"

Pazel nodded. "It comes from the springs of the deep, the same water that flows through the Garden. I don't know much about the Garden, do you?"

"Only what my father told me." Hod's voice was breathless as they hurried through the long cave. "Elohim sent our father Adam from the Garden."

"Do you know of the river that flows from the Garden and becomes four rivers?"

"Yes, I lived near one—the Pishon."

"This river underground is a fifth river, pure from the source in the mountains of the Garden. It flows through crystal minerals and contains all that Elohim intended for water to give us."

"I thought all the rivers were pure," Hod replied.

"The Watcher said all the others are defiled by man and beasts. Only this one has living water."

As he considered this new information, Hod was surprised that such a thing as living water could exist. Water that would keep a man healthy and add years to his life would be prized and sought by all mankind.

"So what purpose did the Watcher tell you of? Is it to share this water?"

"No. I'm supposed to guard the water. As far as my purpose, I'm still waiting."

Pazel sat down on a smooth area near the river and signaled for Hod to sit with him.

"I've been thinking. You've had a hard journey. We will travel through the dark passage after you rest a few hours. I am not tired, so while you sleep, I'll get some almonds, figs, and barley from my stores."

Hod nodded his agreement and stretched out on the smooth spot. While Pazel was gone, Hod thought about how he had left the Pishon alone with little food and water and no one to guide him. Now he had a guide, food, and water. He heard Pazel returning before he saw his torchlight.

"Where do you find barley out here?" He asked the question that had been puzzling him.

"I trade with the people of the west, east, and south—and even the north when I have to—who come this way in search of salt. I am a salt seller, but you didn't know that, did you."

"Where do you get the salt?"

"I scrape it from the walls of one of my caves and put it in clay pots."

Suddenly Hod remembered a trek Jediah had made years before. He had gone far to the west and had returned with many jugs of salt.

"I think some of my brothers have bought salt from you. Do you remember Jediah, a Sethian? He would have traded beans, barley, gourds—maybe walnuts."

Pazel's grin twisted his dark face as he nodded. "Was he old? I remember a man who walked like a youngster yet had a white beard and wrinkled face."

"Yes, that sounds like him. He was almost two hundred when he died."

"How did he die?" Pazel had extinguished the torch and made himself a resting place on the cave floor. His voice reflected his sympathy. "I thought you Sethians lived for centuries."

"Our camp was attacked by nephilim—only three days ago, although it seems as if weeks have passed. Jediah was killed by a behemoth. Many more of us were killed fighting them. They made me flee instead of fight."

"And why you?" Pazel asked.

"I am the youngest of a very large family. And they think the nephilim want to kill me."

As the two young men conversed in the dark, Hod was reminded of nights when he and Chay had lain in the cave talking after the torches were put out. *If somehow Chay was not killed by the Lamechites and if I ever see him again, I will do whatever it takes to make peace with him.*

When Hod heard Pazel clear his throat as if he sensed his sorrow, he decided to change the mood.

"I'm thankful you found me. You said earlier that I saved your life. Well, you have saved my life too. You said you've been here twelve years. How old are you?"

"Nineteen—I'm older than I look. We are a short people, we Cainites, and due to my illness in childhood, I did not grow as I should have."

Hod thought about his family, all the tall, strong men. Some were smarter than others, some were braver than others, some were kind, and some were loving, but this short, happy Cainite who was ready to risk his life for a stranger was as good as any of them.

◁8▷

The Dark Passage

PAZEL WAS CALLING HOD'S NAME SOFTLY WHILE HOLDING THE lighted torch and carrying a sack over his shoulder. Hod awoke immediately and jumped to his feet.

"We ready to start? Is it morning?" He looked up at the dim light coming through the cave roof.

Pazel grinned widely and then laughed aloud. "It was only noon when we met. You took your nap two hours later, and you've slept two hours. I want to be out of the passage before nightfall."

"Sounds good! I need to get moving," Hod agreed. "I'd like to wash my face one last time in that crystal river if you don't mind."

115

"Go ahead but hurry. Remember, the water has the power to heal. If you're sick or wounded or near death, it will heal you, but for everyday use only a small sip will last you for hours."

Without answering, Hod hurried to the river, threw himself on his stomach, and washed the sleep from his face in the clear water. Only then did he cup his hand, fill it with water, and lift it to his mouth. As soon as he drank, he was wide awake and invigorated. The early morning hunger he had felt was gone.

Hod picked up his pack, pulled out the sandals he had packed away when he began running, and then took a moment to put on the footwear. He knew some cave floors would wear the skin off your feet. When ready, Hod hurried back to his friend and clapped a hand on his back.

"You're right! One drink and I feel wonderful! I wish I could share that water with my family."

At these words Pazel grabbed him by the elbow.

"You must be careful whom you tell about this water! That is the one condition I have for sharing it with you. The Watchers told me it is a gift from Elohim to be protected."

Hod reached over and took the hand that was gripping his elbow and looked Pazel in the eye in the dim light. "I promise by my family that I will never share the secret. It's between you and me."

"Good! Now, let's get going. In a while I'll give you your own torch just in case we become separated; however, it's important that you stay close to me."

The old prickle of impending danger tickled Hod's spine. He shrugged his shoulders in an effort to cast off worry. He was, determined to face any test. Now he must be prepared to die if that was his end.

Pazel slowed his pace and pointed toward a passage to the left. Then he reached for a pineknot wedged in a crack in the wall, touched it to his torch, and gave it to Hod.

"We're leaving the sunlight and will soon be in complete darkness. Stay close to me because, as I said before, there are more dangers in this passage than even I know. I don't use it often."

"Why are we taking it?"

"This passage will lead you into a high and distant part of the mountains. You'll come out in a crevice between two mammoth-sized boulders where you will be shielded from enemies."

Hod tried to assess the trustworthiness of his companion. Pazel's face showed nothing but friendliness and good will, no sign that he might be luring Hod to his death. But he still wondered what awaited him in this dark tunnel? "It just occurred to me that I might be foolish to trust you. You admitted sending me into danger. You might be working with the nephilim."

"I detest those dirty giants! If I wanted you to die, I could have killed you while you slept. Besides, you saved my life, so we are now brothers. If you want, I'll go with you and suffer what you suffer."

"Is that the only reason you have for helping me?" Hod demanded as his eyes bored into Pazel's.

Pazel's crooked smile and the hand he put on Hod's shoulder were reassuring. "Maybe this is the work the Watcher spoke of."

In the dimness of the entrance to the dark passage, Hod closed his eyes for a few minutes to ask for confirmation that he had made the right decision. When his eyes opened, he saw Pazel at the river filling Hod's waterskin with the healing water. That was when he knew for sure this was a man he could trust.

"Are we ready to go?" he asked Pazel.

Hod followed Pazel into the passage, which at the beginning was not large enough for both of them to walk abreast. Hod held his torch before him in his right hand, saving his strong left hand to reach for his sword if needed. Meanwhile, he felt the wall to his left as they walked.

They walked silently for an hour or so with no dangers apparent. The only noises were the drip of distant water and the echo of their footsteps returning to them from far ahead. And then another sound began to accompany the echoes. It reminded Hod of the flapping wings of the black crows he used to chase from the fields. They would be feasting happily when he came upon them and raised a boisterous cry to scare them off. Dozens would take flight at once with a concerted beating of heavy wings.

This sound was much the same, yet too distant to be clearly identified. What would crows be doing in a dark, underground passage like this? Nothing that loved the day and the light like those thieving birds of home could live in this utter darkness. His torch shed only the weakest light, and even that was quickly absorbed by the blackness. Any bird that lived here would soon go blind.

"Pazel, do you hear that? Do you hear that flapping sound? What is it?"

"Bats. We must go right through their colony. There is no way around them. Prepare yourself."

In his heart Hod laughed at Pazel's warning. He knew bats from his own cave, had even had one as a pet when he was a boy. They never bothered a human beyond brushing through your hair when they were disturbed and took flight out of the cave. Snakes, giant lizards, pits: these things gave Hod reason to be scared, but he could never fear a bat.

And then they turned a corner. A chill wind whipped down the dark corridor, accompanied by hundreds of immense wings beating and slapping at the young men. Hod's torch went out immediately.

Pazel spun, turning his back on the wind and the wings, and hunched his shoulders to protect his light. Hod lost sight of his companion as he twisted his body in a vain effort to avoid the creatures attacking him. The bats were ten times larger than those he knew. And they were ravenous!

They nipped and clung to the boys, grabbing at their hair, tearing at their clothes. While he fought them off with his dead torch, Hod looked for Pazel and saw him slapping at the bats with his still-lighted torch.

"Keep moving," Pazel yelled.

Hod heeded these words. Knocking off bats that were biting him and clinging to him, Hod stumbled after Pazel, almost falling but catching himself as they stepped into a large cavern with one overhead hole allowing light. When Hod staggered from the passage, the bats let go of him and fled back into the dark.

Pazel hurriedly turned to Hod, who was breathing in short gasps.

"Are you all right?"

"I've been bitten." Hod slipped to the stone floor. "And I lost my waterskin in the tunnel."

Pazel found a cleft in the rocky wall to wedge his torch and then quickly knelt beside Hod. He slipped his waterskin off his shoulder, pulled out the stopper, and brought it to Hod's mouth.

"Here! Drink from mine, but only a sip, and then I'll pour a little over your bites."

An inspection of Hod's back, legs, and neck revealed several widely spaced pairs of fang marks almost as wide as the length of Hod's thumb. He shuddered to think how large the bats, which he had not clearly seen by the weak torchlight, must have been.

As Pazel poured a few drops of the healing water on each wound, Hod studied them a moment, expecting to see an instantaneous miraculous change. Nothing happened at first.

"Now that I have lost my water, we will have to share yours. Will that be enough?" Hod felt guilty to have been so careless with the precious liquid. "I'll run back and find it if you want me to!"

Pazel shook his head and smiled his wide grin. Hod was beginning to sit up straight and stretch his body as he talked.

"So you feel that well, do you? No, I won't let you risk your life. If enough of the bats got you at once, they would kill you."

"But what will we do for water?"

Now his friend stood and reached for his backpack, his torch, and his sword.

"Oh, there is plenty of water in the mountains, and I have more water containers in some of my other places. That water will do for our thirst. You take my waterskin with the healing water and keep it for when you really need it. Have you looked at your wounds?"

Hod looked and could not even tell where the bats had bitten him. Not even a scar remained. "This really is healing water! I'm as healthy as I was before the bats attacked."

"I knew you'd be astounded. Let's move on. There are more dangers ahead before we come to the end."

The two young men hurried through the lighted cavern where Hod saw several openings to more passages and soon came to another small dark opening leading away from the light. Pazel took his torch, touched it to Hod's to ignite the knot, and then with a gesture of his head, motioned for Hod to follow him in.

"This passage is much smaller," Pazel said. When it narrowed, Hod had to turn his wide shoulders and walk sideways to keep up with his friend. Pazel with his smaller size had no trouble negotiating the tunnel.

At times Hod had to stoop to keep from bumping his head on the low rocky ceiling. It was cold but dry in this passage. There was no drip of water along the walls as there had been in the earlier one. Also, it seemed to be going upward, making Hod guess they were now in the mountains. And then Pazel stopped so suddenly that Hod bumped into him.

"What's the matter?"

"Directly ahead is a pit that takes up the entire floor. It will be difficult to get around it."

"Can we jump it?" Even as he made this suggestion, Hod shivered to think of trying to jump a pit in the gloom. How easy it would be to miss the other side and slide down into the unknown black.

"Too wide!" Pazel put his torch between two loose rocks on the floor. "We will have to leave our torches here because it will take both hands as well as feet to climb along the side of the wall. That is the only way to get to the other side."

"What? Leave our torches and go on in the dark?"

Pazel chuckled and patted Hod's back. "I'll go first. Then you put out my torch and throw it across to me. I'll relight it from my flint. Then you can throw me your torch and I'll light it and put it where it will help you see."

"How do you do this when you're alone?"

"Usually I leave my torch to burn out and go on in the dark. As I said earlier, I rarely take this passage."

With no choice but to trust his friend, Hod took both torches and held them out as far as he could to help Pazel find his way.

"Good," Pazel said. "Now watch how I cross. Try to pick the same hand and footholds. And wait until I'm on the other side before you put out your torch."

Pazel stood close to the left side wall, his face only a thumbsbreadth from the rocks. He first reached out with his right hand, far and high until he had a good hold on a rocky knob. Then he reached with his right foot, which found a toehold on the thin lip of floor beside the pit. Hod watched as Pazel's left hand and then left foot followed, finding their own holds. It took only a few minutes for the young man to work his way over, and soon he was standing on the other side, his face barely visible.

Noticing that Pazel's torch was sputtering out, Hod tamped out his own torch on the rock floor, and then tossed it over to his companion. He waited to extinguish the other torch until the first one was burning again, but there seemed to be a problem. He could see the flint sparking and sparking in the darkness of the other side, but the pine knot did not catch.

"What's the matter?"

"There's not enough resin in this wood to catch. That happens sometimes. It's worthless as a torch now."

"So—what do we do? I'll toss you this one and see if it lights, but it looks bad."

"No, I know by the way yours is sputtering that it's nearly used up too. Let me think."

Pazel's voice betrayed some concern, the first since Hod had met him. "If you put your torch in a crack high on the wall, it should give you enough light to cross over."

Hod's stomach jumped at the picture coming to his mind. It would be harder to find hand and toeholds in the weaker light, but he thought he could do it. He was not totally inexperienced in rock climbing.

He and his brothers had sometimes climbed the faces of the rocky cliffs around their home, but never had he felt how much his life depended on how sure-footed he was.

The question most troubling him was what to do with his torch.

"But when I get there, my torch will be back here. I've lived in caves long enough to know never go down a passage without a light."

"We are almost at the end, and this is the last obstacle. I can find my way in the dark, especially since it's a straight shot with no side alleys. Trust me—I know the way. Right now we need to get you over here before your torch dies."

Hod tried to follow Pazel's steps and choose the holds that had worked for him, but he felt as if he were holding on by his fingernails. Then, without warning, the fingers of his right hand slipped from the rock, and he fell to the right, causing first one foot and then the other to let go too.

Only the strength of Hod's left arm—built by the years of chopping weeds—and the secure rock he held kept him from plummeting into the pit. He hung there by his left hand while his body swung away from the rocky face.

"Help me!" he cried, expecting to plummet to his death any moment.

Suddenly, in the near dark of the cavern, Hod felt a strong hand grab his right hand and pull it up to a firm knob, which he immediately grabbed. Then the hand took his right foot and put it on the thin ledge at the opening to the pit.

"Thank you, Pazel. I would have fallen but for you!"

"What do you mean?" his friend asked from the other side. "I haven't moved."

"But—but—someone grabbed my hand and kept me from falling."

Hod quickly looked to his left, where his torch still gave some light. Moving down the passage away from him was a shimmering, silvery figure that seemed to face away as it receded.

"Do you see that?" Hod called. "Is it Remiel?"

"I don't think it is Remiel. But I'm sure it's a Watcher."

Now that he had secure holds on the rock wall for hands and feet, Hod wasted no time crossing the last distance and was soon standing beside Pazel, who threw his arms around Hod's shoulders.

"Thank Elohim, you are safe! I think that was one of Remiel's soldiers who helped you."

"Are they watching us all the time?"

"Maybe. I don't know. They *are* called Watchers. I'm just glad he was there even though I couldn't see him. Are you ready to finish the passage?"

Both young men turned and looked into the blackness beyond the pit. Hod's fading torch, from its spot wedged into the wall, did not penetrate the depths of the other side. Hod swallowed as memories of the bats and the pit sprang to his brain.

Pazel had admitted he did not come this way often, so there could be new dangers.

"Try to light your torch one more time," Hod said.

"It's no use. Don't worry. Keep your right hand on the wall. I'll keep talking, so that you can stay close."

Putting his worries aside, Hod motioned into the dark. "All right. Lead off."

Into the blackness they stepped. Hod's pupils stretched their widest, searching for light, but once they left the pit behind there was no light to be found. Pazel kept up a constant chatter and occasionally paused for Hod to respond. During this final hour in the passage listening to his companion talk about himself, Hod learned how Pazel had made the rocky plain and the southernmost range of the Eden Mountains his home.

No one else lived near, but travelers and caravans had passed by and spent time with him. When a traveling Sethian had mentioned the need for salt, Pazel had told him he knew where it was to be found and would trade for it.

"Since then word has spread of my salt. They come from all around to buy it."

"Where do they find you? Do you have a house where they come?"

"On the mountain—but west of here—is my main cave. It even has a door that rolls to the side. I would take you there if it were not out of your way. And the Lamechites know of it. If they guess you are with me, they'll come there."

Hod was silent and thoughtful. He had put his whole trust in this friendly little man. If Pazel wanted, he could leave him here, or on the mountain, or turn him over to his enemies, but Hod's heart told him his new friend was completely loyal. "Where are you taking me then?"

"To the center of my mountains, closer to the garden. The Lamechites will go there last."

"That's where I need to go! For my mission, I mean."

"Mission? You never said you were on a mission." Pazel's voice was full of curiosity. "I thought you were just running from the Lamechites and nephilim."

In the darkness, Pazel's voice seemed to be bouncing off the walls and coming from behind him. Hod reached out and touched his companion's back to make sure he was still in front of him. He felt his guide stop and knew he had turned to face him.

"Just being certain who is leading," Hod explained. "For a moment, I thought you were behind me."

Pazel laughed. "Yes, the voice plays tricks on you in these passageways. Sometimes when I'm alone, I think I hear a human voice calling to me, a deep moaning voice. It always sounds like it's luring me to my doom. Sounds mad, I know."

"I think being all alone in these tunnels and caves would make you mad. How do you stand the solitude?"

"Guess I'm used to it. But tell me more about your mission while we walk."

Pazel continued moving forward with Hod close behind him. After considering a while about how much he could safely tell his new acquaintance, Hod decided to tell him the whole story.

"When I was born, a prophetess foretold that I would have something to do with the end of the nephilim, so Kron searched for me for seventeen years. When he found me, my family had to run and I ended up by myself. That was when Remiel told me to find my uncle Enoch who lives in these mountains. Enoch will tell me what I must do."

"So you don't really know yet?"

A downdraft of cool, fresh air began to fill the passageway. Hod sucked in the sweet smelling air before answering.

"No, I've no idea what my mission is. I know Elohim is directing me, and I trust Him."

"I hope the prophecy is true." Pazel stopped, causing Hod to bump into him. "The nephilim are so corrupt that they make the whole world evil. I hate to do business with them. I'll do anything I can to help you."

Hod was wondering what it would be like to have to trade with nephilim when his eyes began to see a distant white spot.

"Am I imagining it or is there light down there?"

"We're near the end of the passage. That's daylight. It must be late afternoon by now, and we need to find a safe place to sleep by dark. Let's hurry."

"Have you heard of Enoch?" Hod asked as he hurried behind Pazel.

"I'm not sure, but I have heard rumors of an old man who roams the high peaks. They say he communes with the Watchers—both good and bad ones. But I wouldn't know how to find him."

Now that they had something to move toward, the two young men picked up their pace. The light grew larger and larger until they could see an irregularly shaped opening with twilight sky behind it.

When they crawled through the small hole, they were between large boulders, which they would have to climb before they were completely out.

"This opening is well hidden. How did you ever find it?"

"I found it from the inside out—the way we came—and I only use it when I'm trying to evade someone or something."

They both climbed the boulders and finally stood atop them with hands on hips surveying the view. Hod looked back toward the south, across the rocky plain that had caused him so much effort to cross. It looked like a thin strip between the mountain they were on and the ridge where he had decided whether to go on or back. He could even see over that ridge to the furze-covered land and beyond that where he knew the Pishon rolled by, although he could not see it clearly.

"There's no one in sight," Pazel said.

"We lost them for the time, but we still need to get under cover. You see those large birds up there?"

"Yes, I've seen them before. Those are haraanis, aren't they? What do you know about them?"

Pazel shrugged and gave Hod a puzzled look. "They nest in some of these peaks. There's one of their nests up there."

Hod followed the direction Pazel pointed and saw a large clump of sticks and branches on a small rocky pinnacle nearby. "I think Kron has used them to search for me. Does that sound possible?"

"Maybe. I don't know that much about them other than they are always flying around and they are very strong. I saw one carry off a goat once."

"Let's get out of their sight," Hod urged, and Pazel quickly led him to shelter.

◁**9**▷

Prisoner of the Tower

T HE TOWER OF KRON STRETCHED TOWARD THE GRAY SKY LIKE reaching fingers probing the heavens in search of a way in. High in the uppermost peaks of the northern side of the Eden Mountains, windows and doors had been carved in the limestone many cubits above the ground.

Chay bent his head back as far as he could and whistled softly. "What kind of a place is this? Do all you nephilim live here?"

"That's the fortress. Kron's dwelling. And hundreds of us stay here. Kron lives at the top."

131

"Will they take me way up there?" Chay pointed upward and his legs began to tremble at the thought of climbing up into that towering fortress.

Kodi shrugged his shoulders and looked surprised at the quaver in the Sethian's voice.

"I think so—when Kron wants you, but the prison isn't up there."

"Prison? What's a prison?"

"It's where enemies of Kron are locked up. They'll probably put you there."

Chay looked from Kodi to the sky-high towers. "I've never been that far off the ground. What if I fall and am dashed to death on the rocks?"

Now Kodi laughed and pushed Chay in front of him toward a gathering of nephilim who had come out to greet the caravan.

"Don't worry. You won't be all the way up there. The prison is much closer to the ground and at least five hundred cubits back in the mountain."

The thought of being imprisoned in the dark heart of these mountains depressed Chay so much that he decided the heights of the peaks were not so bad. The more he looked at the rock fortress—even the highest parts—the more awed he was.

"How did you people make this place?"

Kodi puffed out his chest. "Hundreds of Lamechites worked for fifty years carving out the rooms. They are still working to make it even bigger and tunneling back into the depths of the mountain."

An older nephil who had come out of the tower and conversed with Gradrach, now walked over to Chay and Kodi.

"So this is a brother of the one we seek." He did not even look at Chay. "Kron wants him right now. Take him up!"

Kodi led the way up to the mountain while a stocky nephil carrying a spear that looked like a small pine tree followed. The ascent was worse than Chay could have ever imagined.

A stairway—curving and coiling upward—had been carved into the rocks on the outside of the mountain. It was made for nephilim, so the steps were high and deep. Chay had to clamber up each one. One misstep or loss of balance would send a climber plummeting to his death on the sharp stones below.

The nephilim steadied themselves by holding on to a railing attached to the mountain face, but it was too high for Chay to reach, so he was forced to bend forward to keep from losing his balance and falling backward. Terror gripped Chay's stomach. If he had eaten recently, he would surely have thrown it all up.

"Is it as terrifying as you feared?" Kodi asked when they stopped at a doorway where the stairs came to an end more than halfway up the peak.

"More." Chay panted, trying to catch his breath while he could.

The long-legged nephilim traveled so much faster that he had had to hurry to keep up.

He crept closer to the edge and craned his neck to peek down at the piles of rubble he guessed had been dug from the inside of the mountain. A sudden dizziness made him feel as if he were being pulled downward and almost compelled to throw himself off the mountain.

Kodi grabbed Chay's tunic. "Hey, watch yourself! You almost fell."

"Thank you."

He felt a sudden fondness for the young nephil who almost acted as if he cared what happened to him. Maybe his plan to get to know Kodi was working. In this foreign world, the young giant was the closest to a friend he had.

"Follow me through here," Kodi said. "The rest of the stairs are inside."

It took another half hour before they had finished climbing the stairs—dark, but lighted by an occasional torch—and had come to an arched doorway that opened into an immense chamber.

While they stood in the doorway, Chay took a moment to glance around the room. Its ceiling rose so far that he wondered how the small Lamechite workers who had carved it out had been able to reach it.

Along the left wall tall, thin windows let in narrow slivers of sunlight and fresh air; the other walls were lined with over-sized torches that burned like small bonfires.

At a signal from the far end of the room, Kodi marched Chay before him into and across the room to a gigantic gold, jewel-encrusted chair that looked as if it grew from the polished stone floor.

Seated on this chair—Kodi whispered that it was called a throne—was the largest and most impressively terrible nephil Chay had yet seen. His head was thickly covered with iron gray hair that grew down the sides of his face and continued in a beard cut into many sharp spikes. His eyes were black holes in red pools as they stared at the tiny Sethian.

"You are the brother of the fire-hair?" The voice boomed down like close thunder. Chay opened and shut his mouth but was unable to make a sound.

"Speak, Adam's spawn, or I will put my foot on your head and mash you into a puddle of skin and blood."

When Kodi prodded him in the back, Chay forced a croak from his dry throat. "Yes . . . I am his brother."

"Tell us where he is. Kron, king of the nephilim, demands to know."

"I . . . I . . . d . . . don't know. He ran off and left me to fight the Lamechites. He left me for dead."

"Where was he going? What were his plans?"

Chay thought a moment before answering. He could tell the nephilim king nothing because he knew nothing, but he feared that he would be killed if he could not help him find Hod. And what would be the purpose for his death? Nothing but protecting the brother who had not helped him when he needed it.

He assumed Hod was headed for the home of Seth but decided to invent something to say that would lead

Kron away from his family. "I know he was never to go back home. I think he was headed for the Eden Mountains."

"Does he know we seek him?" the voice roared.

"Y—yes, my father told him about the prophecy. He told Hod to run away."

A rumbling growl began to grow from Kron's chest. It built to a crescendo as it echoed from the roof and down to Chay, who cringed and grabbed his ears.

"HOD! A hundred rubies to the nephil who brings me the Sethian called Hod! Bring him to me alive, and I will eat him for dinner!"

Chay shook so much his legs began to crumple. No matter how angry he was at his brother, the thought of Hod being a meal for this king was horrifying. Kodi grabbed Chay by the neck and held him up with less friendliness than he had earlier shown.

Kron's red eyes almost glowed in the half-light of the chamber. "Human, if you bring me your brother, I will spare your life."

"I—I don't know where he is. How can I find him?"

Kron's teeth—a row of fangs fit for a tiger—glinted as he grinned at the tiny human. His laugh held nothing so much as venomous hate.

"My haraanis have spotted him high in the mountains behind us. They will take you there, and you will give him to the Lamechites who are following him."

"Betray him?" Chay was shocked to find out Hod really was in the mountains. "He is my brother!"

"And what difference does that make? Does a dog refuse to fight and kill another dog just because they are brothers? Nature tells us to fight for our survival. I give you the chance to live. Who will live—you or your brother?"

In the heat and glare of Kron's eyes, Chay's brain became clouded. He couldn't think clearly or reason through the questions he was being asked.

"I—I—I d—don't know."

"Throw him in a cell," the giant roared. "I give you one day to decide, and then you will be my feast."

Chay could not even make his legs work, so Kodi and the other nephil dragged him out of the chamber. By the time they reached the cell, he was almost unconscious, but after tossing the prisoner on the hard floor, Kodi let the other guard leave without him, and then came back to the cell.

"Chay," he whispered. "I'll be back with some water."

Kodi returned with water and started to give Chay a drink. Before he could, the other guard returned and stuck his head into the cell. "Kodi! What are you doing?"

The young nephil jumped to his feet and threw the water in Chay's face before hurrying out of the cell and closing the door. "I was making sure that Sethian was still alive. Kron wouldn't like it if he died before he found his brother."

Lying in the puddle on the floor of the cell, Chay heard Kodi's words and knew the nephil would have liked to help.

Chay moaned and turned over onto his stomach. He rubbed some of the water on his face and licked it off his fingers before pushing himself up to his hands and knees. The cell was pitch black, dark as only a cave can be when all sources of light are far away.

Chay moved carefully until he found a rock wall to lean against. The rank smell of human waste proved that this cell was well used.

"Do you have food?" The faint voice came from the other side of the cell.

Chay was relieved to know he had company. "No, I have nothing. Don't they feed you?"

"Not much, mostly meat, which I don't—." The voice was overtaken by a fit of coughing.

"You mean you don't eat meat? You must be Sethian. What are you doing here?"

His cellmate coughed at least half a minute before answering. "I'm a hostage and a Sethian. Are you Sethian too?"

Reassured by the kindness and weakness of the voice, Chay introduced himself to the voice across the cell. "I am Chay, son of Elim, son of Jared. I was captured when the nephilim attacked my home in Garth. Who are you?"

"I am Mathu. We are Kenanites, descendants of the grandson of Seth. Our family grew so numerous that a hundred years ago many migrated to Havilah to mine the gold and precious stones. When the nephilim began to organize and exert control over the earth, they cast their eyes on us and our treasure. We were helpless."

"Did they destroy your people?"

"No, they enslaved us and made us work for them. They take our gold and give us nothing. We barely live off what we can grow in our gardens."

Remembering the ugly land and pitiful hovels he had seen on his journey, Chay shivered to think that this could be the lot of his family someday, now that the nephilim had found them.

"Why are you a hostage?"

"I have a beautiful sister, more lovely than any human woman since Eve." Mathu stopped speaking to cough some more. "Her name is Mehri. The Dark Watcher Azazel, father of Kron, desires her for himself. My family has hidden her where he cannot find her."

"I thought the Dark Watchers only took Cainite women."

"Yes, but my sister's beauty drives Azazel mad. Many of my family have died rather than give her up while I, the youngest son, am held until she goes to the Watcher. I would gladly die to save her."

Chay fell silent. Here was the best example of family love, yet he had been tempted to give up his brother.

I should love Hod as much as this man loves his sister. Am I a coward or a man with no honor?

"Why does Kron keep *you* alive?" Mathu asked.

"My brother. He wants my younger brother—he wants to kill him because of some prophecy. I don't know where my brother is, but Kron thinks I can find him. I have one day to decide to go after my brother or be eaten."

Mathu coughed and cleared his throat, but said nothing. Chay waited, expecting a response, and finally spoke. "What do you think I should do?"

"He is your brother. Do you have a choice?"

"No, maybe I don't. I can't really turn him over to Kron, but I can *say* I will do it to save my own life. I have no idea where he is. I could spend weeks looking for him and never find him."

"You'll have nephilim with you." Mathu's voice sounded tired and weak. "What will you do if you do find him? They will take him to Kron."

Chay paused before answering and ran his hand over his face. "Of course, I would never intentionally harm him."

Throughout the time in the cell, Chay alternated between thinking about how he could get out of this prison alive and talking ideas over with his new friend. Eventually a plan took shape, one he hoped would help him and Mathu escape the cell and Kron. He shared it just before a nephil he did not recognize came for him.

"Mathu, I am going to tell Kron that you have revealed that your sister is with Enoch and that my brother is going there too. I will ask him to let us both go find them for him. I will ask if a young nephil I met coming here can go with us."

His friend was silent a while, and Chay feared he disapproved of the lying involved in his plan. Then he heard Mathu sliding slowly across the floor.

"The nephil who wanted to give you water?"

"Yes. I got to know him on the way here. I think I can trust him, or at least get him to help us. We would probably have other nephilim with us, but we can deal with them when the time comes."

"Do you really think it will work," Mathu whispered. "I'll try anything to get out of here."

"Let me at least try. If he doesn't believe me, we won't be any worse off."

Before they could say more, the door opened and Chay was dragged off. Back through the long, dark halls, they marched to Kron's chamber where the king sat in the same place, looking as if he had never moved.

"Sethian! Have you decided?" The voice beat down on the prisoner, and for a moment Chay doubted that he had the courage he needed to lie to Kron.

He looked up at the monstrous nephil, this being who held the people of the earth in his fist, and knew he would defy him if he could. Kron leaned forward to better hear Chay's answer. His neck was encircled with rectangular gold plates hooked together with gold rings.

Chay clenched his fists and hardened his jaw. His dark brown eyes glinted with determination to make his lie convincing.

"I will, but I need to take Mathu, son of Dolian, with me. I know my brother is going to find Enoch, and Mathu has told me he took his sister to Enoch. If he is with me, we can bring them both to you."

Kron's eyes and burned down on his prisoner. "He will not turn in his sister. He cannot be turned."

Chay shook his head and made his voice as hard-hearted as possible. "He will only know I intend to find my brother."

"And you will give me your brother? Even if you know he will die?" Kron studied Chay's face, trying to read his innermost thoughts.

"I disowned him when he left me to the Lamechites! He ruined my family! I don't want him to die, but I won't die for him."

The king stared at Chay before hissing a final warning. "If you are lying to me, your death will be unbearable. I'll roast you on a spit—alive."

"I know the cost of crossing you. You can believe me." Chay shivered as he imagined the horror of burning slowly to death. No matter what happened, if he ever escaped, he could never allow himself to fall back into Kron's hands.

Kron grunted his satisfaction, straightened up, and beckoned for one of his men. He meant to whisper, but Hod had no trouble overhearing him.

"If I can get the Sethian girl for Azazel, he will be pleased. It's worth the try. I still have Lamechites and Hartagga after the fire-hair too. I will send this one and the other one in the cell on haraanis. With all these looking for this Hod, surely one will find him."

"Who do you want to send with them as a guard, master?" the other one asked.

"Hmmm, that is a problem. No nephil is light enough to be carried by the birds."

"How about Kodi?" Chay interrupted, even though he knew the king was not talking to him.

A frown shot across Kron's forehead. Eyebrows went up, then down. "Silence, human!" Then he looked at his lieutenant.

"Why didn't you think of Kodi? He's the only one light enough. He's ridden haraanis before, hasn't he?"

"Sorry, sir. I'd forgotten about Kodi."

"Well—what are you waiting for? Go get him!" Kron's roar sent the nephil running. "And pick two good Lamechites to go with them."

Mathu was dragged from his cell, fed bread, and generally well-treated after Kron agreed to let him go with Chay. The two Sethians nodded at each other in the semi-darkness before being dragged through long, dark tunnels leading from the northern fortress side of the mountain to the southern side, where they emerged onto a wide, flat area high on the peak.

From this point Chay could see the desert to the south and the ridges beyond it.

The mountains are much less forbidding here than on Kron's side, and there is no sign of nephilim activity. Maybe we will have a chance to get away.

When a deep coughing reminded Chay of Mathu, he turned to study him for the first time in the daylight. The young miner was pale and slim with a concave chest. His eyes seemed too large for his thin face. Chay thought Mathu looked as if he did not have long to live, and he hoped fresh air and sunshine, plus decent food, would revive him.

They had only a few minutes to talk before they were joined by the rest of their squad.

"Mathu, Kron is letting you go with us, but he thinks I am tricking you into helping me find your sister. Don't let any of the nephilim or Lamechites know our plan."

"All right," Mathu stopped to cough for a few seconds. "What are we doing up here?"

"We'll be flying on haraanis who know where my brother was last seen. I'm nervous about heights, but this is the only hope to get out of the tower, and it looks shorter than the way I came in. We'll have to escape when they let their guard down—if they do."

Kodi and two Lamechites came out onto the flat area, causing the two Sethians to fall silent. Mathu kept his eyes on the ground while Chay looked confidently at the Lamechites before smiling at Kodi. "Someone is going to have to teach us how to stay on these birds."

Kodi pointed to the haraani he was about to mount. "See this leather band around its middle. You sit on it and grip it with your knees as tight as you can. Then you hold the reins attached to this strap around its head. You can guide them by pulling on the right or left, but haraanis have a mind of their own. It's hard to make them go where they don't want to."

"What if I can't hold on?" Chay asked.

One of the Lamechites who was close enough to overhear cackled and slapped the nephil on the back. "Then he'll fall off and end up smashed on the rocks below, right, Kodi?"

Kodi didn't laugh at the little man's joke. Instead, he gave Chay an encouraging smile. "I know you're afraid of heights, but you can do it. Just hang on tight."

Chay hesitated a moment and studied the bird he was supposed to ride. Like the rest of the haraanis, it was sitting upright on the rim of a severe drop off. Since it was nearly as tall as he was, Chay wondered how he would get on it, but when he touched the bird, it bent low and spread its wings.

Kodi mounted on the largest of the haraanis. "Remember, Chay, put your legs around him and press your knees into his sides. He'll know you are secure."

Watching how Kodi sat his bird, Chay gripped the leather band, threw his right leg over the feathery back, and grabbed the reins. The bird shifted its weight from foot to foot, and then turned its head to look back at its rider with a black assessing eye.

"Come on, Mathu, mount your haraani," Chay said to his new friend, who was standing back watching the instructions and coughing from time to time. "You can't be more scared than I am, but it's better than being in a cell."

Mathu nervously climbed on his bird, which immediately turned back and pecked him. "Hey! That hurt!"

Kodi looked over at Mathu for the first time, and frowned. He studied this pale Sethian with dark circles under his eyes as if trying to make a judgment about him. He motioned toward Mathu's haraani.

"You have to show him you have confidence. Now watch how I take off and copy me."

The two young men watched as Kodi nudged his haraani with his knees. The bird stepped off the rim and immediately plummeted downward under the weight he bore. They leaned forward to peek over the rim and see if the nephil would survive this flight. Just then the haraani lifted its wings, brought them back down, and pushed itself and its passenger up into the air.

Relieved to see Kodi intact, Chay copied the nephil and soon his bird was also plunging toward the ground and then lifting up in the air. Once their mounts had regained altitude, Kodi and Chay circled the takeoff area. While Mathu struggled with his mount, the Lamechite who had not spoken took off on his haraani, which had an easier time due to the man's slight weight.

"You're next, Sethian," Kodi called down to Mathu, who tried to do what he had seen the others do.

Before he even tried to make his mount move forward, his bird bucked him off and then strutted arrogantly around the takeoff area. The Lamechite who had laughed at Chay caught the reins and brought the haraani back to Mathu.

"Pray to your god," the man said with a sneer. "You'll be flying without a bird before long."

The Lamechite roughly helped Mathu back on the bird and laughed at the clumsy hold he had on the reins. Mathu closed his eyes as the Lamechite prodded the haraani off the rim. The bird stepped off, lost altitude, and then began to climb up toward the others.

"Why are we taking that human?" Kodi shouted to Chay when their birds circled close.

"He has a sister Kron wants. I think he can help us. With you and the Lamechites to overpower them, we can take my brother and the girl back to the king. That should make him happy."

Chay saw Kodi gave him a suspicious look, as if he doubted his willingness to turn his brother over to Kron.

I must be careful not to give away my plan to this nephil until I can find a way to save Hod, Mathu, and myself. I may have made friends with this fellow, but I must never forget what he is.

The last of the group to take off was the jeering Lamechite, who Chay worried would give them trouble before the venture was over. His whole demeanor exuded arrogance and disdain for Sethians. They watched as he confidently hopped on his bird—one almost as big as Kodi's mount—and punched it toward the edge.

The haraani dropped right off, as the others had, and then they saw the Lamechite jerking at the reins. The bird veered sharply upward, rising almost straight toward the sun.

As they watched, they first heard a horrified scream and then saw the man falling head over heels with arms and legs flailing until he hit the ground below.

"How do *you* like flying?" Mathu called after him right before he hit the ground below.

Chay guessed the Lamechite had taunted Mathu. He looked one last time at the body so far below, shuddered, and then put it out of his mind. He did not plan to fall off his haraani. Kodi, who had been watching the man's fall, shook his head and shouted to Chay.

"That man was riding Keoaw, the most strong-willed of the haraanis. That bird doesn't like being controlled. Someday I'll train him, and he'll make a good mount."

The birds headed southeast and after some time began a circling search of the southern side of the mountains. It seemed their keen eyes were trying to find Hod or the Lamechites who were following him.

As he tried to see what he could detect below, Chay leaned to the side and looked down at the mountain peaks. Immediately, he shut his eyes and clutched at his haraani's neck.

"Why do I always find myself up high?" he groaned as his bird squawked a protest. Chay tried to loosen his hold.

Instead of looking down, he turned his eyes to the right where Kodi was riding his haraani with the ease and enjoyment of a child on a goat. His nephil friend was grinning from ear to ear and waving one hand in the air.

"I'm glad you're having fun!" Chay yelled.

"I am. Isn't this great?"

By this time Mathu had caught up with them, and it struck Chay that he was beginning to look more comfortable on his bird than Chay was.

It's time to get over this childish fear of heights. You've been on a behemoth, on the side of a mountain, and now many cubits off the ground on a bird. Live for the moment and have fun. Who knows if you'll even be around tomorrow?

◁10▷

The Deceiver

NOT ANOTHER CAVE?" HOD GROANED WHEN HE SAW THE cavern Pazel found. It had a low, wide opening and did not seem so much a cave as a deep, horizontal cleft in the rocks. No passages opened up to other caves beyond.

Ignoring his friend's protest, Pazel laughed and pushed Hod into a space barely high enough for a Sethian to stand up straight. "Just this last one, I promise—at least for now—and then we should be traveling in the open until we find your uncle."

"Do you think the Lamechites are on our trail?" Hod asked.

"If they aren't, they will be. It is probable that one of those haraanis saw us, and they'll get word to Kron. Once the Lamechites get a scent, they never give up. And with Hartagga helping them, they'll find us for sure."

Hod bumped his head on the rocky ceiling and stooped a little as they moved farther back into the cavern. "Will we be safe enough in here?"

"I think so. You must stay far back in the cavern where you can't be seen from above. There's more room against the back wall. The ceiling is higher, at least."

As they had not stopped to eat on the way, only satisfying their hunger by chewing on figs, Hod was hoping Pazel would suggest they eat. But he was disappointed in that hope.

"I need to leave right now if I am going to find some water and be back before dark," Pazel said. "You rest. I'll get more food too. When I get back, I will make us something to eat."

"How long will you be gone?"

"An hour at the most. Remember that Hartagga can pick up your scent from the air. Stay in the back of the cavern!"

Hod waved Pazel off with a grin. "Wake me when dinner is ready—and be careful."

He found a comfortably smooth place on the stone floor and stretched out. After two days of traveling, much of it running, his body craved rest, so he leaned back, put his folded hands behind his head, and prepared for a good doze.

When a low moaning sound woke Hod from his nap, he thought it might be Pazel, injured and trying to get back to the cave. He sat up and looked quickly toward the entrance of the cave. Then, realizing the sound was coming from behind him, he whirled around and grabbed his sword. In the dim light he saw no one—nothing at all.

Hod did not let lack of light stop him. On his hands and knees, slowly and determined to make no sound, he crawled toward the back wall of the cavern. The moaning grew louder, and now he thought he could make out words.

"Oh, won't someone help me? Oh, me, what can I do? So alone! So alone."

Hod froze. Someone was nearby, someone in need of help. He listened intently before moving again. This time his knee dislodged a loose rock and sent it skittering across the stone floor.

"I hear you. Oh, oh, I know you're there. Friend, kind friend, please help me." The voice was soft and deep and very weak.

Convinced that someone was trapped in the cave, desperately in need of help, Hod moved faster but soon discovered he was at the end of the shallow cavern. The floor ended at a wall that ran up to a ceiling at least an arm's length above his head. He saw he was right in his first assumption that the cave ended here. But where was the pitiful voice coming from? It seemed to be behind the wall, yet the rock should block all sound.

Whatever the situation, someone needed help. He would find out!

Hod worked his way along the wall with his ear close to the rock. The voice grew louder and louder until he was sure it was directly on the other side. He thought it might be coming through some small opening or window in the seemingly solid stone.

"Who's there? Can you hear me?" he called.

"Yessss," the voice hissed, a dying sound, Hod thought. "I hear you. Are you going to help me? I am so alone."

"I'm coming. Hang on!"

Finding no opening along the floor, Hod looked higher up the wall. "There must be some way through this rock," he muttered.

He stood and felt along the upper wall. And then he found an irregularity in the rock, an alcove or indentation about six handsbreadths square and one handbreadth above his head. He reached into the alcove and found that it was filled with loose stones.

Hod began shoveling the rocks out onto the cave floor until he had opened a window into another cave. He hefted himself up onto the alcove and began to wriggle into the hole. It was a tight fit, but he was able to stick his head and shoulders into what seemed to be a spacious room.

The smell was acrid and disgusting, like no cave odor he had ever encountered. Hod wrinkled his nose and thought of a rotting animal carcass he had once accidentally stepped on in the woods.

"Please help me," the voice said, and Hod looked into the gloomy cave for a body to match the voice.

He expected complete darkness, but there was a diffused light—as if it were passing through a linen cloth—coming down in one narrow shaft from some kind of opening in the rocks above. Hod's eyes followed the beam from the ceiling to a deep den many cubits below the spot where his head and shoulders protruded from the wall.

His head instinctively recoiled when he saw—halfway lighted by the shaft—a black or dark green head the size of a boar. The head was watching him from topaz eyes while licking dry lips with a long, thin forked tongue.

"You came," the voice sighed. "What a kind young man you must be. Will you come down and talk to me?"

Hod jumped back from the hole when the giant snake head darted up at him. But he was still worried about the old man who had called to him, so he crawled back and, with only his head protruding from the hole, tried to scan the depths of this immense pit for the hapless soul who must be trapped with this serpent.

"Where are you?" he called. "I can't see around this snake. Have you been bitten?"

The head moved back and forth on a level with Hod, its tongue flicking in and out. Hod was sure it was smiling at him.

"No one here but me. So lonely, so lonely."

When he saw the words were coming from the serpent, Hod jerked back so quickly that he banged his head on the rocks above him. He jumped out of the hole and flattened his body against the cavern's back wall, his heart beating hard against his ribs.

Animals don't talk. At least no animal I've ever known. And then he remembered the stories his father had told him of the old serpent in the Garden. He had talked and walked on legs too before he was cursed. His father had said this serpent was rumored to be still alive in the mountains somewhere.

I've found him, Hod thought, and his heart pounded faster.

"Come back. Please come back," the deep, sonorous voice pleaded. "I'm so lonely. At least talk to me and tell me what is going on in the world. I've been here for centuries, all alone."

Slowly Hod inched his face up to the opening and peeked into the serpent's den. The head was not in sight, so he hitched himself onto the ledge and squirmed his torso halfway in. By the shaft of light, he saw that the serpent's head was reclining on its body, a body consisting of coil after coil of blue-green tubes covered with overlapping scales.

"Who are you?" Hod tried to sound braver than he felt.

"Dracon. The first man called me Dracon, but no one uses my name anymore. Who are you?"

Seeing that the serpent had relaxed and was not threatening him, Hod decided it would do no harm to tell about himself. "I am called Hod, descendant of Seth."

A hissing and then a rustling as of scales sliding on stone caused that old prickle along Hod's spine. If this was that serpent, he could be an enemy.

"I never met Seth although I once was a good friend of his father and mother. You could say I was their best friend." Dracon's voice became more chatty and companionable.

Hod leaned in a little further. "I know who you are. You're the serpent from the Garden, aren't you?"

"Yesss. So you've heard of me.

"You are part of the story of our beginning," Hod explained. "Every Sethian child learns about you."

Dracon smacked his lips. "How nice to be remembered. I've always loved Sethians. It's been years since I've tast . . . that is, talked to one of your tribe."

The voice began to remind Hod of a friendly elder relative spending time with a child. He remembered those days at Elim's knee when he listened to the old stories.

"Do they prosper, the line of Seth?"

Hod cast off his earlier foreboding. The warmth of the voice comforted this young man who missed his family.

"The Elimite family has lived away from most of the Sethians all my life, so I can't tell you much. I know the Elimites are facing dangerous times."

"Dangerous times?" Dracon purred. "So these are dangerous times for you? Is that why are you here in the Eden Mountains?"

"Yes, I suppose so. I'm looking for a relative. Actually you might be able to help me since you live here."

"Perhapssss, but I don't get out any more. I only know what I learn from visitors, and I don't have many of those. What is your question?"

Even while doubting the wisdom of trusting the serpent, Hod plunged into his purpose for leaving home.

"The nephilim want to kill me. I need to find my father's brother Enoch so he can help me. I was told he lives in these mountains. Do you know where he is?"

Dracon's head rose and bobbed slowly up and down. "I have talked with that one. He visited me once many years ago. Why do you want him? He is a very stubborn man who cannot be reasoned with. I do not think you will like him."

"Nevertheless, I must find him."

"He said he lives above the great gushing spring, the gateway to the deep, the source of the mother river. I wish I could take you, but, you see, I have outgrown the opening—where you are now."

Hod glanced up at the place in the cave ceiling where the diffused light was coming from. "Is that hole above not big enough for you?"

"Alas, no," Dracon sighed. "But I am glad to have it, for it gives me light—and sometimes food."

"Food?"

Dracon's chuckle echoed and reechoed through the cave. "My friends the haraanis drop little gifts for me from time to time. Tasty little tidbits, I must say. Here comes one now! Look up!"

Instinctively obeying, Hod looked toward the ceiling and saw a bulge made of sticks and straw drooping through the hole. He realized that this material was the reason the light was obscured as it entered the den.

The bulge slowly broke open and a light brown object—looking much like an ostrich egg but as large as a pig—dropped straight down toward Dracon, who deftly moved his wide open mouth to catch it. Hod realized that the bulge was the underneath side of one of the huge nests he had seen on a high place above the cavern.

"Mmmm! I never get tired of haraani eggs, especially the ones about to hatch. Do you like eggs, little Sethian?"

Hod had recoiled at the sight of Dracon swallowing the egg, which he could have sworn was in the process of hatching. The thought of eating an animal made his stomach turn.

"No, we Sethians do not eat meat."

"I know," the serpent's voice held a note of contempt mixed with pity. "Because He did not say you could. I've heard that myth before. You should understand that is a complete misunderstanding of His intent. I was there, so I know."

"I've never eaten animals. Why would I want to?" Hod argued.

Dracon's body slithered back and forth on itself while his head drew ever closer to Hod's face. The unblinking topaz eyes, which he now saw had vertical opaque black pupils, seemed to widen as they concentrated on the human.

"He knew that the first men were too protected by their time in the Garden to digest the rich, succulent meat of animals. He never intended for you people to make it a law."

Hod was unconvinced. "How do you know?"

"Did He say, 'Don't eat animals'? No! Didn't He kill one of the innocent animals in the Garden to make clothes for the man and woman? It was His plan for one animal to kill and eat the other, from small to large, from dumb to intelligent, all the way up to the wisest ever created."

"Man?"

Dracon chuckled again and weaved back and forth, never taking his eyes off Hod. "How typical of a human to think so. Your ancestors thought they were the pinnacle of creation too, but if it had not been for me, they wouldn't have known wrong from right."

Hod felt so ignorant in the face of this creature's age-old wisdom. It was obvious the serpent meant himself as the one who was superior to mankind, and he might be right for all Hod knew. Maybe humans did think too well of themselves. He searched for a way to refute Dracon's ideas.

"But we have a soul," he finally said, thinking this would put an end to the creature's claim of superiority.

"Why would I want one if it means eternal punishment?" If the serpent had eyelids, he would surely have winked at Hod, but he could only stick his long tongue straight our before flicking it over his face and back into his mouth.

Hod could not think of an answer at the moment. The belief that he had a soul was bedrock of his faith, taught to him by his mother from early childhood. He could not imagine the emptiness of life without it. But this was the first time he had ever heard it suggested that the soul was eternal.

"Next you'll be bragging that you are made in His image, I suppose." Now Dracon's voice was sly and insinuating and aimed at cutting Hod's beliefs out from under him.

"You're right! I am and you're not."

"And what good has it done you? Better to be like me—or as I once was before He cursed me and made me crawl like a worm."

Dracon's voice was growing in strength and volume. Louder and louder, it expanded until it filled the room and battered Hod's ears. He could not imagine how he had thought he sounded like a sick old man.

"I was not created in His image, yet I was the most beautiful animal in the Garden."

Dracon's head was inching closer and closer, and becoming larger and larger until Hod was frozen by its golden eyes.

"And then in one day He cut me down and cast me out. And why? All because of a woman, an afterthought! Don't trust Him. Someday He'll turn on you too."

"But you disobeyed Him!"

"Who says so?" Dracon hissed. "Who says He can tell me what to do? I do what I want to do!"

"But Elohim—."

The serpent's head flattened into a hood as he interrupted with a sizzling hiss. Steam seemed to rise with the creature's breath.

"Don't say that name! He ruined my life! Trust me! Listen to me! I am the wisest of the wise. I can tell you the secret of eternal life."

Stunned by the brazen audacity, Hod could only whisper. "Secret?"

"Humans long for it. They so fear death and extinction."

Dracon moved closer, as if sharing a confidence. Everything about him exuded sibilant menace.

"There is a tree. . . ."

Caught like a mouse in the eyes of the serpent, Hod was unable to move.

"Do you want to become immortal?"

Without warning, the giant head darted at him. Fangs like daggers came at his chest, but he could do nothing, not even call on Elohim. Just as the fangs were about to strike, a strong arm from behind jerked Hod back.

He heard Dracon's head smash into the empty opening and fall back into his den. Hod turned and, blinking his eyes as if waking from a dream, looked into Pazel's puzzled face.

"What was the matter with you? I called and called, but you didn't seem to hear me. Sorry for pulling you back so quickly. Are you all right?"

Shaking with relief, Hod leaned against the rock wall and then slid down to the floor, his head on the knees drawn up before him. Sweat streamed from his head and down his back as if he had been laboring in a field. His mind was just beginning to come to grips with how close he had come to death.

"You're in bad shape. What did you see in that hole?" Pazel asked. He looked up at the opening, which was well above his head.

Hod grabbed his hand. "Don't climb up there! Don't look! It's something evil!"

Hod stood to his feet and began shoving the larger rocks back into the hole. It came to him that someone before him had also tried to block the entrance to the serpent's den. When he had closed Dracon away from reaching them, Hod pulled Pazel farther down the cavern.

"I'm not going to tell you what I saw there, but I think it's the source of the voice you have heard in the caves. You must believe me when I say it was evil in its oldest and most deceptive form. Promise me that if you have to come back to this place, you'll never remove these stones. Evil lives there and must stay there."

Pazel was silent in the darkness as he considered Hod's words.

"I'm curious, but if it is this bad, I will promise not to ever open that hole, unless I have no choice. Now, I'm hungry. Let's make us some supper."

◁11▷

Reunion

FOR FOUR DAYS HOD AND PAZEL SCALED STEEP PEAKS, scrambled over tumbled boulders, and enjoyed an occasional mountain meadow, but they had not yet found any sign of Enoch. They had probed the heights of the summits; indeed, today Hod stood on a protruding rock from which he could observe the whole world as a great panorama.

Looking to the south, he saw the land he had crossed only a week earlier. Far to the east he knew was the land of Nod, home of the Cainites, a land distant from the Eden Mountains. Pazel told him the hills of

164

Nod were filled with the iron ore from which the Cain-ites created weapons and tools. To the west was the wild land of Havilah, known for its riches and home to both Sethian and Cainite pioneers.

And then to the north—he had left that cruel land until last—Atlantia, the chosen home of the nephilim, stretched like a wound upon the earth. Pazel told him that the voracious appetites of the giants devoured all plants and animals within their grasp.

"They tear everything down and never replant," Pazel explained. "They eat every animal they find, but never breed more. That's why they are always foraging and raiding. They have decimated the behemoth herds."

There was very little green to the north. Looked down on from the mountain heights, the land was a mixture of brown and black blots and blotches inter-spersed with plumes of smoke.

Hod hoped his mission would not take him to this degraded country that lay on the back side of the moun-tains. He had no desire to see this ruin up close or to get near enough to the nephilim for them to lay hands on him.

He left the height and followed his companion, who was searching for a safe place to spend the night. The sun was close to setting behind the western peaks when Pazel declared that he had found a protected grassy spot. They climbed a narrow defile going up a small slope and entered a circular, rock-surrounded nook.

"So far the Lamechites have not caught up with us," Pazel said. "But I know they are out there. They will have to climb this slope to reach us. I'll put some loose stones in their way. When they slip on them, the rocks will roll down the hill and make a great deal of noise. We'll have time to prepare."

"How do you know they're still following?"

"I told you they never give up. Did you notice the haraanis are still around?"

"Yes, I did. I think I saw one of their nests in that last cave—the one I won't talk about," Hod added when he saw that his companion was about to ask more about what he had seen in the serpent's cavern.

Pazel shrugged. "They can be nasty, those birds. They're as big as a horse. I'm thankful the nephilim are too heavy to ride them, but sometimes their allies the Lamechites fly on them."

"Do you think they've seen us?"

"Maybe, but I don't know. If they want to find us, they will. They can see a rabbit from high in the sky. I think they were just looking for the Lamechites. They might have a message for them from Kron."

Once they were sure no enemy was near, Hod and Pazel settled down on the grassy patch, lying on their backs and staring up at the stars spread across the sky like the jewels he had seen in the waterfall cave.

Since emerging from the dark passage and climbing so high in the mountains, Hod had learned how different the world could be from his old home. So high up, they were above the nightly mist that rose from the ground. Here the air was clear and drier, although it still had a refreshing coolness.

Despite the possible dangers, each young man eventually drifted off to sleep.

Several hours later the sun had just emerged from the distant eastern horizon and begun to wake the sleeping travelers when a sliding and scrambling noise forced all drowsiness away and sent them to their feet. Pazel's plan had worked. Somewhere down the small slope something was approaching their grassy spot.

"It's them," Pazel whispered, motioning Hod to move behind some higher boulders. "Have your sword ready. We can defeat the two Lamechites if Hartagga isn't with them."

Together they backed up to a large stone, drew their swords, and watched the only spot an attacker could come from, the top of the slope they had climbed to reach their campsite. Once the crashing sounds had revealed their presence, the Lamechites must have given up any attempt at surprise.

Only a minute or two later the two armed Lamechites stood twenty paces from the young men. The rising sun behind them made black silhouettes of the enemy even as it shone directly into the eyes of Hod and Pazel.

When he saw their quarry temporarily blinded, the first of the two Lamechites ran straight at Hod, his crescent-shaped sword held aloft. Screaming curses as he ran, he did not waver from his target. Hod crouched slightly and hefted the sharp nephil blade, which he reckoned was stronger than the Lamechite sword. His eyes never left his assailant, and then when the man was almost to him, Hod stepped quickly aside and swung his weapon into his opponent's path.

The sword bit into the man's chest, stopping his progress. Blood dripped down his side, but the Lamechite did not fall. Instead, he turned on Hod, who had whirled around into an immediate defensive stance.

"Finally we meet, fire-hair. You've made me follow you many miserable days. I'm going to make you pay for what I've gone through!"

The defiance of the badly wounded man surprised Hod, yet he chose not to answer as he readied himself for the next move. The second Lamechite had stood back watching. Now he stepped forward to help his partner.

Pazel had moved close to support Hod, but when he saw that Hod was handling the first assailant, he circled around to head off the second and smaller enemy.

Balanced on the balls of his feet and ready to parry any attack, Hod watched every move his adversary made. After hesitating and seeming to weigh the power of his opponent, the Lamechite suddenly charged at Hod, evidently intending to use his smaller size to run up under Hod's sword and stab at his abdomen.

Instinctively, Hod swung his sword in a circle, knocked away the thrust with an upward motion, and then brought his weapon back down at his enemy. This blow cut into the Lamechite's neck as easily as if it were a sapling. The sharp nephil blade cut from shoulder to torso before Hod could halt its movement.

For a moment, he was frozen in horror at the sight of gushing blood and ripped flesh. It took the sound of his friend in combat with the other tracker to focus his mind. Pazel had evidently been keeping his opponent away from Hod.

Enraged, the Lamechite ran at Pazel, slashing wildly back and forth with his sickle-sword and forcing Pazel to leap out of his way. The Lamechite turned with him, still slashing, and the sharp curved blade sliced through the little salt seller's belly, which opened up like a melon.

Pazel fell back on the ground and instinctively reached for his torn stomach in an effort to hold in the protruding organs. The Lamechite, seeing that Pazel was mortally wounded, wheeled toward Hod and for the first time saw his slain cohort.

"You may have killed my cousin, fire-hair," the Lamechite snarled. "But you have not yet faced Niute."

The small man came at Hod the same way he had attacked Pazel, with his curved sword slashing a deadly arc. Hod knew sidestepping it would be impossible. Instead he raised his sword over his head and brought it straight down just as the curved sword neared him.

Iron rang against iron, but the Lamechite blade was no match for Hod's weapon. When the sword fell from the man's hand in two pieces of broken metal, Hod ran forward, his sword pointed straight at his body. The Lamechite began backing up, as fast as he could, and then, when he came to the top of the bank where Pazel had placed his trap, the man lost his footing and fell backwards.

Hod hurried forward in time to see the Lamechite roll over and over down the slope, try to get to his feet, and then fall back. Realizing the man had injured his leg, Hod watched until he was sure the Lamechite offered no threat.

Just at that moment, Hod heard the roar of an enraged monster, loud but not too close. He looked for the source and saw Hartagga on a nearby peak standing on hind legs, roaring, and swinging his arms toward Hod.

Knowing it would take Hartagga half an hour to go down the peak and then climb this summit to reach him, Hod ran to Pazel, who was holding his abdomen together with his hands while blood oozed through his fingers.

"Pazel! What can I do?" Hod's cry of anguish echoed back at him from distant peaks.

"The water," his friend whispered, and Hod ran to get the waterskin he had stashed with his pack.

Over the days since they had left the caves, Hod had tried to save the healing water, but occasionally, when he was very tired, he had taken a few sips for rejuvenation. There was still three-fourths of the fluid left. He ran back, cast no more than a glance at the dead Lamechite, and then knelt beside his friend.

"Help me push everything back inside," Pazel whispered when Hod started to give him a drink. "And then pour the water on my stomach."

Without speaking Hod gently pushed Pazel's intestines back into his abdomen before pouring the water generously up and down the wound. Afterward, he gave his friend several swallows. Having done all he could, he sat back on his heels and watched.

When Hod had been injured, he had not even thought of the bat bites while they healed. He had concerned himself with their next steps, with getting up and moving, and before he knew it, he was whole. Now he intended to see what would happen.

His friend lay prone on the ground with closed eyes and his hands over the wound. The bleeding stopped immediately. Then Pazel's groans ceased and he seemed at peace. As Hod tried to concentrate on the slashed skin, slowly, very slowly, the skin on either side of the wound began to seal, pull together, knit, and grow until nothing remained of the cut.

Awed by the sight before him, Hod reached a hand out to feel the like-new skin that had replaced the gaping wound. Pazel lay a while before sitting up, and then sat a little longer before standing and stretching.

"If I had not seen that and experienced it myself, I would say it was unbelievable," Hod said. "Do you feel well—well enough to walk? Hartagga will be after us soon."

Pazel sat and then stood up. "I thought I heard him. I hoped it was just my injury making me imagine things."

"No, I saw him on a peak just across that last chasm. He'll have to go down and come back up, but he's headed our way. That last Lamechite is still out there—and angry—but I think his leg is broken."

Pazel collected his sword and backpack before motioning with his head. "Let's get going then. We need to find someplace safe."

171

The two friends scrambled over the boulders rimming the grassy glen where they had spent the night. They checked the sun's position briefly to decide which direction was east and then moved that way as quickly as they could.

Hod's sandals were worn thin by the days of tredding rough stone, and his tunic had become ragged and thin in spots. He wondered when he would be able to replace these things or even have a day to rest his body.

Behind them they occasionally heard rocks shifting and rolling downhill as if set in motion by a heavy body. These sounds quickened their pace, causing them to rush forward with no clear idea of where they were heading. They tried not to follow the easiest path in hopes of finding a place to hide from the monster behind them.

"Down here," Pazel said and slipped into a wide crevice between two monolithic blocks of granite.

Hod followed without question. The crack in the rocks, no wider than Hod's shoulders, enlarged slightly once they were in. Before he had gone five paces, Hartagga's roar at the opening of the crevice made Hod hurry his steps. Hartagga would never fit in here, but he would be able to wait outside for them to come out, effectively trapping them in the crevice.

The further they went, the more Hod thought the crevice offered a good hiding place. It continued on into the rock and after a while was covered by a great slab of stone, which protected them in case Hartagga tried to reach them from above.

"Wait, Pazel, wait." Hod stopped and looked back. At the opening to the crevice, Hartagga's large black snout was trying to push its way in. He bellowed out his frustration as his long arm and sharp claws reached as far as they could.

"We can't go back out that way," he said when Pazel stopped at his call and looked back. "Do you think there could be another way out?"

"I don't know. This crevice shows no sign of closing up. We'll have to go on and see what is ahead."

Soon Hod realized that their steps were going downhill as if they were walking down a huge sloped rock. The slivers of sunlight coming through cracks between the top slab and the granite walls kept them from total darkness, yet it was still difficult to see where they were going. For balance Hod kept one hand on the wall to his left.

His toes gripped the bottoms of his worn sandals as he strained to maintain his footing. Suddenly Pazel cried out and fell backward, then went sliding down the slope before him. Hod stopped immediately for fear he would also fall.

"Pazel! Are you all right?" he called out although he could not see what had happened to his friend.

"I'm a little bruised but in one piece. It's a short fall."

The healthy sound of Pazel's voice allayed Hod's concerns, but he still was not sure what he should do now.

"What's down there?"

"It looks like a wider space way down in the rocks and with nothing overhead, so there's plenty of light. Try to come down without falling."

Hod pulled off his sandals, put them in his backpack, and then, hoping the tough soles of his feet would grip the granite better, attempted to work his way down the slope.

But halfway down, the incline was so steep that he could not prevent his body from falling back and sliding the short distance to the bottom. Hod was surprised when he landed on his feet right in front of Pazel.

"What now?" he said.

"Let's keep on going," his friend said. "There's nothing else we can do."

As they continued walking, they were relieved to find the crevice growing wider and wider until it eventually became a broad open area—almost like a corral—surrounded on three sides by walls of granite. The two friends walked side by side down this wide path, curious about where it would lead.

"Listen," Hod said. "How quiet it is!"

"Yes. Not even the sound of a scurrying lizard." Pazel pointed at a high summit not too far off. "There is the highest peak in the Eden range. We might have to climb it."

"Do you think Enoch is there?" Hod wondered how anyone could live in that highest of altitudes.

Pazel wrinkled his brow and thought a moment.

"No, but it will give us a good view. At least we can look down from that peak and see if there is someplace he could be."

"All right. Lead on."

They had just reached what looked like a gateway out of the stone corral but was really a narrow place where the circling rock walls almost came together, leaving enough space for a man to walk through.

A sudden loud flapping of multiple wings coming from the west—behind them—made both young men jump to the wall and flatten their backs against it. Approaching across the rock-rimmed clearing, they saw four of the huge haraanis, but now each bird held a rider, and the largest held what was surely a nephil.

"Draw your sword, Hod! You take the nephil and I'll hold the others off."

"Stand beside me." Hod's heart began pounding. "We'll face them together and take them as they come."

With fierce determination, the two stood ready to do battle, to die if they must. The great birds glided, wings wide-stretched, to landings in the clearing. Hod did not take his eyes from the rather short nephil who dismounted and stepped forward to face the drawn swords. He looked at Pazel a moment before turning to Hod. Blue eyes locked with the green eyes for a moment before the nephil glanced from Hod's red hair to his drawn sword.

"Fire-hair! You are Hod, son of Elim, are you not?"

"Who are you? What do you want of us?" Hod moved his sword forward.

When the nephil stared boldly at him, Hod's temper began to rise. He was ashamed of the desire to stick his sword in the giant's chest without further converse. Then the nephil held out his hands.

"I have no weapon drawn, Sethian. Neither has your brother."

"My brother?" The words had just left Hod's mouth when Chay came running toward him from behind one of the birds. Hod could only stare as his brother grabbed him in a warmer hug than he had ever given before.

"Hod! You're alive! I hoped you were all right."

Hod looked his brother up and down. He could not understand what Chay was doing here. "And I was sure you were killed by the Lamechites when I left you and the others."

"No, I was captured and taken to Kron."

Chay and Hod gripped hands while studying each other. Hod looked at his brother's companions again. What was Chay doing in the company of a nephil and a Lamechite?

"Who are these others, and why did you come here on those birds?" Hod looked at the nephil as he spoke.

"I have much to tell you," Chay said. "First, this is Kodi, a nephil I came to know on my journey to Kron's tower. And this is Mathu, who was my cellmate in the tower's prison. Kron sent us on the birds to find you and bring you to him. That Lamechite is a guard."

Chay's words stunned Hod. This change in his brother's situation was incomprehensible. Chay knew the nephilim wanted to kill him. Why would he agree to turn his brother over to the king of the nephilim? For the moment he was unable to speak.

Before Hod could answer, Pazel—who had stood silently behind him—grabbed his arm and turned him around.

"Let's get out of here. Your brother is working for Kron."

When Pazel began to run, Hod took off after him through the gateway and into a green meadow they found on the other side. He wanted to trust Chay, who was calling for him to stop, but he could not risk capture.

Soon he heard the rest of Chay's group running after them. Hod ignored his brother's calling voice and followed Pazel across the meadow and into a grove of slender white-barked trees. The two wove their way through the trees, darting and dodging in an effort to lose their pursuers.

The woods ended at the bank of a rivulet of clear water running over smooth pebbles. The stream was narrow enough to jump, but on the other side the bank was up against a sheer rock wall—there was nowhere to go.

Hod and Pazel stopped, looked up and down the stream and then back behind them. Chay and his companions were not far away. Escape was impossible.

Hod and Pazel had run with their swords in hand, so when they turned, they were ready to fight.

"Hod," Chay tried to catch his breath enough to talk. "Would you fight me? Your brother?"

"You come after me with a nephil and a Lamechite and say you are going to take me to Kron? And you're surprised I'm ready to fight you?"

As Hod spat the questions at his brother, bitterness ripped at his soul. The nephil, grim-faced now, drew his dagger and stepped to Chay's side. The Lamechite stood behind him, also with drawn weapon. Emotion crackled in the air between the two sides. No one knew how it would end. No one wanted to start anything.

And no one expected the voice that would solve the stalemate.

"Are you young people intending to kill each other —even though two of you are brothers, two are cousins, and two are childhood friends?"

Hod, Chay, Kodi, Pazel, Mathu, and the Lamechite all turned to look at the old man who stood on the narrow bank across the rivulet. He seemed to have appeared from the air.

"Who are you? And how do you know about us? I know this is my brother," Hod said to the old man. "But cousins? Childhood friends?"

The man's long white beard moved as he smiled at them all. He pointed at the nephil. "Why, young Kodi there is the son of Pazel's aunt, and Mathu played with Kodi when they were children. They loved each other then. And, Hod. You love your brother, don't you?"

To the surprise of those standing with him on the bank of the rivulet, Hod suddenly waded through the shallow water and stepped up on the bank beside the old man.

"Uncle Enoch! You are Enoch? I have been looking for you for days."

"Hod, Hod! I knew you were coming. Bring your friends and come into my home."

Enoch beckoned to the others with his right arm and held on to Hod with his left hand. Then he stopped and pointed at the Lamechite.

"Not you. You must stay outside."

"What? I won't let these Sethians out of my sight!"

The Lamechite began to wave his curved weapon at Enoch.

"We'll do what the old man says," Kodi said to the Lamechite.

"I'll keep an eye on our prisoners. You take the haraanis back to Kron and tell him where we are. You can come back and find us later."

"Yes, sir," the Lamechite grudgingly agreed, "but I don't like it!"

Enoch pointed at the little man again. "Tell Kron these are protected by Watchers. You cannot touch them while they are with me."

The Lamechite quickly looked around as if expecting a Watcher to appear, and then turned and ran back toward the rock corral.

Enoch and Hod stepped through a nearly invisible gap made by an overlap in what looked like a solid wall on the other side of the rivulet. When Enoch and Hod disappeared from sight, the others were mute with surprise but followed obediently.

Beyond the wall, a beautiful garden opened up before them. Hod thought this must be close to what the original Garden had been. Hearing the others splashing through the stream and up onto the bank, Hod leaned over and whispered in Enoch's ear. "Uncle, one of them is a nephil."

"I know," Enoch whispered back. "I'll tell you something you might not know. Elohim loves him too."

◁12▷

Enoch's Garden

K ODI AND MATHU STUDIED EACH OTHER SURREPTITIOUSLY AS they followed Hod into Enoch's garden. Chay paid no attention to them while he hurried to catch up with his brother and uncle, and Pazel was studying the area outside and around the gateway as if he knew he would later have to take them safely away from this place. So the nephil and his childhood friend fell into step side by side.

"The old man said we played together as children." Kodi squinted his eyes thoughtfully while he searched his memory. "I grew up in Havilah with my grand-father. You must have been one of the Sethian children. I do not remember you."

"I remember you quite clearly. In fact, I heard about you only a few weeks ago."

Kodi cocked his head to the side and looked down at the human next to him. "Who spoke of me?"

"An old Cainite named Juban. He said he is your grandfather." Mathu put his fist to his mouth and coughed deeply.

Memories that had been suppressed by the in-fluence of the nephilim flooded back into Kodi's mind. His grandfather's was the loving face he saw in his dreams. He remembered being held in arms that were strong and fatherly. And he remembered the day when two nephilim took him away.

Since that day no one had put an arm around him, hugged him, or even smiled at him. Nephilim had no use for such human emotions, and—as he was often re-minded in the kingdom of Kron—he was a nephil.

The day was forever burned in his memory. He had been playing at mining, digging in a hill and piling small gold nuggets in a bowl. His grandfather had been filling his sack with larger chunks of the yellow rocks. Kodi remembered that the mine they were working was not near any others, so he supposed no one else from the community had witnessed the scene.

Two extremely tall men dressed in animal skins cov-ered with iron plating had been seen around the com-munity that day. Everyone was talking about how the men poked their noses into every house and mine—pushing the people to increase their gold production—and asking questions.

That day the old man had insisted Kodi go with him out to the mine. When the two nephilim approached them, his grandfather had tried to make Kodi hide, but it was too late. He had been seen.

"Old man, this boy is a nephil," one of the giants had said. "It is not fitting that one of the gods should be digging in the earth like a slave."

"He's not a nephil," Juban had answered and reach-ed for his grandson, who could easily look down on the old man's head. "He is a Cainite and a grown young man—almost eighteen. If he were a nephil, he would be taller."

The nephilim had laughed at the old man. One of them knocked him down with a glancing blow from a fist while the other snatched Kodi from him. He still remembered the blood on his grandfather's head.

"Don't try to lie to us," the second one said. "Look at the breadth of his shoulders and the size of his arms. From his height he must be eight or nine years old. We know one of us when we see him."

The memory of his grandfather dragging himself to his knees and begging the two nephilim to leave Kodi with him was suddenly as fresh as yesterday.

"Please, please don't take him. He is all I have," the old man had said.

But the nephilim had only mocked him and pulled the ten-year-old away with them.

Now, five years later, Kodi swept away the tears in the corners of his eyes with the back of his hand before the Sethian noticed his weakness. The one thing the nephilim had tried to knock into him was to cleanse himself from all emotions, crush all feelings. The tears he had shed so frequently when first taken had been rewarded with blows. He had not cried in four years.

"I remember now. You were the boy who told the others to let me play with you." The warmth in his heart shamed Kodi. "You were nice to me when they thought I was not grown up enough."

Even though he was a nephil, Kodi had the emotions of any adolescent. He had been taken from his grandfather and thrown into a world where love and friendship did not exist, where loneliness became his normal life. Now that he had rediscovered his friend, he was tempted to let his stifled feelings come out.

He smiled tentatively at Mathu. "I'm glad to meet you again. Maybe someday I can go back to Havilah and see my grandfather. He is still living, isn't he?"

"He was two weeks ago when they took me hostage."

Kodi nodded. "I know about that. Kron wants your family to tell him where your sister is so he can give her to Azazel, the Watcher."

"The *Dark* Watcher. He wants to take my sister as he did your mother." Mathu's voice was flat and bitter.

"My mother? Are you saying Azazel is my father?" Kodi cried. "If so, then Kron is my brother."

Mathu regarded the friendly nephil with pity. It had never occurred to him that Kodi might not know his own parentage.

"Sorry to shock you. I thought you knew."

"No, Kron never told me, but then he doesn't talk about personal things. It explains why he has been good to me."

"'Good'? What do you mean by 'good'? He's a monster!"

Kodi's surprised expression when he looked at Mathu showed how unused he was to hearing anyone speak against the nephilim.

"Kron taught me to be a proper nephil. He said he wanted me to be his right arm. He took me in from the first and has taught me the way of the nephilim. I guess he helped me because I am his brother."

"Did he love you like a brother should?" Mathu asked.

Kodi tightened his lips and lifted his shoulders. "Kron does not understand love. It's not the way of the nephilim to talk of love, but he must care about me if I am his brother."

Mathu noted the lonely longing in Kodi's voice and reflected on how hard it would be to be under the influence of Kron every day. His own experience with the nephilim king had been terrifying. He couldn't imagine having Kron as a brother. Mathu looked at Kodi a moment and thought he saw some remnants of his childhood friend.

Unlike other nephilim Mathu had known, Kodi had an open, pleasant face. His eyes, which crinkled with good humor, were nothing like the fiery eyes of his brother.

They had fallen behind Enoch and his nephews, all of whom had left a little grove and entered a clearing. Enoch stopped and beckoned to the lingerers, so Mathu and Kodi hurried their steps until they caught up with the rest.

Enoch indicated a ring of smooth rocks resembling giant mushrooms. "Let us all sit here and talk."

Pazel, far behind Kodi and Mathu, also hurried to join the rest who were obediently taking seats on the mushroom rocks. No one spoke a word as they waited for their host's words, yet each one was full of questions.

Hod and Chay wondered if Enoch would settle the hostility between them, Pazel wondered if this nephil was really his kinsman, Mathu wondered how he belonged here, and Kodi wondered if this man who knew so much could help him find out what world he belonged to.

"I know you have questions for me," Enoch began. "But first, I want to ask Chay why he has come here with a nephil to take his brother back to Kron."

"I never intended to give Hod to Kron. I told Kron I would bring back my brother and Mathu's sister, but I just told him that so we could escape him."

Kodi jumped to his feet. "You used me to help you get away? I'll be in trouble with Kron if I don't return with Hod! I should have known not to trust a Sethian!"

Chay left his rock and walked over to put a hand on Kodi's arm and look up at his troubled face. "I hoped you would help us. I got to know you on our journey and thought you might let us go."

While Kodi loomed above Chay, one hand on the hilt of his dagger and his face angry and humiliated, Mathu spoke up from his seat beside the nephil.

"The Kodi I knew as a boy would not be the cause of anyone's death—or the capture of my sister."

Kodi looked quickly at Mathu. His brow creased and his lower lip trembled, but he said nothing. Everyone was aware there was a struggle inside him, and all sensed he was not a normal nephil.

"Mathu's right," Chay said. "You're not like Kron."

While the young men tried to convince Kodi to help them, Enoch sat by and watched. Hod, whose life and death were being debated, noticed that his uncle seemed fascinated by Kodi. The old man soaked in every look on the nephil's face.

Eventually Enoch, without moving from his seat, called to his guests. "Please take your seats. I understand what Chay has done. I regret that he had to lie, but that is not the problem. Elohim has sent Hod to me for a special mission. It is His plan for all of you to help Hod—yes, even you, Kodi."

The protest Kodi had begun died on his lips. Something about the old man held him as if he were frozen. In the last five years, he had discovered what it meant to be enthralled to a powerful personality.

He had never been able to say no to anything Kron asked of him. But Enoch's power was as light compared to darkness.

"Kodi? Will you help Hod do the will of Elohim?" Enoch asked.

Kodi knew this was the most important decision he had ever made. For once he was being given a choice instead of being commanded to obey. And this choice of following Kron and the Dark Watchers or Enoch and his god, Elohim, would change the course of his life.

All were silent while Kodi thought through this decision. "Kron will kill me for this. But I would rather be on your side, Enoch, especially if Chay, Mathu, and my grandfather are on that side."

"Good! The next question I will answer is from this young Cainite Pazel, although he has not spoken it. You wonder if Kodi is truly your cousin."

Pazel grinned, but shyly this time. "Well, I know nothing about my family, so I can't deny it. I remember that I had a grandfather once who left when I was very small."

Enoch walked over and put a hand on Pazel's shoulder as he explained the boy's history. "Your grandfather Juban fled Nod to keep Kodi from the nephilim. He sent word to your father to join him after your mother died, but your father was killed on the way."

"Yes, I remember my father's death, but how do you know all this?"

"The Watchers see everything. They are my friends and tell me much of what they have witnessed in the happenings of humanity. They told me about you, and that they had saved you. You and Kodi share the same grandfather. He is your cousin, and I am happy that you meet each other at last."

Mathu had been listening with intense interest to Enoch's words, but when the old man mentioned the Watchers, Mathu coughed and half raised a hand.

"Do you know anything about Dark Watchers?"

"Yes, the other Watchers revealed to me the end of this perversion caused by the Dark Watchers. I was sent to Azazel to tell him that a great destruction will come in the days of my great-grandson. I told him that all their children, the nephilim, will be wiped off the earth."

"Whew!" Hod said. "I'm sure he didn't like that."

"No, he was furious. He and his son Kron are doing all they can to prevent it from happening—or at least to be sure mankind perishes with them. Now I must tell Hod of his mission. I will talk with Hod and Mathu first. The rest of you wait here."

Wondering why he and this stranger he knew nothing of were chosen and why his uncle was leading them so far from the others, Hod followed through an almond grove and into an area where the ground seemed to fall away a feet paces ahead. Only the blue-gray sky was visible beyond that.

"Stop! There's a cliff ahead here," Enoch said. "Stay close to me and walk slowly."

Hod, obeying the command without question, slowed his steps to match Enoch's. He noticed that Mathu seemed unable to move at all and had stopped several paces back. Hod slowly shuffled toward the edge where he could now see a panorama of vertical cliffs running to the right and left in a circle as large as half of Garth. The three of them stood directly across from a steep-walled gap in the cliffs, a gap far off and just wide enough for the broad river that flowed through it.

The cliff they stood on was so high that the trees below looked like grass. The walls of the circular cliff sloped inward so that no one would be able to climb down them, even if they had not been so high from the ground. He realized the eastern end of the Eden Mountains were really a ring of sharp spires and steep precipices sheltering this huge green bowl.

"What a view!" Hod cried. "Come closer, Mathu, and look at this!"

The young Sethian miner forced himself to move up a little and then crept closer to the edge, even closer than Hod had gone, and peered at the green floor far below.

"What is that down there?"

Enoch smiled like someone dreaming of heaven as his eyes moved hungrily over the green circle below them. "It is the Garden. I wanted you to see what we have lost. You see the river that runs through the center? Its source is a spring welling up from the deep and gushing through an opening in the cliffs directly below us."

Hod and Mathu tried to look down but both were overcome with dizziness. While his companion quickly jumped back, Hod went down to his stomach. With his head hanging over, he could see straight down the sheer cliff to the immense burst of crystal clear water shooting from the rock wall about halfway down. Many cubits beneath the spring's outlet, the water formed a large lake, which opened at the eastern end into a river that cut through the Garden and flowed out the gap.

Seemingly unafraid of the proximity of the precipice, Enoch bent down toward Hod and pointed out into the green space.

"There in the middle of the Garden—do you see— the tall tree towering above the others. That is the Tree of Life."

Hod whistled. "If they had not sinned, they would have eaten that fruit and lived forever. Imagine not growing old! No death! But how wonderful it must have been to live there!"

"My family does not talk much about the Garden," Mathu said. "But I have heard of the Tree of Life. Could I ask you why you brought me here with Hod? I've been wondering."

"I brought you two first because you are righteous young men. It is to you first I must speak."

"Why do you call me righteous? I don't feel righteous." Hod looked down at the dusty ground beneath his sandals. "I mean, I try to be, but I know what's inside me."

Mathu's eyes watered as he looked at the old man. "I know what Hod means. I've had hateful thoughts about the nephilim. I've wanted to kill them. I'm sure I'm not righteous."

Enoch stood between the two young men and looked from one to the other. His voice was so down-to-earth and confidential that they almost forgot who he was. "You might find this hard to believe from all you've heard of me, but I'm not righteous in my heart either."

Mathu turned a quizzical look on Enoch. "But you just said we were righteous. And surely you are!"

While the two young men watched, Enoch raised his arms as if he were pronouncing a blessing over them.

"No human can be righteous. Our hearts are black, and each of us knows it. Hod, when Elohim called you, you believed and did what He said. When you believed Him and obeyed, that was all he expected of you. He knows your heart, you see."

"What about me? What have I done?" the other said.

"You believed Elohim would save your sister. You trusted Him and followed where He led. He knows you are ready to lay down your life for your sister."

Hod shivered and looked at Mathu to see what he would say but saw only a man looking down at his feet. "So He knows we are not righteous, but He . . . ."

"Counts you as righteous in His eyes because you obeyed His call," Enoch finished the sentence.

Hod thought about this puzzling idea a moment before deciding to accept it even if he could not understand it. "What is our mission?"

Enoch put a hand on their shoulders and led them away from the edge of the precipice. They walked with him around his garden home as he explained the plan.

"Mathu has a beautiful sister named Mehri," he began, and Mathu looked at the old man with questioning eyes. "She is hidden in a glade on the western slope of these mountains, hidden from Azazel, who desires her."

Mathu looked at Hod and nodded. Neither spoke as Enoch continued.

"What he does not know is that it is the plan of Elohim. He has revealed to me that Mehri will become the grandmother of one who will save mankind from the destruction of earth—many years from now. The nephilim will perish in this catastrophe, but the remnant of Adam will survive if Mehri is saved from Azazel.

"I know her daughter will marry my grandson Lamech. When he is an older man and she is a young virgin, she will marry Lamech and give birth to the last righteous man of the first world."

Now Hod whispered. "What does He want me to do?"

"You will go to the glade and bring Mehri first to me, and then to the home of Seth, where she will be safe. Our forefather still lives within sight of the Garden. No Dark Watcher dares come so close to the cherubim or the flaming sword."

For a minute Hod remembered what his father had said about the land just beyond the gate to the Garden. Adam, the first man, had stayed as close as he dared to the only home he had ever known. His children had been born there and one had died there.

As man's numbers increased, they had moved farther and farther from the Garden. But Adam had stayed there until his death the same year Hod was born. And Seth had stayed there, also, and was known for looking at the cherubim every day to remind himself of the consequences of sin.

"I will do what Elohim asks—I have been doing so for a fortnight, but I am sought by many enemies." Hod looked at the ground as he shook his head and then looked at his uncle. "The nephilim want to kill me. Everyone with me will be in danger."

"You were chosen to save the girl. After that, Kron will leave you alone, at least for a while."

"How can we safely travel the mountains?" Hod protested. "I was followed all the way here by a bearlike monster, Lamechites, and haraanis. Remiel saved me from death once—maybe twice. Will he or other Watchers protect me during this mission?"

These words brought an understanding smile from Enoch. He looked at the young men with eyes of compassion that seemed to wish he could save him from the troubles ahead.

"Not always. They will be watching, but it is not the will of Elohim for them to interfere in all the difficulties of our lives. He wants you to do this task yourself. You will have your friends to help you."

Hod sighed and thought of what he had already suffered since leaving home. Remiel had helped him, but at other times he had fought his own battles or been saved by others like his brothers and Pazel. And his brothers had died protecting him with no help from the Watchers.

"You are never on your own, my son. Elohim is with you. He is strengthening your arm for the battles ahead."

Enoch took Hod and Mathu to a bench beside a bubbling spring, gave them some bread and a cup to fill with water, and then went back to the rest of his visitors.

As soon as his uncle was gone, Hod turned to Mathu. "I haven't heard how you came to be here with Chay. Where did you meet him?"

This question brought a laugh from Mathu, who looked sideways at Hod and coughed a bit before speaking.

"You will find this hard to believe, I think. We met in Kron's prison."

"Prison?"

"You are like your brother. He had never heard of a prison either. Come to think of it, neither had I until I ended up there."

Mathu took the cup and knelt at the spring to fill it. "Are you thirsty?"

"Yes, very, but I didn't even think about it until now." Hod took the cup Mathu offered before going back to his question. "What is Kron's prison?"

"A prison is a place where bad people lock up their enemies. I was in a cell—a small room with no light and little food. I had been there two weeks when Chay was put in with me."

"So Chay ended up with the brother of the girl I was sent to save?" Hod asked the question as much to himself as to his companion.

"Yes—I guess it was a coincidence."

The coinciding of the threads of Elohim's cloth, Hod thought, but to Mathu said only, "Tell me how you came to be captured."

"After Remiel took Mehri and my mother to safety, Azazel came for her. He was furious when he learned she had gone while he had not been able to see what was happening."

Hod shivered at the thought of being pursued by a fallen celestial being. He hoped they would never turn their wrath on him. It was bad enough to have the nephilim after him, and they had no supernatural powers.

"What did you do?" Hod asked.

"We tried to go on with our lives, but the nephilim began to persecute my family, trying to force us to tell where Mehri was. Four of my brothers were tortured to death. When that didn't work, I was taken hostage to try to force us to give her up."

"Were you ever tempted to tell?"

Before answering, Mathu began to chuckle. "After so many have died for her, could I value my life above hers—or theirs? I truly didn't know where she was, but if I had, I would never tell."

Both young men fell silent as they sat side by side at the spring. Mathu was thinking of his beautiful sister and probably wondering if they would be able to bring her safely to Seth. Hod was thinking of his sister at home. He also thought about his brother and the division that had come between them lately. He hoped that this time with their uncle would bring peace between them.

When Enoch returned for Chay, Pazel, and Kodi, he showed them a smooth patch of grass where they all—even the old man—sat cross-legged in a close circle.

"I sense that you three are all lost or confused about Elohim." As Enoch spoke, he looked from one to the other and met each pair of eyes with serious concern. "I am here to answer any questions you may have."

Pazel, always quick to speak up, responded first. "I was saved by a Watcher many years ago, but since then I have had no word from Elohim. I have often thought that I was not good enough for Him because I am a Cainite."

"You are a son of Adam," Enoch said. "Your people have suffered from the sin of Cain, not because you are guilty of his crime but because his character flaw has been passed on by blood and example. However, you grew up away from your people, so you did not learn bad ways."

"So," Pazel's eyebrows rose as he spoke. "Being alone was good for me?"

"Of course. Elohim prepared you to save Hod, guide him to me, and help him with his mission."

The little Cainite grinned his merry grin and threw his shoulders up in a nonchalant shrug.

"Oh, well. I never minded being alone that much. And I had the whole mountains as my play yard."

Enoch squeezed Pazel's arm before turning to Chay. "What question do you have for me, nephew?"

"I don't see that I am part of some divine plan." Chay scowled and grabbed up a handful of grass from the ground in front of him. "Hod was the anointed one, but I'm the one who was captured, tied up, dragged up a mountain, and thrown in prison."

"You resent your younger brother, don't you?" Enoch asked in a gentle yet matter-of-fact voice.

"No! Oh, maybe I do. He was always the center of attention. Nobody noticed me."

Enoch sat directly across from Chay, yet he was close enough to lean forward and take his hand.

"I never thought of this before now, but I believe your father may have felt the same way about me. Our parents held me above him. I never understood why he was not close to me."

Chay's head came up in a swift, sudden move. He met Enoch's gaze with wide eyes.

"My father only told us that you were a special man who walked with Elohim. He never spoke ill of you."

Enoch nodded, seeming to say this was natural. "Someday you will think this way of your brother too."

◁13▷

The Iron Fist

THE DAYS WITH ENOCH WERE THE CLOSEST TO ADAM'S GARDEN any of these young men would ever come. They had rested from their rigorous travel and filled their stomachs with olives, figs, almonds, and bread. With the old man's help, they had repaired their sandals and mended their tunics.

Most importantly, they had filled their souls with food and drink from the wisdom of Enoch. After the old man showed Chay, Pazel, and Kodi the Garden that first day, he took them over to the spring where Hod and Mathu waited.

"Now, my young friends, I suggest you regain your strength here for a few days before you depart on the mission Elohim had given you. You are the five fingers of the iron fist needed for the dangers ahead."

"Five fingers?" Hod exclaimed. "So that was what Remiel meant when he told me I would not have to do this mission by myself. He told me there would be four others and together we would make an iron fist."

"Hod and Mathu will explain your mission. Come find me as soon as you have eaten and drunk your fill, and I will show you where you can sleep." With these words, Enoch left them alone.

During the next three days, Mathu and Kodi spent much time together discussing their childhood and re-establishing their friendship. Pazel liked to sit with them and learn about the family he did not know.

Hod, however, avoided the young nephil. After spending four weeks learning to fear his giant enemies, he did not trust Kodi. He was surprised to sometimes see his uncle walking with him and engaging in what seemed to be earnest conversation. He wondered what Enoch found to interest him in this misfit.

Another person Hod had not made his peace with was his brother Chay. The day when they first saw each other and he saw that his brother was with Kodi, Hod had been confused. He had always loved him even when he knew Chay resented him, but could he trust him to be faithful on this so very important mission?

On their last day the old man gathered them as one to give his final words. All of the young men who had suddenly become part of a mission for the Creator became silent and intensely focused on Enoch, even leaning forward when he spoke as if drawn by a lodestone.

"Kodi is the only one to ask me if it is true that I walk with Elohim. Is this what is told about me?" Only Hod and Chay nodded.

"Yes, you two sons of my brother Elim have heard that. I suppose it is one way to view my relationship with Him."

"How do you know He is with you?" Hod asked.

"Well, every day He talks to me in the peace of my little garden."

Pazel blurted out the question some of them may have thought. "What does He look like?"

The young man blushed when Enoch chuckled at his words. Hod elbowed Pazel and gave him a black frown.

"No, no. Don't be angry with him for asking questions." Enoch looked at Hod and then at his friend. "Little Cainite, no man can look on Elohim and live. It would be like staring at a million suns."

"But . . . ," Pazel started to speak before stopping when he saw Hod glaring at him.

Enoch, however, seemed to read his mind. "But how can I walk with Elohim when I cannot see Him? I feel Him beside me as I walk. I hear His voice just as I hear yours. But, oh, what a voice!"

"What does He sound like?"

No one reprimanded Pazel this time. Indeed, they all wanted to know.

"Human language does not have the words to describe it." The old man sighed, shook his head, and lifted his eyes to heaven, before turning brooding eyes on his visitors.

"It is my wish that each of you spend his life close to Elohim, but, alas, humans are separated from Him by such a wide gulf that we cannot find our way to His side."

"But you found your way!" Hod blurted out. "What made you different?"

Enoch cocked his head to one side and studied his young questioner for a moment. "I always had a curiosity and a hunger for Elohim and spent many years at the knee of Adam learning the truths of the beginning. When he became too old to work in the fields, he taught the children."

Hod pursued the question that most interested him. "What made you different from the other children, though? They all learned at his knee."

"Several of us asked Adam what it was like to walk in the Garden with Elohim. He said he talked to Him and walked with Him first thing upon awakening. He said he was consumed with the desire to be with Elohim, that he thought about Him all the time, that his heart almost burst because it was so full of Him. He said Elohim was more important than food or water or air."

The young men looked at each other and their eyes were wide with the thoughts Enoch was sharing. At the moment each of them wanted this experience—this state of being.

Perhaps it was understandable that Chay, the one among them with the most rebellious heart, spoke now. "With such a closeness to Elohim, how could Adam disobey Him?"

"Our first ancestor told me that after his wife was given to him, he began to think of her more and more. His love for her began to take first place in his mind. He still walked with Elohim, but his heart was divided.

"He told me that he knew she was wrong to eat the fruit and that he knew she would die because of it. Deceived by the serpent, she took her bite out of pride. He took his bite out of love for her. He purposely disobeyed. If she must die, he would die with her."

Tears gathered in their eyes, and their throats constricted painfully. All the young men's thoughts were on the first couple's tragedy and pain. Eventually Pazel broke the silence—and the serious mood—with a teasing joke.

"Are you saying that wives keep men from walking with Elohim?"

The laughter following his quip drew them all closer. Even though none had yet been married, all except Kodi and Pazel had witnessed the struggles in the marriages of their parents and siblings. The nephil looked confused but said nothing.

"No, I'm not saying that, young man," Enoch replied. "Elohim gave Adam his wife, perhaps for a test as well as for a mate. I married when I was only a few years older than some of you, and I loved my wife. I did my best to walk with Elohim as I grew up. I prayed, I sacrificed, I memorized all that my forefathers could tell me about Him. However, it was not until after my wife died at Methuselah's birth that I heard His voice.

"When I was no longer distracted and when I needed Him desperately, He came to me. It was not until He walked with me that I walked with Him. I married again, but I had learned who came first."

Enoch left them after this—to spend time with Elohim they supposed. The five young men turned to each other to share their thoughts and feelings on what they had heard. Hod wanted to explain the mission, but would not do it with Kodi there, so he stayed with Enoch's words.

"I would like to walk with Elohim. Wouldn't all of you?"

Chay rolled his eyes and snorted. "You would! I think it's arrogant and prideful to even aspire to that. Enoch's right. Elohim has to find you."

These words stung, and Hod felt like snapping back, but before he could, Pazel spoke. "I wonder if it is even possible for a Cainite to walk with Him."

"If it's impossible for you, what hope is there for me?" The other four looked up in surprise at the longing in Kodi's voice. "If I wanted to worship Elohim, how could He have anything to do with me? I am the son of Azazel!"

All looked at Kodi with pity, yet none of them had any idea what to say in response to his question. Finally Hod—who trusted the nephil the least—spoke his thoughts.

"Enoch told me that Elohim loves you. Take comfort in that thought."

Kodi looked at Hod. "Thank you. That's something to think over."

ξ

THEY LEFT WHEN THE FULL MOON SHONE ITS BRIGHTEST, TWO hours before midnight, when the haraanis were sound asleep in their mountain eyries.

Pazel, the mountain dweller, was the first to slip between the offset walls of Enoch's retreat to stand on the bank of the spring-fed rivulet. The plan was for him, because of his sure-footed skills, to first scout the area for signs of Hartagga or the Lamechite they had left behind.

Pazel bounded easily across the narrow stream before crisscrossing through the sparse woods that separated Enoch's home from the rocky corral where he and Hod had met the others. The trees were shorter and more widely spaced than the forests of the lowlands.

Oversized paw prints marked the far bank of the stream. Evidently Hartagga had paced back and forth, patrolling the entrance in hopes of finding Hod. At the upper reach of the rivulet, he found where the prints led back into the woods. Seeing no human prints, Pazel concluded the Lamechite had not returned. Noiselessly, careful not to step on even a twig, he moved through the grove from tree to tree, always ready to climb if necessary.

A growling snore coming from a wallowed out space between two slightly larger trees alerted Pazel to the proximity of the beast. He crept close enough to see it sleeping noisily in the moonlight. Pine needles, fallen branches, and moldy leaves were piled in a ring around him as if they had been scratched and dug up from the woodsy floor.

From the condition of the spot, Pazel concluded that Hartagga had made his bed here for the nights they had been with Enoch. He assumed from the fact that the creature was sleeping that it did not expect them to be leaving their refuge at night.

Pazel backed out slowly, holding his breath and trying to make no sound to alert the monster, but, unable to see where he trod, he put one foot on a dry twig, which snapped like a whip crack. The Cainite froze in place. His eyes stretched wide, and his ears strained for any sound from Hartagga.

His eyes never moved from the black fur hulk half buried in the leaves. At first the beast did not react. But then, as if the extreme silence itself awoke it, the huge head reared up and a muted roar came from his wide jaws.

Hartagga's black eyes rolled around his environment warily as his snout snuffled and grumbled and bit at the air. But then his head flopped back on his bed, and he lay motionless. Pazel realized the beast was still wrapped in sleep and had reacted to the sound but not awakened.

Turning so that he could watch where he stepped, Pazel slowly worked his way back to the group. When they saw him, the other four slipped through the stone gap and, without a word, followed the leader as he took them away from Hartagga.

They continued to go single file and slowly until they had cleared the grove and the meadow and arrived at the opening into the stone corral. Pazel waited for his companions to move past him before following them into the rock corral.

"Wait here and don't talk. I'm going to go back and listen for sounds that Hartagga could be following. Once he's awake, he'll scent me and be after us straightaway."

Pazel walked to the grove and stood listening for any sound that would warn of Hartagga. Ear turned toward the north, he waited for anything to break the silence. Then he heard a rustling that became a crunching of leaves and limbs. Hartagga was awake and would soon scent the human who had come so close to him as he slept. Everyone heard the far-off roar just as Pazel came running back into the arena.

"Run!" Pazel yelled. "He's awake and knows I was there! He'll be after us soon. Run as fast as you can for the other side of the open area. We must get into the crevice!"

"Let me lead. I'm faster than you," Hod shouted over his shoulder as he ran.

They all ran full out behind Hod directly toward the crevice he and Pazel had used to escape Hartagga days before. Behind him he heard the slap of sandals moving rapidly across the stone ground and the panting of lungs gasping for breath in the thin air.

At first that was all he heard. And then Hartagga's bellowing roar and claws clacking on stone joined the sounds, still at a distance but closing quickly.

"Faster!" Hod ordered and was surprised when he was passed by Kodi—carrying Mathu on his back.

Hod realized that his brother's cellmate was weak from lack of food and from the cough he had contracted while in captivity; however, he did not expect a nephil to show such concern.

Hod sped up to stay with Kodi so he could show him the passage. When Hartagga's growls grew closer, Hod chanced a look over his shoulder to make sure Chay was keeping up. His brother trailed Pazel by quite a bit; in fact, Hartagga was only five lengths from catching him. Hod slowed his pace until Pazel was even with him.

"Lead them to the passage. I'm going to help Chay."

Hod stopped and pulled his sword. He knew the others would want him to protect himself, would think he was vital to the mission, but he was determined not to desert his brother again. When Chay reached him, Hod signaled him on with a sweeping gesture and turned to face Hartagga. Chay halted too even though he had no sword.

"If you're going to face this monster, so will I."

"Then come on. Maybe we can outrun him together."

Hod grabbed Chay and pulled him along with him. The others were already in the passage, which he knew would soon narrow into a thin crevice.

"Here, here, this way." He led Chay farther and farther up the ever narrowing passage. "A little more and he won't fit between the walls."

By now the enraged animal's hot breath surrounded them and his roars could be felt on their backs. Expecting the monster to pounce at any moment, Hod slowed, pushed Chay ahead of him, and turned while extending his sword. Hartagga reared up on his hind legs and lunged for them but only succeeded in wedging himself tightly between the rock walls. Struggling to move, Hartagga tried to reach for Hod, who watched as the monster bellowed angrily at the brothers just out of reach of its claws.

"We're safe," Chay crowed and slapped Hod on the back. "He'll never get out of there."

Hod shook his head, unable to share his brother's optimism.

"He'll get loose. That beast never gives up."

Without another word he inclined his head in the direction the others had gone and then led the way down the passage. They helped each other up the slope he and Pazel had slid down and soon met up with the rest, who were gathered at the opening out of the crevice, the spot where they had escaped Hartagga three days ago.

"Did the beast catch you?" Pazel cried.

Chay gave the Cainite a disbelieving look. "Yes. In fact, he ate us. Can't you tell?"

Pazel, not minding Chay's acid tone, burst into laughter. "You look unchewed to me!"

The usually grouchy Chay glared a moment before beginning to laugh along with Pazel. Soon both were laughing until tears ran down their cheeks. The other three stared at them as if they had lost their wits.

But then first Mathu, then Hod, and eventually Kodi, joined in the tension-relieving mirth. When they had laughed themselves out, Hod returned to business.

"We left Hartagga stuck between the rocks, but he will no doubt get himself out before long. We must get on with our journey. Enoch said that if we climb to the peak shaped like a pine tree and circle to the western side, we'll see what he called a 'boulderfall.' He said there is a long groove from the top of the mountain, filled with very large round stones that look as if they were poured out by a giant hand."

Pazel nodded eagerly and motioned the others to follow. "I know the place. I can lead us there, but it will be rugged traveling."

"Enoch said we can crawl underneath the boulders," Hod explained. "There is supposed to be enough space underneath to work oneself down the mountain."

Chay and Mathu were shaking their heads as if to show their doubt of the wisdom of trying this path. Pazel, however, thought a moment before speaking.

"I didn't know there was room under the boulder-fall for a human to crawl, but if Enoch said there is, I believe it. Let's go!"

An hour later the group had almost reached the top of the steep, stone peak. While they climbed the rocky ground, no one spoke unless absolutely necessary. Each was aware that Hartagga could come clambering up the slope any moment, and if he did would find them totally vulnerable with no place to hide and nowhere to fight.

When Pazel reached the top, he stopped, turned, and leaning with one hand against the tree-shaped spire, looked back down at his companions. Hod was not far behind him, Chay perhaps ten paces behind his brother, but Mathu seemed to be struggling and coughing farther down the mountain. Pazel wondered why Kodi was not helping Mathu.

The young nephil was nowhere in sight. Pazel immediately shared his worry. "Hod, look back! Kodi isn't with us!"

Hod's head jerked around. He looked down the mountainside, his eyes scanning from right to left for any movement or unusual sight. There was not a clue to the disappearance of Kodi. His earlier concern about trusting a nephil surged back with increased force, and he glared at his brother.

"Where is Kodi?"

"I don't know," Chay said, looking back. "He was behind me last time I looked, but that was a while ago. Don't worry. He'll catch up with us."

Hod scowled as he scanned the area below them. "I never trusted him. The nephilim are our enemies. I don't know why you brought him along."

The two brothers squared off eye to eye and in their faces all the grievances and rivalries of their life together could be seen.

When he answered, Chay spoke through a clenched jaw, but his voice was under tight control. "Kron would never have trusted me to go without a guard, and the other nephilim were too heavy to ride the haraani. If we had to have a nephil, I'd rather have Kodi. Besides, Enoch trusted him."

Pazel and Mathu, who had finally caught up with them, said nothing as they watched the brothers' confrontation. Everyone held his breath until Hod finally spoke.

"I guess you made the right choice. He's better than a Lamechite or another nephil, but I still don't trust him. Where is he?"

Mathu stepped between the brothers, looked at Hod, then at Chay.

"I trust him. He carried me when I couldn't run, and then put me down at the bottom of the slope. I told him I would be all right. He said he had to do something and would catch up later."

All of the young men turned and looked back to the bottom of the long, steep slope they had just climbed. They watched the tall boulder they had walked around before starting their ascent to see if Kodi would emerge from behind it. But it was Hartagga, not Kodi, who shambled around the boulder, snuffling the ground as he came, and, looking up, bellowed at them.

"Let's get moving!" Pazel shouted, and they all turned and followed him around the pine-shaped rock and down the other side of the mountain. "There's the boulderfall a hundred paces down."

They hurried after Pazel, stopping when they came to the long, narrow stream of boulders that looked as if they had been poured from a gigantic bag until they flowed all the way down the mountain.

"Wait here while I try to find a way to get below the rocks," Pazel said.

The other three young men looked from the Cainite back to the summit above them, shifting nervously while Hod held his sword at the ready. Pazel was working his way from boulder to boulder at the beginning of the line of rocks. Finally, he looked back at his companions.

"Here is a big enough space to get into, and it looks like there is room to move farther down. Come on."

No one questioned him as each waited for the one in front of him to climb into the space. Pazel had already crawled several cubits down the mountain by the time Chay, who insisted on being last, was able to drop through the opening.

"Take my sword if you're going to face the monster," Hod said, turning to his brother.

Chay took the weapon before looking up the mountain. When he saw Hartagga coming around the spire, he almost dove under the huge stones. "He's after us! Move farther in, so I can get out of his reach."

Hod squeezed as close as he could to Mathu to make room for his brother in the space under the boulders. Chay pressed close, pulled his feet up to his body, and kept the sword at his side.

None spoke as they listened to the breathing and snuffling sounds of the giant beast. They could hear him searching for them, trying to understand how they had eluded him. Eventually his nose found the opening they had entered.

"Can you move farther?" Chay hissed. "He'll reach me if he stretches his arm in."

When all four moved far enough to be out of Hartagga's reach, Hod took time to study this place his uncle had sent them. Beneath them was the rough, stone face of the mountain. They were lying in a vee-shaped groove running down the gradual slope while above them large boulders, piled randomly, made a roof over the groove. Looking past the others and farther down the groove, Hod saw some rocks blocking the way and wondered how they would make it past them.

"He can't get at us here." Pazel finally broke the silence. "There is some space between the boulders above us but not enough for him to reach in. We'll have to watch out for bigger gaps as we move down."

"I'm thankful these boulders are piled too deep for Hartagga to get to us," Hod said. "By keeping moving, we'll always be ahead of him if he does start digging."

With Pazel leading the way, the four young men began crawling down the mountain. The rough stone scraped at their palms and knees, yet they hardly noticed. For a while they could hear Hartagga snuffling at the spaces between the boulders as he kept up with them. Sometimes they were forced to squeeze under or around the low hanging stones Hod had noticed, yet they were able to keep moving.

"Stop! I think we have reached the end of this passage." Pazel halted and turned to look back at his companions. "This boulder ahead of us totally fills the tunnel."

"What do we do now?" Chay called from behind them all.

Pazel, able due to his small size to turn in the tight space and look at the others, motioned for them all to move closer. "There is a space to the lower left of this boulder. By squirming around the stone, I think I can get out."

"I see light coming around it," Hod said. "But if Hartagga's out there, he'll tear you apart before you can take five steps."

"I haven't heard him lately. Maybe he has given up." Pazel looked at Hod first and then at the others, his eyes asking their opinion.

Chay answered first. "We can't stay here forever. We have to do something."

They all fell silent and listened for any sounds of the great beast. No sniffing, growling, grunting, or scratching could be heard. Of course, they knew he could be watching out of earshot.

"I'll stick my head out and look around," the Cainite said. "If he's close, I'll jump back in here, and we can figure out how we can fight him. If he's not there, I'll look for another way to get under the boulders farther down."

With no other ideas, the other three nodded. Hod put his hand on Pazel's shoulder and squeezed it.

"I'll come out far enough to watch. If you're in trouble, I'll come to your aid."

Pazel's shaggy black hair moved slowly up from behind the large boulder. His head turned right then left. Seeing nothing to fear, he stood up straight and turned to look behind him. Hartagga was nowhere in sight, so he climbed up to the flat rock surface on his left and moved stealthily on down the boulderfall looking for another space big enough to get under the rocks and go on down the mountain. Several paces down he found what he was looking for and signaled for Hod to come.

Hod turned back to his companions before following Pazel. "He has found a place to get under the rocks again. Stay here until I go and then come one at a time. Chay, give me my sword."

Chay obeyed and, as soon as his brother left the tunnel, tapped Mathu on the leg. "I want to be ready to help Hod. Can you move up enough so I can get past you?"

With some squeezing and maneuvering, Chay was soon up in the opening watching Hod, who was now almost to Pazel. Since neither Chay nor Mathu had weapons, he was not sure how he would help his brother but knew he would do whatever was necessary.

Just then Chay heard Hartagga's roar behind him and whirled to see the monster running down the slope toward him. Involuntarily and instinctively, Chay ducked back into his hole, expecting the monster upon him any moment, but Hartagga ignored the older brother for the younger.

"Hod, watch out!" As soon as the animal passed him, Chay clambered out from the rocks and started after him, not caring that he was unarmed.

When Hod turned, sword in hand, to face the charging beast, Chay knew his brother's weapon would be no match for the sharp claws and teeth of the attacker. He had no idea what he would do, only knew he must protect his brother, with his bare hands if he had to.

Hartagga was almost on Hod, and Chay was too far away to make a difference when a spear from far to the right of the boulderfall blazed like a lightning bolt toward Hartagga's chest. Following close behind the spear, the missing Kodi ran toward the beast with drawn dagger.

Momentarily halted by the spear, Hartagga looked at Kodi, who threw himself on the animal, jerked its head back, and slashed its throat with a decisive stroke of his dagger.

When Kodi let go of him, Hartagga slumped to the ground, jerked convulsively, and then was still.

Chay ran to Kodi and grabbed his blood-spattered friend. "I knew you had not betrayed us! I knew it!"

"Of course, I didn't! I've been keeping an eye on Hartagga. But I knew we had to kill him to save Hod."

Hod, stunned by all that was happening, also ran to the nephil. Suddenly the tall, blond young man did not disgust him at all. He grabbed Kodi's hand in a warm grip. He saw his heart, and it was good.

"I'll never doubt you again—friend. I'm glad you are a part of our iron fist."

◁14▷

Finding the Glade

WITH THEIR NEMESIS DEAD, THE BAND OF TRAVELERS FELT FREE to rest and share a meal.

First, they each walked around the shaggy furred carcass. Hartagga had fallen away from the boulderfall on the smooth rocky area where they could easily walk around to study the body. They were astounded by the length and sharpness of his teeth and claws.

Kodi looped his finger in the animal's loose, golden collar and pulled it out from its neck to study the clasp holding it closed.

"Should we take the collar with us?" Pazel, who was also scrutinizing the golden band, asked the group. "It's worth quite a bit in trade."

Kodi looked at his cousin, nodded, and then bent down to use his dagger point to pry open the lock on the collar. "You might as well take it."

"Wait!" Chay put a hand on Kodi's shoulder. "Will Kron's anger be worse if the collar is gone? Maybe we shouldn't antagonize him. I don't want to take unnecessary chances just because someone is greedy."

Pazel's dark eyes showed shame and hurt. "I don't mean to be greedy, and I don't want to make the situation worse."

"How can it be worse?" Kodi asked. "Kron wants to kill Hod and now Chay and probably Mathu. Let Pazel take the collar. He knows these mountains so well that he can hide it and get it later."

Hod made the final decision. "Good idea. Pazel, it's yours. Now, let's eat."

While the little Cainite took the collar Kodi gave him and stowed it in his pack to hide later, the others found a flat place farther down the mountain and spread out the food Enoch had provided.

Four of them had filled their waterskins with the pure water from Enoch's spring, but Hod—who was protecting the last few mouthfuls of healing water in his skin—drank from Pazel's waterskin.

No one had yet noticed the nearly empty waterskin Hod carried, but when he saw Kodi looking at his waterskin, Hod decided to distract him.

"Kodi, tell us why you left us and how you followed Hartagga."

The nephil put down his food and eagerly began his
narrative. "First, I saw Mathu was doing all right, so I
fell back to be the rear guard, as I have seen nephilim in
Kron's army do. Then, because I began to wonder what
Hartagga was up to, I decided to go back and check on
him."

"Weren't you afraid he would attack you?" Chay
asked.

Kodi shook his head and pointed back at the dead
animal.

"Not at all. Remember, that monster was Kron's pet,
and I lived with Kron. Hartagga knew me, so he never
thought of me as being with you. Anyway, he would not
have killed a nephil."

They all looked back at the carcass a moment as if
trying to make their memory of the ferocious beast fit
with Kodi's words. The idea of the animal as someone's
pet was ludicrous. Pazel finally spoke for all of them.

"You mean in the nephilim world he was cute and
cuddly?"

"Hardly!" Kodi threw back his blond head and
laughed loudly at this idea. Then he grew serious, glancing once more at Hartagga. "I've seen him kill and eat
enemies of Kron that the king threw to him for fun. No,
he was terrifying even though I knew he would never
hurt me."

Now Chay chuckled. "I can see you nephilim
scratching his belly before he chewed on leg bones."

Seeing his usually sour-tempered brother joking around with a nephil, Hod had to admit to himself that Kodi was good for Chay. He was beginning to see another side to his brother, and he liked that side. When Kodi gave Chay what he intended to be a light slap on the back but that almost made him fall on his face, Hod joined in their laughter.

"You think that's funny, do you?" Kodi said. "Only Kron petted Hartagga. No one else would have dared. Anyway, when I saw him coming after us, I let him see me and acted as if I were going the other way. He look-ed at me, but then went on after you four."

"Why didn't you kill him right then?" Chay com-plained. "You could have saved some skin off our knees and hands, not to speak of a painful lump on my head where I ran into a boulder in that tunnel thing."

"Since I only have a dagger, I made myself a spear from the trunk of a thin aspen. It took me almost an hour to make it and then get a point sharp enough to pene-trate Hartagga's fur. After that I ran to catch up with him.

"When I saw you had gone under the boulders and that he was following you above the rocks, I stayed with him but off to the right behind that ridge paralleling the boulderfall. He never even scented me."

"Well, we're all glad you did follow him," Hod said. "And glad you were ready to act."

Pazel grinned from ear to ear. "I'm glad you're so accurate with a spear!"

"Very true. If not for your skill, Hartagga would have ripped me apart." Hod gripped Kodi's shoulder tightly.

Then Hod turned to his brother and put a hand on his shoulder. "You probably saved Chay's life too, for the idiot was rushing to help me with nothing but his bare hands for weapons."

Chay shrugged and look embarrassed, but Hod gave him a searching look and continued. "Thank you, for trying to help me. If not for Kodi, we would have died together, but you were ready to die to help me and that means much. I'm sorry for my fault in any trouble between us."

"Forget it, Hod. All that bad feeling was in another life. We have a mission to complete. Let us only think of that."

Mathu had been silent during all the earlier conversation; however, at the mention of their mission, he spoke up.

"I'm eager to see my sister again, to see if she is safe. What are our plans now that the beast is dead?"

"We go on," Hod said. "Just above the boulders instead of under them. Kodi mentioned Lamechites coming along, so we still have to be careful.

Kodi nodded. "Yes, the one I sent back when we went into Enoch's garden will return. I'm surprised we haven't seen him already."

They all stood and began packing up the rest of the provisions in their backpacks.

Then they started down the fairly smooth rock slope just beside the boulderfall. Hod motioned for Pazel to lead the way before taking second place. Kodi once more took the last spot. They made rapid progress even though now they laughed and talked as they walked.

Hod was happy to see the lighter mood in his companions, yet he knew that the most difficult and important part of his quest still lay ahead—returning to Enoch with Mehri.

It would be harder to travel with a girl. She would not be able to endure the hardships they had, she would probably slow them down, and she would be a target of their enemies. He sighed to think of what could lie ahead.

For another hour they moved easily down the mountain with no obstacles or enemies to worry about. The sun was a ball of fire hanging above the top of the highest western peak in front of them when suddenly, coming directly at them from the orange globe, an oversized bird—a haraani with outstretched wings—swooped down on the troop.

"That's Keoaw. He's looking for Hod." Kodi waved at the haraani, which circled very close overhead. Eventually it flew back toward the sun.

"What now?" Hod asked Kodi. "What does this mean?"

"They saw Hod. I think we have at least a half hour until they come—probably with Lamechites." Everyone turned to Kodi as he spoke.

"Maybe we should go back under the boulders," Hod suggested.

"You four move on down the hill as quickly as you can," Kodi said. "I'll keep up with you up on that ridge and watch the sky for the haraanis. I should be able to give you five minutes warning."

"You won't fit under the boulders. What will you do if we go back under?" Hod suddenly felt concern that the young nephil might suffer because of them.

"I'll find a place to hide on the other side of the ridge. You all get going. It will be full dark in two hours."

They did as Kodi suggested and moved quickly down the mountain. Trusting the nephil to warn them of approaching enemies, no one took the time to look at the sky for haraanis. The sun had dropped behind the highest peak when a sharp whistle from behind the ridge brought them all to a stop.

Kodi's head was visible above the ridge, but soon his entire body appeared and hurried down to the boulderfall.

"I see three haraanis coming with riders. Get into the boulderfall quick!"

When Pazel could not easily find an opening to the passage under the rocks, Kodi pushed a smaller boulder aside with an ease that impressed the others and held it while his friends slipped into the tunnel.

"Thanks again, Kodi," Hod, the last one to enter the passageway, clapped the nephil on the back.

Kodi smiled. "I've got to get out of here, but I'll be watching the Lamechites and the boulderfall. I'll be there when you need me. Now get moving!"

When Hod was safely down in the tunnel, Kodi replaced the huge rock as gently as he could, but still all the boulders above the others shook and trails of rock dust sifted down on them.

Pazel, Mathu, Chay, and finally Hod moved as quickly as their sore hands and knees allowed. The rocks above them were piled three deep as they neared the bottom of the mountain, and there was no sign of an egress from the narrow passage they traveled. The density of the piled boulders overhead kept all but the dimmest of filtered light out.

After crawling under the rocks half an hour, the group came to an opening large enough for only Pazel to squirm through.

He looked back at the others. "You all stay here under cover while I go out and look around. Maybe Kodi will see me and come out from his hiding place."

The other three took the opportunity to stretch out as best as they could and rest their tired bodies. Outside Pazel glanced around for some sign of a pursuer. Seeing nothing to worry him and no evidence of the nephil, he walked toward the ridge Kodi was supposed to be behind. He saw a gap in the rocks and was just walking through it when he came face to face with three Lamechites.

"Hey!" The man Enoch had turned back, grabbed Pazel's shoulder. "Where is the fire-hair?"

Pazel's first reaction on facing the enemy was to run, but, on second thought, he decided to brazen it out.

"Yes, I guided him up the mountain; however, I left him with the old man."

"What are you doing here?"

"Uh, well, I was heading over to Havilah to visit someone."

The other two Lamechites crowded around him. One, who eyed him with suspicion, poked Pazel with his forefinger. "Do you know who killed Hartagga? We found him up the mountain with his throat slit."

"No, I don't know anything about it."

The other Lamechite grabbed Pazel by the tunic.

"I don't believe you. Maybe you killed him yourself."

"No, really . . . ."

"Maybe you took his collar, though," the leader said.

Now Pazel was beginning to get worried and to wish that he had never taken the golden collar or at least had taken the time to bury it. He began to back away from them slowly. When the second man grabbed his pack, Pazel shrugged it off, left it in the man's hands, and ran for the boulderfall.

Back in the tunnel, Hod, Chay, and Mathu heard running sandals and then Pazel's voice whispering at them.

"Quick! Everyone start moving as fast as you can! The haraanis did bring Lamechites!"

Nobody hesitated. Nobody asked any questions. Mathu began crawling as fast as he could with Chay and Hod right behind him. Pazel deftly slipped through the hole and started after them. He had not gone far before he heard the voices of the enemy discussing him, so he paused to listen.

"It looks like he's hiding under these boulders," said the third Lamechite, who stuck his head into the opening. "He's crawled some way in."

"We aren't after him, even if he did kill Hartagga," the leader said. "We'd better look for the fire-hair."

Pazel held his breath but kept moving. Maybe they would go off and leave them. But the suspicious man was not so easily put off. "I smell the scent of others here. Two Sethians, at least."

While the leader hesitated as if thinking this over, Pazel crawled as quickly as possible. Even though he was getting farther away, he could still hear the suspicious one.

"I think it's the scent of the fire-hair."

The leader must have agreed because Pazel soon heard them all entering the tunnel and coming his way. The Lamechites were not all that far behind, yet he knew he could stay ahead of them.

After a few minutes, Pazel reached his friends, who were not moving fast enough. It was evident that at this pace the enemy would soon catch up with them.

Pazel stopped, turned, and kicked with all his might at a loose rock he had noticed on the edge of the passage. He kicked and kicked at the little boulder until it broke loose, fell to the rocky floor, bringing with it a cascade of other stones that partially filled the tunnel.

That will slow them. But we will have a hard time getting through this tunnel on our way back. Hopefully we can travel above ground safely by then.

"Keep moving, friends," he called to the others. "I've slowed them down, but we still need to move fast!"

They moved in the near-darkness more by feel than by sight. Eventually they could tell the slope was leveling, meaning the groove beneath them was flattening and the boulders above them were nearer the rocky floor. At times they had to flatten their torsos on the ground and scoot through on their stomachs.

"This is getting tricky." Hod stopped and looked back at his companions. "If we don't find an opening out of here, we'll be stuck. I don't think even Pazel can get under that next boulder."

Mathu was taken with a fit of coughing that racked his thin frame and couldn't say a word.

Behind Mathu, Chay snorted loudly. "I should have known. All this ripping away of skin for nothing. We would have been better off sticking with Kodi."

The three young men looked at Hod. He had heard Chay's words and felt responsible for getting them into this situation. Meanwhile, Pazel looked around at the boulders with the eye of the one whose job it had been to find a way down the mountain.

"Have you tried pushing at some of the boulders to see if any are movable?" Pazel asked. "I don't think they're as big or piled as high as those higher."

"I tried," Hod answered. "But these around me are too big to move."

Just then scrambling sounds coming from back up the passage convinced them that the persistent Lamechites had moved the fallen rocks and were still in pursuit.

Hod looked at the boulders nearer him. He picked one with enough room to get under, lay on his back beneath it, and then bent his knees to his chest so that he could put the soles of his sandals against the boulder.

With all the power of his youthful, muscular legs, Hod pushed at the rock and was relieved when it moved a bit. "Come on, Chay. The two of us should be able to shift this one."

Chay squeezed past Mathu and came to his brother's side. The two of them, side by side on their backs with their legs bent, pushed the boulder and were able to lift it about a handbreadth. Their eyes met.

"Now!" Hod cried.

As one, they threw the great stone away with their legs and feet. The sound of the heavy impediment to their freedom bouncing and then rolling away from the boulderfall brought muted cheers from the other two and relieved smiles from the brothers.

Chay was the first one to pop his head and shoulders through the aperture they had made. The sun was no longer visible behind the western peaks. In the waning light, he could see Kodi's head sticking up above the ridge.

His nephil friend was staring right at him and had obviously seen the boulder ejected from the pile. Although he was silent, Kodi was motioning for him to come to where he was. When Chay didn't move, Kodi repeated his motion with great urgency.

"Kodi is right over the ridge," Chay whispered to the others. "He wants us to hurry to where he is. Let's go!"

Chay put his hands on the rocks above, pulled himself out of the tunnel, and ran toward the ridge. One at a time each of the others did the same. As fast as they could, they scrambled up the ridge and threw themselves over it.

Kodi reached over and pulled Mathu back. The young miner began to cough. "Get down! And try to be quiet. The Lamechites are behind you in the passage."

While Mathu smothered his cough with both hands, the others stayed well below the rocky ridge.

Pazel turned to Kodi and put a hand on his arm. "The Lamechites saw us when I looked around about half an hour ago. They followed us into the passageway."

"Yes, I saw that from here. I was sure they would catch you, but there was nothing I could do to help. How did you avoid them?"

"Pazel kicked in the boulders," Chay said. "It slowed them down at least."

"Quick thinking!" Kodi told Pazel, who grinned his big grin, pleased with the compliment from his cousin.

Kodi peeked over the ridge and then motioned with his hand for the others to stay down. "They're out and sniffing around. Their noses will lead them here soon. Follow me."

Without questioning, the others followed the nephil as he led them perpendicular from the ridge. They jogged quickly several hundred cubits to the south along a fairly flat area in the foothills of the Eden Mountains. Rock gave way to thin soil covered with shaggy grass and short trees. Once they entered the woods, Kodi turned to the west and back into a hilly area, what looked like true forest.

When he stopped, they all slowed, glad of an opportunity to catch their breath. Mathu was immediately consumed with a fit of coughing. Kodi waited until the miner had control of his coughs before addressing them all.

"I'm sure we have a good lead on them. I don't think they are near enough to hear Mathu. Let's rest and decide what to do. I've never been into this area. Have you, Pazel?"

"Once or twice. I know there are some pretty woods, glades, and waterfalls around here."

Mathu nodded eagerly, tried and failed to speak, and finally got out a brief phrase. "Mehri . . . Mehri's in a glade . . . with a waterfall."

"Then we must be near it," Hod said. "I don't know how we'll find it, but I have faith that Elohim will lead us to it. I suggest we keep walking, though. Lamechites are slow but sure trackers."

Pazel's shaggy black hair wiggled as he looked at Hod. "I'm not disagreeing with you, but I can add a strategy to our looking. I hear a brook not far from here. If we follow it downstream, it could lead us to Mehri's waterfall."

"Faith is fine, brother; however, I'm with Pazel on this." Chay's usual contrariness did not bother Hod this time, for he also thought the Cainite had a good idea.

So the group followed Pazel to a swift-running brook where they all bent and slaked their thirst before looking to him for direction. He was listening with a cocked head, his left ear turned downstream. As one they held their tongues.

"I hear a waterfall, very close. Follow me!"

They walked along the bank of the brook for no more than a quarter of an hour. Suddenly, the land dropped away and the water fell fifty cubits straight down to a pretty grassy area. It was twilight, but Hod was still able to scan the land below.

"There are signs of people down there. Look at that little thatched arbor to the right. Someone has made that. Mathu, what do you think?"

"It could be them. My mother helped make thatch for the roof on our hut. She would know how to do it."

"What do we have to lose?" Pazel said, tossing his head. "Let's find a way down."

As Pazel searched, he circled the woods to the left, staying on the edge of the heights. "We can climb down this vine-covered area here."

The four lighter travelers climbed down the thick vines with only a little trouble, except for Chay who stopped a few feet from the top and looked down, way down to the ground below.

"I'm getting dizzy," he called up to Hod, who was waiting to go next. "You know how much I hate heights!"

"You can do it, brother. Look up at me and keep moving down. You'll be there before you know it."

"All right." After taking Hod's advice, Chay was at the bottom in minutes. Mathu and then Hod worked their way down the vines with caution.

Only Kodi, the heaviest, struggled with the descent. As he moved down, vines tore loose from the cliff face and threatened to dash him to the ground. Using his great strength, Kodi let go of the loosened vines and grabbed at tree roots and protruding rocks as he needed to. Eventually even he had reached the bottom safely.

The young men looked around before starting across the glade stretched out before them. The knee-high, wide, dark green blades of grass were cool as they brushed against their legs.

A shallow stream from the waterfall rippled over rocks and smooth pebbles. When they reached the stream, the group could see in the moonlight the thatch-ed arbor they had spotted from above.

"There it is—over there," Hod cried.

Across the stream and another grassy area, a small open arbor covered with a thin roof was the only evi-dence of human habitation in the entire idyllic glen. The arbor was nestled among thick pines that waved above it like guardians of precious treasure.

Mathu stood still, watching almost without breathing while the others chatted casually. Suddenly the young miner waded into the cold water, which came only to his knees, and with eyes glued to the thatched roof waded back out of the stream and continued on a straight line toward his goal.

"Mother! Mehri!"

He broke into a run while his friends stood on the other side of the stream watching the unfolding scene. Two women had arisen from mats under the arbor. One was running toward Mathu while the other followed more slowly. When the one they guessed was Mehri threw her arms around him, Mathu grabbed her up and spun her around and then turned to hug his mother.

"Let's go meet Mathu's family," Chay said before wading into the stream.

The others followed him and soon all were close to the thatched-roofed arbor. Mathu held his mother's and sister's hands and turned them toward his friends.

"This is my friend Chay. He helped free me from Kron's prison, and this is his brother Hod, who will explain why we are here in a minute. Here is Pazel, a Cainite who is Hod's guide in the mountains."

As each was introduced, he greeted the two women. All of them were stunned by Mehri's raven-haired beauty, so no one could say more than "hello" to her.

"And here is someone you know, Mother." Mathu took Kodi by the elbow and pulled him forward. "This is

Juban's grandson Kodi, my old playmate. He is helping us."

"Kodi, you've grown. I'm glad to see you again." Neva looked up at the nephil. "Mehri and I are pleased to welcome all of you to our glade. Would you come share a meal with us while you explain what has brought you to us?"

Neva smiled softly and indicated the arbor, which was floored with mats woven from rushes.

After sparse rations since leaving Enoch, all of the young men eagerly accepted the invitation and were soon relaxing under the arbor.

◁15▷

Taken

"HAVE YOU BEEN SAFE SINCE YOU CAME HERE?" MATHU ASKED his mother and sister while eating dinner. "Has there been any sign of the enemy?"

His mother shook her head as she offered food to the young men. "We have been perfectly safe. We only see the Watchers when they bring us food. And as for that, there are plenty of fruit trees around here for us to enjoy, so we haven't seen them often."

"I thank Elohim for protecting you." Mathu could not get enough of watching his mother and sister. A few days ago he had never thought he would see them again and now they were together sharing food. "Have you heard from our father and the rest of the family?"

"No. Mehri and I have had no contact with them. I'm sure they have no idea where we are, but it is for your sister's protection."

"Mother, you do not know this, but four of my brothers have given their lives to protect Mehri."

Neva's hands flew to her mouth. "Oh, no! Who? Who died?"

Mathu's companions were quietly eating as they watched the conversation between this mother, son, and daughter. Each of them had empathy for their friend and sorrow for his situation.

Before Mathu could answer his mother, Mehri—who was standing at the time—burst into tears and began to collapse to the ground. Without thinking, Hod jumped to his feet and caught her before she hurt herself. Then he helped her to sit beside her mother.

"Who died?" Neva repeated.

Mathu held both her hands in his and looked her in the eyes. "The four older than I, Davi, Ziti, Berl, and Case."

When a deep cough began to rack Mathu, his mother quickly put an arm around him. "My son, you are not well. You must lie down for a while."

"Yes, I will. I used the last of my strength to run to you."

Coughing again, Mathu let his mother take him to a pallet. The young man, pale even in the moonlight, was struggling to breathe. His friends watched him with concern and wondered if he would be able to continue the mission.

"Your mother is right. You need to rest. Also, I'm worried your coughing will bring the Lamechites down on us." Hod knelt and put a gentle hand on Mathu's back as he spoke. "They might have found the waterfall by now."

Neva was hovering over her son as he rested. "If only I could help him. I wish I had my healing herbs."

When he heard these words, Hod looked at Pazel and pointed at his nearly empty waterskin. Pazel nodded slightly, helping Hod make up his mind.

"I have some water with invigorating qualities left in my skin. Neva, let your son drink the rest of it. It will help with his cough."

Hod deliberately downplayed the efficacy of the water since Pazel wanted to keep the fifth river secret. Mathu drank the last two swallows of the water, thanked Hod, and then coughed again immediately after speaking. Perhaps only Hod and Pazel heard the difference in the depth of this cough.

Chay quickly spoke to Neva. "I was in a cell in Kron's fortress with Mathu. He was there much longer, and the air was damp and unhealthy. I think that is why he has the cough."

"Can you tell me how Mathu got away from Kron?"

Chay explained their escape and then turned to Hod.

"My brother can tell you of his mission from Elohim that brought us here. Hod, tell them."

"All right. Enoch said I am to take Mehri back to his home and then on to the home of Seth where she will be safe from the nephilim and I suppose find a husband."

Hod leaned close to Neva and gazed into her eyes with serious intensity. He knew it would be hard for her to understand why they would take her daughter into danger only to save her.

But Neva's reply surprised him. She offered no argument or complaint. "Did Enoch tell you Elohim's plan for Mehri?"

"Yes, he said Mehri's daughter would marry Enoch's grandson many years from now. The son of that union would be the last righteous man on earth. He said by then the nephilim will have corrupted the whole earth. Elohim will destroy all his creation except that man and his family, who will be protected by his righteousness."

They all looked at Hod with wide eyes filled with horror. Each thought of the evil and decay he or she had witnessed and wondered how much worse the world would be in a few more centuries.

Neva hugged her arms and shivered as if a chill wind were blowing over her. "Yes, we heard some of that from Remiel. I'm glad I am an old woman and do not have to witness these things. But I grieve for my children, grandchildren, and those after them. To think only one will be saved."

"And his family," Mehri said and laid a hand on her mother's knee. "They will be your descendants."

"I *am* thankful that some of our family will survive after the catastrophe."

Neva stood and began to put away the food. "When will we leave?"

"Mother, you cannot go with us." Mathu had risen when no one was looking at him. As his mother looked shocked, he gave his friends a pleading look. "It is too hard and dangerous for my mother. We need to take her home first."

"Mathu, you're standing. Do you feel better?"

Mehri ran to him and threw her arms around his neck. The young miner gently took his sister's arms from his neck, stretched himself, and took a deep breath. All noticed that color had returned to his face. Everyone but Hod and Pazel showed amazement at Mathu's sudden good health.

"What was in that water, Hod?" Chay asked. He rose and went to stand over his brother, his eyes demanding an answer.

Hod did his best to give a nonchalant shrug. "You'll have to ask Pazel. He gave it to me."

All eyes turned to the Cainite, who looked up at the sky before gracing them all with his customary impish grin. "It came from a river I know of here in these mountains, hidden away and unknown by all but Hod and me. That's all there is to it."

Chay shook his head and glowered at Pazel. "That's not all, and you know it. What's in that water? Why is Mathu suddenly well when he seemed on the point of death a few minutes ago?"

"I don't know," Pazel insisted. "I just know it makes you feel better."

Even as he admired the way his friend evaded telling the others all about the water, Hod felt he must clarify this matter.

"You really don't know why the water helps, do you, Pazel?" he asked.

Pazel's grin disappeared and he looked Hod squarely in the eyes. "No, I don't. I know only that it has healthful qualities."

"I'm just thankful we had some of the water left to help Mathu," Hod said when he was assured he had heard all the truth Pazel was free to tell. "Now we need to head back to Enoch. We don't have time to take Neva home. We must get Mehri back to Enoch before the enemy finds her here."

Silence fell on the group as they pondered this problem. Finally, Pazel stood up and cleared his throat.

"If you think you can find your way back to Enoch without me, I'll take Neva home. I'd like to meet my uncle, anyway."

"I'm not sure we can afford to lose you. You will be useful when we leave Enoch and head down the eastern slope," Hod said.

"I know a quicker way through the mountains, but it's too hazardous for any but me. I'll be there shortly after you."

Hod listening with a cocked head, cut his eyes from Pazel to Neva, and then to Mathu.

"That's a good idea. Let's rest a while and leave a couple of hours before dawn. Those Lamechites might be sleeping then."

Chay looked around the clearing and then up at the waterfall at the other end of the glade. "I think we should tear down and hide this thatch roof. If the Lamechites follow us to the waterfall, they'll see the thatch in the moonlight and know we're here."

"I agree," Hod said. "If the women will keep an eye on the area above the waterfall, we'll start now."

In only a few minutes — with great help from Kodi — the young men had torn down the shelter and carried all the parts off in different directions in the trees. Pazel went over the ground to make sure no sign remained of human habitation.

"Now we should move back into the trees to rest," Hod advised.

Each of the company found his or her spot. Mathu pulled his sister and mother into a hidden place under a hanging willow tree. He sat against the trunk, quite wakeful after his drink of healing water, with his arm around the two dearest people in the world to him. Neva snuggled on one side and Mehri on the other.

Mathu, when he heard the deep breathing of slumber from his charges, spent some time talking to Elohim. He thanked Him for the safety of his sister and begged for continuing protection during the rest of the mission.

"Father Creator, You see all and You have each of us in the palm of Your mighty hand. I know that You have a purpose for me in this mission. You have rescued me from imprisonment, have healed my sickness, and have brought me to my mother and sister. I ask You to let me have a part in the continuing protection of Mehri."

Chay was lying on the ground not too far from his friend Mathu and could make out the words of prayer. He was moved once again at the depths of family love shown by his cellmate. A prayer came to his mind, but Chay chose to voice it silently.

Elohim, I am surely the least of this company my brother calls the iron fist. I see that You used me to free Mathu, but other than that, I have been a dragging weight on this mission. I never chose to be here, yet I accept Your will. Help me to understand You and do my part.

Hod, exhausted by the tension of the day and confident that he was in the will of Elohim, fell immediately into a deep and peaceful sleep.

Kodi, meanwhile, paced the perimeter nearest the clearing, watching for any approaching Lamechites and determined to prove his loyalty to his new friends.

As he walked, he found a prayer coming softly to his lips. "Elohim, Father of my ancestors Adam and of Cain, please let me know that I can worship you. Help me throw off the influence of Azazel and Kron. I want to be a normal human. Please do not abandon me."

While the others prayed or slept, Pazel scouted for an easier way out of the glade. He returned at midnight and woke Hod to tell him his good news.

"I found a gradual slope up to the level of the waterfall. Then we can go on north of here and come out below the boulderfall. Mehri shouldn't have any problem with this route."

"How about the Lamechites?" Hod asked. "Any sign of them?"

"Yes, I climbed a high rock and saw them getting nearer the waterfall. They are probably there by now and trying to figure out where we've gone."

At these words Hod moved to the end of the woods and scanned the glade with worried eyes. "I don't trust them. They could be crawling through the grass right now. Maybe we should move out."

Those awake nodded in agreement. They woke the women and began picking up their weapons and back-packs. Mathu and Mehri both went to their mother to bid her farewell. Pazel took this moment to have a parting word with Hod.

"I plan to see you again, my friend," the Cainite said as he took Hod's hand. "But in case something prevents me, I want to tell you how thankful I am that you included me in this great adventure."

Hod gripped his hand and returned the infectious grin. "I think it was Elohim who included you, and I'm thankful He did. You are a good friend!"

"You are the only friend I've ever had," Pazel's grin faded and for once he was completely serious. "I'll help you whenever you need me."

"I think you have three more friends now." Hod looked at Kodi and Chay and then over at Mathu. "Be careful, and I'll see you soon."

ξ

MEHRI HELD HER BROTHER'S HAND TIGHTLY AS THEY WALKED through the woods in the darkness. Occasionally a break in the trees revealed a full moon overhead, but only a few filtered shafts of moonlight illuminated their steps.

Her mind kept straying from the perils ahead to her mother, who right now should be well on her way home. It was comforting to think of her mother back with the family where she could truly grieve for the loss of her sons. However, Mehri was already missing Neva's presence.

At least I have Mathu. How could I go on without him? She squeezed her brother's hand and then smiled when he squeezed back.

"How far is it?" she whispered to Mathu.

"It was a day's journey coming, but we crawled much of the way under boulders. If we can stay above ground, we should move faster."

Even though Mathu had whispered his answer, the redheaded man called Hod turned back and hushed them. By now they had come to a place where the trees stopped and a rocky slope before them was illuminated in the moonlight.

They all waited there while Hod turned to Mehri. "I know you are just wanting information, but we don't know where the enemy is, and we must not alert them to where we are. We must be quiet."

"I understand," Mehri said. "I wasn't thinking."

Mehri smiled up at the young leader of these boys — or men. She wasn't sure what to call them. They were very young, yet they carried mature responsibility.

Hod was very nice-looking, she thought. His thick red hair, something she had never seen before, gave him an air of daring emphasized by his greenish eyes and dark eyebrows. She also liked the light reddish freckles scattered across his nose.

He was still looking at her as if her opinion was important to him, and then he whispered softly.

"Mehri, we are going to climb this rocky slope with the boulderfall in the middle. While it's dark, we'll move as quickly as we can, for when the daylight comes, we might have to deal with haraanis, Lamechites, and even nephilim."

"All right. I'm ready," she whispered back.

"Are you strong enough to walk very fast uphill? If not, Kodi can carry you."

No one could tell in the moonlight, but Mehri blushed at the thought of being carried by the nephil giant. Where Hod was warm, friendly, and appealing to her girl's heart, Kodi was breathtakingly handsome. For some reason, he was not as tall as the nephilim she had known. He had golden hair, sparkling blue eyes, and a square jaw.

Most nephilim had cruel eyes and mouths, but Kodi had a gentle smile and kind eyes, both of which she attributed to his ten years with his grandfather Juban.

The thought of being carried by this majestic young nephil was much too embarrassing.

"No, I'll keep up. No one has to carry me." Her eyes glanced over at Kodi and then back to Hod.

Kodi immediately added his assurances to the leader's words. "I carried Mathu some and, even though he is skin and bones, he's much heavier than you. You would be like a sparrow to carry."

"Thank you," she insisted. "It won't be necessary."

Mehri was glad no one pushed the issue. Instead they took her at her word and hurried down onto the rock slope. Since the moonlight was so bright in this area, they moved to the far left of the boulderfall where they hoped to stay in shadows cast by tall stones or promontories found intermittently.

With no one daring to speak, they walked as fast as possible. Mehri knew they were pacing themselves to her steps and made herself almost run up the slope. Halfway up the slope, Mathu silently pointed to the carcass of a huge animal lying outstretched on the rocks. Without slowing his step, Mathu whispered a few words in her ear about the monster.

During the nighttime hours they made good progress and had almost reached the top of the slope by the time the sun peeking over the eastern summit began to blind them.

"Look, Mehri, see that pine tree-shaped rock at the top of the slope?" Mathu pointed toward the pinnacle of the hill. "That's the summit. We start down toward Enoch's garden on the other side."

Before she could answer, Mehri had to stop walking and try to catch her breath. "You . . . mean . . . we're almost there?"

Her brother stopped with her, allowing the other three to move on ahead of them. Mehri noticed that Kodi took several more steps before he also paused and looked back at them.

"Almost," Mathu answered. "I think it took us an hour to get from the garden to the pinnacle yesterday, but that was climbing and I'm afraid I slowed them down."

"What caused your sickness?"

"I lost a lot of weight in prison because I would not eat meat. And then I developed that cough."

Mehri gave her brother a warm smile. "But you are quite well now! You climbed that slope with no problem and pulled me along when I lagged."

"You're right! I feel fine! That water Hod gave me truly did invigorate me."

By this time Kodi had walked back to them and whispered, "We should keep moving."

Mehri looked up at Kodi. He was so tall and strong. Between the love of her brother and the protective strength of this young man, she believed she would be safe. Somehow she felt that either one would give his life for her.

"I was just telling Mathu that he isn't weak at all. It's as if he has been healed. That water is very powerful."

Kodi studied Mathu a moment before gesturing for them to keep moving. They started off after Hod and Chay, who were waiting at the pinnacle. Kodi's long strides quickly took him ahead of the brother and sister.

Suddenly Chay pointed behind and beyond them. "Here they come! Lamechites!"

Three of the small, dark men had come from the ridge to the left of the boulderfall, not far behind Mehri and Mathu, and were running up the slope toward them. Each one held a curved sword, and when they saw they had been spotted, each began to emit a high pitched cry.

This was the first time Mehri had seen the vicious and filthy men. She clutched at her brother's tunic just as one of the Lamechites reached them, grabbed her arm, and swung his sword at Mathu, cutting a long slash down his arm.

When Mehri let go of her brother, the man began dragging her down the slope, but Mathu lunged at him, caught him around the neck with his good arm, and choked him in the crook of his elbow.

The Lamechite kept a tight clutch on Mehri's dress while he struggled to free himself from Mathu. She immediately grabbed the material of her robe in both hands and pulled until it slipped from the man's grip.

Now free, she turned to see if she could help her brother, but he merely vigorously shook his head.

"Run, Mehri, run toward the others!"

Knowing that what he was doing, he was doing for her, she obeyed instantly. As she ran, she passed Kodi running back to help her brother.

Chay also was starting down toward the Lamechites. Mehri tried not to worry about her brother as she hurried toward Hod, who grabbed her arm and started to lead her down the other side of the peak. Just before they dropped out of sight, Mehri heard her brother cry out. She pulled away from Hod, took a few steps back up the slope, and saw her brother's bloody body on the ground.

Kodi was slashing at the Lamechite who had hurt Mathu. She saw the small man fall on the ground as Kodi turned to the next one. Chay was involved in a desperate battle with the third man, using a curved sword he snatched from the fallen man.

"What about my brother?" she asked Hod, who had grabbed her hand. "We should go back and make sure he is all right!"

"You're the most important one now. Kodi and Chay will take care of Mathu if they can. Our entire mission is to keep you safe. If they get you, all is lost."

The young girl's face showed her despair as she let Hod lead her on down the mountainside. They still heard sounds of battle coming from the other side of the pine tree rock, but these noises were fading.

They were near the bottom of the slope when Mehri felt her foot slip off a stone and into a crevice just large enough to grip her sandal tight.

"What's the matter?" Hod asked.

"I've caught my foot." Mehri wiggled the stubborn sole. "Give me a minute."

Hod was looking nervously at the sky when she glanced over her shoulder and noticed his concern.

"What do you see?"

"Haraanis," he said, pointing north. "Headed this

way. I see Kodi and Chay topping the pinnacle, so they must have taken care of the Lamechites. These birds could be bringing more for us to deal with. I can't tell."

Aware how serious her situation was, Mehri worked frantically to free her shoe, but she could neither free it nor get it off her foot. The haraanis were nearer, she saw with another quick glance—in fact, they were almost on them.

"Let me try!" Hod said and knelt on the rocky ground to work at the sandal.

When, after a minute, the sole popped loose, Hod jumped to his feet and helped Mehri up.

"We must hurry," Hod cried. "They're almost here!"

Mehri glanced back to see haraanis aiming straight at them as if they knew exactly who she was. She froze for a minute while the eyes of one bird stared directly into her eyes and held her gaze. Hod grabbed her hand and tried to pull her with him.

By the time the riderless haraanis reached them, Kodi and Chay were nearly down the slope. The first bird ignored the paralyzed girl, grabbed the back of Hod's tunic, and immediately tried to lift off with him in its claws.

Mehri paid no attention to the other bird, which had been staring at her so intently. Instead she slapped at the first, trying to get it to let go of Hod. But then the second haraani snatched the back of her robe and began flapping its wings to take off.

"Someone get him off me!" Mehri was so much lighter than Hod that this bird had no trouble lifting her.

Panicked and terrified, Mehri felt her feet come off the ground. Realizing by the time she was five cubits off the ground that she hung by the fragile fabric of her robe, which she could feel tearing, Mehri clutched the smooth, plated legs above her and held on with all her strength.

Down below her, many cubits now, she saw Kodi and Chay fighting the haraani that had grabbed Hod. Then she saw the haraani get away from them and fly upward. The two young men she had left behind in her ascent were shouting and pointing at her, but Mehri knew they could do nothing to help her now.

The bird holding her was flying north, and she had to look back under her arm to see that the three men were safe. As she soared overhead, she looked back on the other side of the pine tree pinnacle and saw Mathu still lying in the same position.

He died for me just as he said he would the day mother and I left for the glade. Oh, dear, sweet brother! Will I see you again after this life? Is this the end?

Mehri trembled with cold and fear in the high altitude. She knew the haraani was taking her to the tower of Kron. Would Azazel be there, she wondered? And if he was, would she be strong enough to say no to him?

Down below her dangling feet, the mountains appeared as swirling lines, patterns, and oddly shaped circles. It seemed as if the bird flew a long, long time, and Mehri's arms began to ache. She wanted to let go and wait for the talons to tear through her robe. It would be a relief to join her brother.

But she would not allow herself to give up. Elohim had a purpose for her life, so she could not throw it away.

Mehri raised her head to look ahead and gasped at the immense black peak directly before them. She expected the haraani to fly higher to surmount the summit, but instead the bird dropped lower and lower until it landed on a flat area some way down from the top of this mountain.

Before landing the haraani released its hold on Mehri's robe. As soon as she saw she was close to the surface, she let go of the bird's legs and dropped, then fell on the flat rock, seemingly a landing area for the birds. She got to her feet as quickly as possible, but the haraani had landed close to her and watched to make sure she did not try to escape.

Mehri saw a doorway cut into the rock and debated whether or not to attempt a run for it; however, before she could move a tall figure emerged from the opening.

"Azazel!" she cried before collapsing in a faint.

ξ

WHEN SHE WOKE UP, MEHRI FOUND HERSELF IN A BEAUTIFUL windowless room lying on a soft bed draped in scarlet cloth. Along stone walls more scarlet cloth hung in rich drapings. One small torch, placed high on a wall and well out of her reach, lighted the chamber.

At first she thought she was alone, but when she looked around, she saw the same tall figure standing against the drapings and watching her hungrily.

"How did you find me?" Mehri was surprised that she felt less fear or intimidation than the first time she met Azazel.

"I sent two haraanis indwelt by Watchers. The haraanis are useful but need guidance sometimes."

Mehri's face mirrored the horror she felt in her heart. "It was a Dark Watcher carrying me?"

"Of course. We can take any form that is useful to us since we do not have earthly bodies." He sounded friendly and reasonable and totally nonthreatening. She almost forgot who he was.

"What do you really look like?"

Azazel glided toward her, causing Mehri to pull back. He sat beside her and took her hand, and when she tried to pull it away, his grip became like iron.

"My dear, I want to marry you and make you my queen. I am using this body, so that I can be your husband, but you will never see me otherwise. I will be this man and turn my back on my true self—all for you."

As Mehri began to sink into his clear eyes, she felt a strong pull to be his wife. His spirit was drawing her to him. "But I could become the mother of a nephil! I don't want that!"

"The children of Watchers and human women are human because we are in human bodies when we are with our wives."

"But—but I have known nephilim in Havilah and they are all giants—they are not human!"

Azazel smiled—an icy smile, Mehri thought—and then patted her hand with a hand that was very warm.

"This is too complicated for the human mind, but I will tell you anyway. Within the human body, too small to be seen by your eye, are myriad tiny spirals containing the plan for each body. We have learned to disrupt His plan and change it our way."

Mehri shook her head and pushed him away. "How can you change people from what they should be?"

"Of course not. We interfere in the beginning, before they are born. First, we make them all boys. Then we make them taller."

Mehri thought about Kodi and wondered what his beginning had been.

"I met a nephil who was different from the rest—Kodi. He was with the group of men who took me from my hiding place. He was more like a human than a nephil!"

Azazel eyes narrowed into dark slits. His jaw tightened a moment before he answered.

"He is my son. I changed his plan to make him bigger and stronger, but I thought he had died after his mother. By the time Kron found him, we had lost ten years when I would have made more changes in his spirals. It was too late by then, so he will always be a lesser nephil."

Mehri suddenly felt that she should protect Kodi from this being's wrath. "But he did bring me to you."

For a moment Mehri missed the gallant young nephil who had wanted to help her. She was glad he had not had the changes made to him. She was glad he was a human, at least fathered by a human body, and she hoped he would be able to escape the influence of Azazel and Kron.

"So, my dear, remember, you must want to be with me. Will you come with me and be my wife?"

Mehri jumped to her feet and, knowing her bravery was due to the sacrifice of her brother, cried out at the top of her lungs.

"Never!"

Azazel immediately slapped her to the rock floor. "Then you will stay here until you change your mind — or I change mine."

Mehri, still sprawled on the floor, was pale but for the bright red hand print on her cheek. Azazel stood over her, his foot back as if he considered kicking her.

"And if I don't want you anymore," his foot relaxed. "I'll give you to Kron. He doesn't have to wait until you are willing!"

◁16▷

The Rescue

HOD, CHAY, AND KODI, AS SOON AS THEY HAD BEATEN AWAY THE haraani trying to carry off Hod, looked up to see Mehri hanging from the talons of the other bird at least thirty cubits in the air.

Her back was toward them, and she was headed northwest. All three of the young men were horrified and ashamed that they had let this happen to the young woman they were supposed to protect.

"They're going straight to Kron." Kodi straightened his shoulders. "We have to go get her."

Chay shook his head and turned toward the east where Enoch lived, only an hour's walk away. "How can we? I've seen that tower! To even get to it, we would have to walk all the way around to the north side of the mountain. We can't do it without getting caught."

"There is another way in," Kodi insisted, looking his friends earnestly in the eyes. "We can do it. I know every corner of Kron's fortress, and I can move around without attracting attention—as long as I stay away from Kron. He thinks I'm out catching Hod."

"Fine for you! If you get caught, you can explain yourself. If I get caught, I'll be the king's dinner." Chay kicked a rock, crossed his arms, and turned his back on the other two.

Hod had listened to Kodi and Chay with interest. This was the first he had heard of Kron's threat to eat Chay. Despite the bad blood there had been between his brother and him, he was not going to let Chay die.

"But I have to go after her," Hod finally said. "She *is* the mission. If she does not become the grandmother of the last righteous man before the catastrophe, humans will be wiped off the earth."

He watched as his words sunk in to the others. For Kodi, he knew, the catastrophe meant the end of his type. He wondered how Kodi would face this choice. For Chay it meant risking a horrible death for the good of mankind.

For Hod there was no choice. He was committed to this mission, but it was his mission more than theirs.

"I'm going with you," Kodi responded first.

"Thank you." Hod turned his eyes from Kodi to Chay, the question in his eyes.

Chay rolled his eyes toward heaven in his characteristic way. "I suppose I have to go."

The young leader stepped toward his brother and put an arm around his shoulder. "I can't let you die because of my mission."

"I have an idea that might save Chay, yet he can still help us," Kodi said.

Hod nodded without speaking.

"I used to explore all the tunnels, and I know one dug years ago by Lamechites helping Kron search for a way into the Garden. It is extremely long but not long or deep enough to reach the Garden.

"They abandoned it when they came out not far from here. They are good diggers but pretty bad at figuring out what direction they are going."

"What about Chay? How will this help him?"

"About halfway up the tunnel is a large room where other tunnels branch off. It has an air shaft and will make a good place for Chay to wait for us. If we make it back that far and need help, he can help us fight."

Hod turned to Chay, who seemed relieved at this plan. "Does this sound all right to you?"

"Yes. I want to help but don't want to get too close to Kron."

Knowing they had no time to waste if they were to find Mehri before she was hurt, Kodi took his dagger, Hod the nephil dagger he used as a sword, and Chay the sickle-sword he had taken from the Lamechite. They followed Kodi as he zigzagged back and forth, up and down over the boulder-strewn mountain.

"We still could have a Lamechite following us," Kodi explained. "No sense taking chances."

Within an hour the three comrades had climbed the mountain to the place Kodi remembered as the opening to the tunnel. He stopped at a full thorny bush, seemingly growing by itself in the field of rocks. Kodi grabbed the bush, unimpeded by the thorns, and easily pulled it up by the shallow roots which had found soil deep beneath the surface stones.

"After they gave up on this tunnel, the Lamechites filled up the entrance with loose rock. When I came upon it, I dug it out to find out what was beyond. Then I transplanted this bush to hide the opening."

Chay gave his friend one of his infrequent smiles. "Good thing you were an adventurous nephil!"

"Yes, I guess it is. If I am not with you when you leave, follow that path to the left. It leads directly to Enoch's home."

"I hope that doesn't happen," Hod replied. "We need you now that there are only three fingers left in the iron fist."

"Here is my old torch still on the floor. Looks like no one else has been here since I came out this way and went back another way. Now you two hurry on in. I'm going to try to hide the entrance."

The tunnel was large enough to stand, so they were able to run almost through the straight passage. The sense of urgency they shared propelled them forward, and before long they reached the chamber Kodi had spoken of. Chay saw the hole above, evidently drilled by the Lamechites to let in some light and air.

They all immediately took a deep breath of the fresh air. Then Kodi pointed to one of the two passages leading away from the chamber.

"We'll go this way. It's a long, straight tunnel, and we won't have any fresh air until we get out of it. I'll put the torch out near the end where the passage takes a slight bend east. They'll be able to see us coming if I don't."

"Where in the fortress will you come out?" Chay asked as thoughts of Kron's throne room caused him to shiver.

"Near the prison cells—almost level with where we are now. They wanted to come out halfway up the cliff over the Garden, so they started at the deepest part of the prison block."

Chay felt slightly sick to think his brother might end up in one of those cells. "Do you think Mehri is in one?"

"I don't know," Kodi replied. "But I expect she will be higher up in a cleaner place. I've some ideas for finding her. Don't worry about your brother, Chay. I'll leave him in the tunnel while I search. Now, you make yourself comfortable. You'll hear us coming, I expect, but it might be an hour or two."

The trip through the long tunnel was uneventful. Hod felt no fear as he wondered what was ahead of him. It crossed his mind Kodi could betray him to win Kron's approval; however, he had seen too much goodness in the young nephil to expect this to happen. With his superior strength, Kodi could have grabbed him and dragged him to the nephilim king at any time, yet Hod knew he would not. Kodi truly was not an ordinary nephil.

When they reached the bend in the tunnel, Kodi extinguished his torch, signaled with forefinger to lips for Hod to remain silent, and then finished the short stretch to the main part of Kron's fortress.

Kodi stepped out of the tunnel and looked around the immediate area before turning to Hod.

"There's no one around. You move back about ten cubits so no one can see you. Wait for me here. I might be in a big hurry when I get back, and I might need help. Give me at least half an hour and be ready!"

ξ

WHEN KODI LEFT HIM, HOD WAITED FOR A FEW MINUTES BEFORE he gave in to a strong feeling that he should look around a little bit outside the tunnel. He knew it was dangerous, but he felt compelled to do it.

He moved to the very end of the tunnel where he carefully poked his head into the dimly lighted passage outside the tunnel before pulling back. There was no one around.

Hod stood there a moment or two pressed against the wall, his heart pounding, trying to talk himself out of leaving the tunnel. The wide space outside looked deserted. It was also very dark.

It would be easy to slip out, stay close to the wall in the shadows, and explore some of the fortress. With a burst of decision, Hod stepped out of the tunnel and worked his way around to the doorway that seemed to open into another narrow hall. Again Hod peered into this hallway, and—seeing that it went to the right or to the left—chose to go to the left.

Unaware that he had gone the opposite direction of Kodi, Hod tiptoed down a narrow hall. He noticed several low doorways blocked with wooden panels bolted shut on the outside, and from these doorways came a terrible odor. From what he had heard Chay and Mathu say about the prison, Hod was sure he had happened upon that area.

He tapped softly on one of the doors. "Anyone in here?"

"You know we're here," a deep voice grumbled. "Why don't you leave us alone?"

"Who are you?"

There was a long pause with no answer, and finally the grumbling voice chuckled before falling silent.

Hod knew he might be juggling fire as he continued to talk to the unknown man behind the door, but something told him to go on. "I'm a friend."

"Maybe you *are* a friend. We're Cainite brothers."

"Why are you here?"

"Kron locked us up because we tried to hide our sister from Azazel."

Finding this story completely believable, Hod pulled two sliding iron bolts holding the door in place and pushed the panel to the side. Two very dirty, very thin men stepped from the darkness. There wasn't much light in the hallway, but even that little bit made them squint and shield their eyes.

"How long have you been here?"

"Months, I guess," the older-looking brother said. "They used to badger us every day about our sister Dani, but they've left us alone the last few weeks."

"Follow me, and be very quiet. I came with friends to rescue the girl Azazel wants now. I can show you a way out."

He led them to the tunnel and looked around to be sure they were still unobserved.

"Follow this passage. It's a very long tunnel, so don't get discouraged. It will come to a chamber where my brother Chay is waiting. Tell him who you are and that Hod let you out. He'll understand because he was a prisoner here too until a few days ago."

The elder man took Hod's hand a moment. "My name is Zuph. This is my younger brother Tagg. We will never forget you, friend. Thank you."

"You're welcome. My brother will tell you which way to go when you are out. Now hurry."

Hod listened as the footsteps moved as quickly as they safely could in the dark. Before long they would find Chay and he could direct their steps toward home. Hod knew their destiny was out of his hands. He waited more patiently now, believing his early urge to explore had been a leading from Elohim to free the two Cainites. And now he had no more desire to explore the tower.

ξ

As soon as he left Hod, Kodi began to act the part he had decided on. He strolled nonchalantly through the halls of the fortress, nodding at fellow nephilim and scowling at any lurking Lamechites so they would not note him as different from any other nephil. It was not hard to go back to the unsmiling demeanor he had learned to put on during his years with Kron. Indeed, it was hard to smile in this place.

But he had to avoid Kron, who expected him to be bringing Hod to him.

"Kodi, when did you get back?" Gradrach, looking as evil as ever, came face to face with Kodi at a corner.

"I came in today to report to Kron." The first thought that came to his mind was liable to get him in trouble, Kodi knew, so quickly tried to cover. "I've got the fire-hair."

Gradrach grinned his usual hungry grin. Kodi wondered if this nephil would want to see Hod. "Good! Kron will be happy."

"Hey, I saw the haraanis grab the girl Azazel was looking for."

"You're right. They did! Kron has her stowed away in the upper cells—the ones reserved for 'special' guests." Gradrach laughed and gave Kodi a knowing wink.

Kodi shivered at the hidden meaning in that wink. He knew Kron had cells where he kept women he had captured for his personal use.

I must find Mehri before they hurt her. I can't bear to think of that sweet girl in the hands of Kron, or worse still Azazel. Pazel said he was saved to help Hod with his mission. Maybe I was taken from my grandfather to save Mehri from the Dark Watchers.

After this Kodi kept to back corridors and unused passages in an attempt to avoid meeting anyone. A tiny secret stairway, made by Lamechite workers to facilitate construction and too small for ordinary nephilim, helped him climb to the floor where the special cells were.

It wasn't hard to guess where Mehri was being held. Two armed Lamechite warriors stood guard on either side of the doorway, and the corridor outside was awash in the light of many torches.

When he spotted the guards, Kodi hesitated, but then, realizing they had seen him, walked boldly toward them with the arrogant swagger typical of nephilim and so intimidating to their underlings. He did not recognize either of the guards and could tell they did not know who he was.

"Men!" he snarled. "How is the prisoner this morning?"

Snapping to attention, the Lamechites chimed in unison, "Sir, fine, sir!"

"I'm going in to see for myself." Kodi was reaching for the door pull when the older guard spoke up.

"We were told no one was to go in, sir."

Kodi pulled his eyebrows into a straight line, put ice in his blue eyes, and tightened his gentle mouth into a hard line. "They did not mean me—I am Azazel's youngest son."

The older Lamechite immediately opened the door for Kodi. "Sorry, sir, we didn't know."

As he swaggered into the room, Kodi realized that he did not know if he was Azazel's youngest son. But he hoped it was true, for he hated to think of another child born this way.

He immediately looked around the room, which was dimly lighted by a half-consumed torch high on a wall. Below the torch was a bed covered in crimson—with no one on it. Kodi was wondering where she was when a soft voice called out.

"Kodi, thank Elohim you came!" Mehri came running from behind a draping where she was hiding and threw her arms around the young nephil.

"I knew someone would come. Where are the others?"

"Hod is waiting in the tunnel we used to get here. Chay is waiting halfway down to help us when we get there." Kodi, realizing he was holding her hand, let it go.

"My brother is dead, isn't he?" Mehri held his eyes with hers.

Kodi cleared his throat and lowered his voice to a whisper. "Yes. He died for you."

She shut her tear-filled eyes without speaking.

"What has Azazel done to you?" Kodi asked.

"Only threaten to give me to Kron if I don't agree to marry him. But he is horrifying! Be careful—he could return at any time. Can you get me out of here?"

As he watched this young woman, Kodi knew he, like Mathu, would give his life to save her. He also knew he could be more help by staying alive. He quickly ran through some possible strategies in his mind.

"I have an idea. I'll have to fool your guards, though. Stay close to the door after I go out because we may have to run fast."

Kodi immediately opened the door, stepped out, and closed it behind him.

"I need one of you to go to Kron right now and tell him the girl wants to speak to him!"

The younger Lamechite hurried off without asking questions. Kodi stayed beside the other guard. "How long have you been working in the fortress?"

"Two years. I used to be a scout, looking for food growers and herds to raid for the nephilim. Now I'm working in the fortress. Better on these old legs!"

"Is the other guard related to you? He looks like you."

The Lamechite broke into a smile, and for the first time ever it occurred to Kodi that these inferior creatures had feelings too.

"Yes, he's my son. I'm training him to be a guard."

Kodi knew he needed to act quickly to take this man out. For Mehri's sake he should kill him. But now he thought about the young Lamechite returning and finding his father dead. He couldn't do it.

Acting on an instant decision, Kodi waited until the guard turned his back on him and then used the end of his dagger to deal a knockout but not mortal blow to the older man's skull. As soon as he fell, Kodi opened the door, grabbed Mehri's hand, and began running with her, pulling her back down the corridors and stairways he had used to get here.

"I didn't kill that Lamechite. As soon as he comes to, he will tell them what I did. We must hurry!"

Within half an hour, he had reached the tunnel where he had left Hod. Kodi hurried Mehri into the passage and around the bend where Hod stood.

"You made it! Mehri? Are you all right?"

"I'm not hurt, thanks to you two." She reached out and took one hand of each man. "Shouldn't we keep running?"

Before speaking Kodi took his flint and lighted the torch, and then handed it to Hod. When he saw both of the young Sethians looking at him, Kodi shook his head.

"I'm not going with you. You know the way, and you'll have Chay to help you get to Enoch. I can help you more by staying here. I'm going to do my best to throw them off your trail."

"Are you sure? We need you," Hod said.

"I'm sure. You just get Mehri to safety."

"Thank you, Kodi," Hod said holding out his hand. "You are the only good nephil. You are more than that. You are a man. I hope to meet you again."

As Hod and Mehri hurried to escape, Kodi stood a moment watching the torchlight disappear in the distance. Then he turned and hurried back through all the back passages and stairways he had taken before. When he drew close to Mehri's empty cell, he saw no one but the older Lamechite still unconscious on the floor.

He had known Kron would not come immediately upon being summoned because he would consider such a response beneath his dignity. When he decided to stay behind, Kodi had hoped to get back before the king arrived and the guard woke up.

I guess I hit him harder than I meant to. How am I going to explain this all to Kron? I'll have to convince him I was knocked out too.

After checking that the Lamechite was not dead, Kodi used the butt of his own dagger to hit himself in the skull hard enough to raise a bump. Then he used the sharp point to draw some blood from the bump. By this time the older man was moaning, so Kodi sprawled out face first on the cold stones and pretended to be unconscious.

He heard the guard struggle to his feet and stagger groggily around the hall. Then Kodi could tell the guard had gotten on his knees beside his sprawled body. With his ear to the floor, Kodi could hear approaching footsteps at a distance and was sure it was Kron. And then the older Lamechite began to shake him.

"Sir? Sir? Are you all right?"

Kodi groaned in feigned agony and got to his hands and knees. "I'm alive, but if I find those Sethians, I'll kill them!"

He put one hand to the bump on his head, and pulled it away covered with blood. When Kron, just rounding the far corner, saw the two injured men, he bellowed.

"What happened?"

Kodi stood bolt upright as he had been trained to. "I brought back the fire-hair and left him tied up near here. I wanted to tell the girl I had her brother too and she had better cooperate.

She agreed but said she wanted to talk to you. When I came outside, a Sethian gang jumped us."

"A gang? How many were there?" Kron roared.

Kodi thought a moment as he invented his story on the spot. "At least six, I think. They followed me when I captured the fire-hair. They knocked out this guard from behind. I was fighting them, but one jumped on my back and bashed me on the head."

Kron's red-rimmed eyes almost blazed as he jerked open the cell door, stomped in, and then came running back out.

"She's gone. Get the best trackers. We're going after them before Azazel finds out. Kodi, you stay here."

I've done all I can, the young nephil thought, knowing that arguing with the king was useless. *Chay and Hod will have to do the rest.*

ξ

AS HOD AND MEHRI RACED THROUGH THE PASSAGE, THE TORCH he held aloft streamed black plumes of pine-scented smoke and left telltale trails for anyone following to scent.

Hod paced his steps to Mehri's but was surprised by how fast she could run. They had almost reached the chamber where Chay waited when they heard an un-earthly roar echo down the tunnel. It came from behind them, and it was filled with rage.

"It's Azazel!" Mehri cried and tried to run even faster.

Hod began almost pulling her along with him. From behind them they could feel a power almost sucking them backwards. As it grew stronger and stronger, they both began to feel as if they were running through a muddy newly-plowed field.

"He's dragging us toward him!" Hod refused to stop. He refused to be drawn away.

Suddenly the suction stopped. Hod and Mehri fell on their knees, but then jumped up and continued run-ning. They were almost to the chamber now. In fact, Hod could see his brother's shadowy form standing at the end of this tunnel.

Just before they ran into the chamber, a strong wind, filled with a sickening stench, almost blew them to their knees again.

"You cannot escape me!" The voice was in the wind that enveloped them.

"Where is he? Is he here?" Hod spun around and swatted at the air around him. He felt as if unseen hands were grabbing at him with sharp claws.

Chay snatched the torch from Hod, and then grab-bed his elbow. "What's the matter?

"Azazel is after us! He's all over us!" Hod kept on slapping at the air around him.

"I don't see anything," Chay said.

The two brothers suddenly became aware that Mehri had let go of Hod's hand and was being pulled back toward the tunnel by an unseen force.

"Help me! Please! Don't let him take me!"

Both young men ran toward her, only to be thrown back as if they had run into a stone wall. Hod jumped up and ran toward Mehri again. This time the force around her picked him up off the ground, held him a moment high in the air, and then dashed him to the stone floor.

Chay ran to Hod, who was barely conscious, and knelt down so he could hold his head on his lap. "What can I do? He is taking her back!"

"Call . . . on . . . Elohim," Hod whispered.

Chay looked from his brother's white face to the agonized face of the girl he could not save. *What can I do? Elohim is my only hope.*

"Creator, help us!" he prayed aloud. "We are lost without You!"

The instant the prayer left Chay's lips, a loud whooshing sound filled the chamber. He looked up and saw a translucent figure, almost as tall as the cavern they stood in. A beautiful face looked down on the humans below.

"It's Remiel," Hod breathed.

"Take the girl and run as fast as you can. I will fight this battle for you." The thunderous voice made the brothers tremble, but Hod used Chay's arm to raise himself to his feet.

Suddenly freed from the force that had held her, Mehri came running to them. Each brother took one of her hands, and the three ran for the exit tunnel. Behind them they heard an enraged Azazel shrieking at the loss of his intended bride.

Horror at the sounds behind them sped the three down their path. Screams and bellows, which they knew came from Azazel, mixed with terrifying thuds of heavy bodies being slammed into walls. The rock walls around them began to shake as if a mighty earthquake were ravaging the whole of the Eden Mountains. Bits of rock and dust fell from the top of the tunnel.

When they gone a short way, Hod stopped and made the other two stop with him. "Chay, you go on with Mehri. As soon as you're out, head back down toward Enoch's garden. I'm going back to see what is happening."

"Going back?" Chay and Mehri cried in unison.

"Yes, I have to see. I'll just take a look from the tunnel and then run."

Chay was shaking his head but let his brother push him toward the exit. He knew he should insist Hod come with them, but lately he had conceded that the younger brother had become the leader of the older. He obeyed and soon he and Mehri were running hand and hand down the mountainside.

Hod ran back toward the chamber faster than he had run leaving it. The rocks around him still shook from time to time with the force of heavy blows, but he didn't care. Just as he reached the end of this tunnel, the sounds and movement ceased. Hod peered into the dimly lighted room.

Inside, two titanic figures were locked in a tight struggle. Remiel was as large as a mammoth now, and Azazel was just as big. They were barely visible, yet they shone with translucency that lit up the chamber.

Hod gazed intently in an effort to make out the state of the combat. The more he looked, the more he was sure that Remiel was holding the ferocious Azazel, preventing him from going after Mehri. The Dark Watcher's face over Remiel's shoulder was distorted with hate and rage.

And then Azazel saw Hod. The scream the Watcher gave out blasted Hod's ears so that he threw up his hands to protect them.

Remiel turned, his face strained with the effort of combating evil, and looked directly at Hod.

"Run! Don't stop!"

Hod instantly obeyed, turning and running like a deer through the tunnel and out onto the mountainside.

He took only an instant to get his bearings before heading off down the mountain toward the safety of Enoch's home.

◁**17**▷

The Iron Fist Restored

T HE IRON FIST IS BROKEN, HOD THOUGHT, AS HE WALKED through the sparse woods that meant he would soon reach the rivulet next to Enoch's garden.

Mathu is dead. Kodi is back with Kron, although I know he was faithful to us as long as possible. And my friend Pazel? He said he would return, but who knows what obstacles may prevent him.

Still the iron fist had done its job. It had brought Mehri to Enoch, even if one had to die and one remain behind. If—as he expected—Chay and Mehri were now with his uncle, then the hardest part of the mission was over, at least Hod hoped it was.

When he finally reached the rivulet, he looked around and marveled at how peaceful the scene was with no great animal or any Lamechites to threaten them. Hod stepped across the stream, and then quickly went through the break in the rock wall.

No one was nearby when he entered Enoch's garden, but he did not let that bother him. Hod moved toward the area where Enoch had his small house, listening all the while for sounds of his uncle or brother.

Eventually he heard weeping coming from the direction of the cliffs, so he turned and quickened his steps to see what the trouble was.

"Chay! Mehri! What's wrong?" he cried out when he saw them standing near the cliff's edge. Hod hurried toward them. "Where is Enoch? Is he sick? Has he been harmed?"

Pulling Mehri with him, Chay turned to his brother. "Enoch was talking to the two Cainites, and Mehri wanted to see the Garden down below, so he told me to bring her here."

Hod knew his jaw was hanging open and made himself close it. "You mean the Cainites came here with you?"

"Yes, they were so grateful to you for freeing them that they wanted to help us. They waited for us outside the tunnel."

If Enoch gives his blessing to Zuph and Tagg, they would be a great help as we travel through Cainite country. And if Pazel came back we would still have five fingers in the fist.

"Why were you crying?" Hod looked directly into Mehri's beautiful eyes.

For the first time, he felt as if those eyes were deep pools and he was falling into them. He had never thought about girls much. Most of the girls he had grown up with were his sisters and cousins. His mother had told him that one day they would find him a wife from another Sethian branch, but most men did not marry until they were close to thirty, so he had not spent any time contemplating his future spouse. This girl, however, made him give this subject some thought.

"It is so wonderful down there," she said. "I saw colors of flowers and trees I never knew existed. I was crying because it breaks my heart to think we can never live there."

Hod shyly took her hand and turned the young woman toward Enoch's house. "You will have to settle for my uncle's garden. It's very pretty."

Mehri nodded her agreement. "I've already seen that it's lovely. I wish we had such beauty in Havilah."

"I told her she will like living in Seth's home too," Chay added. "From what I have heard, you can see through the gateway and into the Garden from there."

"If you don't mind looking past the cherubim!" Hod laughed lightly.

"I *want* to see cherubim!" Mehri replied, and then laughed along with him. "Remember, I've spent a few weeks with Watchers. Now I would like to see other heavenly beings."

Chay contributed a small smile to the joking yet shook his head. "Not me! I can live my whole life without seeing heavenly beings!"

By now they had reached Enoch, who turned when he heard Chay's words. The old man looked his elder nephew over with a penetrating eye.

"You've never seen a Watcher, my boy?"

"No." Chay shook his head and answered with a hint of sarcasm. "I haven't had that honor."

Enoch's eyes twinkled, showing his understanding of Chay's true heart. "If you come back some day, I will try to fix that. Now, come talk to the new members of the mission."

"New members? Do you mean Zuph and Tagg are really going to go with us?" Hod hurried over to the two Cainites and clapped a hand on the elder one's shoulder.

"We are!" Zuph exclaimed. "We owe you our lives, and from what Enoch just told us, you will be going our direction. We will be glad to do anything we can do to help you get to your destination."

Hod's eyes sparkled as he looked around at Chay and Mehri. "These two will be of value now that we have lost three of our company."

"But Pazel said he was coming back," Chay added.

Enoch swept one arm wide to take in the whole group. "In the meantime I want you all to stay here for at least five days. Zuph and Tagg need to gain strength before they face a journey. And I sense Hod has some unanswered questions. He and I need to have time to talk things over."

Hod stared at his uncle a moment. It was true that he had been full of questions a few days ago, but all he had been through in the last two days had washed his concerns away. There was one thing, though, he would like to know.

"Has the prophecy about me been fulfilled?"

Enoch's eyes were serious as he gave Hod a long look. "Almost. When Mehri is safe at the home of Seth, you will have made clear the way for the destruction of the nephilim and the survival of man in the great flood to come. But there was more that the old woman told only to me at your birth."

"What . . . what was it?"

"She told me that you and those with you would destroy Kron. This will happen the year I disappear."

"Disappear?" Hod gasped. "What does that mean?"

"I don't know; however, I do not believe it will be soon. You must complete this mission. Kron will wait for another day when you are older."

ξ

ANOTHER DAY, WHEN THE YOUNG PEOPLE SAT EATING WITH Enoch, they began discussing the eating of meat after Zuph said he was hungry for some mutton.

"My father said we didn't eat meat because it is an unthinkable sin," Hod remarked.

Zuph's head jerked up and a defensive scowl wrinkled his forehead. "We've always eaten meat. Our forefather Cain set the example. I don't think I'm sinning."

"When I was captured by the nephilim," Chay broke in, "the only food they offered was roasted sheep, and I ate it because I was starved. It was good too!"

All of the young people looked to Enoch. Since this was a matter very confusing to them, each wondered how Enoch would explain or solve the contradiction.

Enoch paused a minute to let them think about this matter, and then took a deep breath before speaking.

"Elohim has given me insight into this subject. He did not forbid eating of animals, but He did not specifically allow it either. The day will come, at the dawn of the second world after the great catastrophe, when He will give us the animals for food."

Chay shook his head, revealing his frustration with his inability to understand his uncle. "Then if it's all right to eat meat, why did our parents teach us not to. Were they ignorant of the will of Elohim?"

"No, they were not ignorant. They were doing right. They were being tested and not just for obedience to prohibitions but to going beyond that. Our ancestor Seth passed the test—he did only what Elohim said 'yes' to. He passed this down to his children."

"How about us Cainites?" Tagg asked.

"Your ancestor Cain struggled with obedience." Enoch stood over Zuph and Tagg. "Once he had killed his brother, I suppose the whole eating meat subject just did not seem important. He passed this down to his children."

Zuph stood up and rubbed his long beard with a rough hand. "So we are condemned by our actions."

"I'd rather say we are saved by our obedience," Enoch winked at Zuph. "And it's never too late to obey."

ξ

DURING THEIR STAY WITH ENOCH, HOD SPENT TIME TALKING with Zuph and Tagg about the country they would be crossing after they came down out of the mountains.

"Directly east of the Garden is the home of the oldest Sethians," Zuph said. "But we will come down the northeast side where many Cainites live. The city Chonoch—named for Cain's oldest son—is farther east in Nod. All the Cainites live north of the River Gihon, the one that flows east many cubits before curving south."

Hod nodded as he pictured his river, the Pishon, which turned directly south shortly after leaving the Garden. He had heard about the other two—the Tigris and Euphrates—but he had never expected to see them. Before this adventure was over, he would see them all.

"I know the western side of the mountain is a gradual slope, but this eastern side, what is it like?" Hod asked. "I mean, what are we facing?"

"Steep drop-offs, tight ravines, narrow shafts, no open areas, and difficult footing," Zuph answered. "We could use some rope."

But no one had rope. And there was not time to make any.

"We'll have to get along without it." Hod was nervous when he saw Zuph look at Tagg and shake his head, so he added, "Or maybe there is a way around this steep side?"

Zuph pointed north. "There is an easier way, but it's too far north. Nephilim country!"

"Well, then, let's figure out how to do this without rope." Almost before Hod had finished speaking, the long-absent Pazel strolled up to the group.

"Pazel!" Hod and Chay called out in unison.

"Who are these men?" Pazel asked as he nodded at the strangers he certainly recognized as Cainites.

Hod introduced Zuph and Tagg to Pazel. He explained how they were going to help with the last leg of the journey as well as what had happened to Mathu.

"That's terrible about Mathu. I'm glad we gave him the last of the water so he was strong enough to help his sister." Pazel's grin disappeared. "Where is Mehri? I would like to tell her I'm sorry for the loss of her brother."

"She's with Enoch. You'll see her in a while. Right now we're trying to figure out how to go down the eastern side of the mountains without rope."

"Rope?" Pazel cried. "I have a lot of it hidden a few hours from here. Let me rest a bit, and I'll get it for you before we leave."

While they all smiled their relief at this news, only

Hod reacted to Pazel's final two words. "You don't have to go with us, now that we have Zuph and Tagg. You've helped me so much, but now you can go back to your home if you would like to."

"I'm not ready to go back to my lonely, boring life. Maybe I'll find my family if I go to Nod. Maybe I'll find a wife."

"All right. But we're leaving in two days. You need to rest some."

"Rest? What's that? Seriously, I'll go get the rope tomorrow morning. By the way, have you seen any har-aanis or nephilim since you've been here?"

"No, but they stay away from Enoch because the Watchers protect him. I have scouted outside a little, and I saw the birds high overhead. They'll be after us as soon as we leave. It won't be easy."

"I don't expect it to be!" Pazel said. "I want to help."

ξ

BEFORE THEY LEFT ENOCH'S MOUNTAIN HOME, HOD FOUND much time to listen to his uncle and learn some of what the old man had learned from Elohim. In spare moments, when the others were otherwise occupied, he would try to learn all his uncle had to share. On the final day, he asked the last question on his mind.

It was late the afternoon before they were to leave when Hod saw Mehri leaning against a tree six paces from the edge of the cliff. She seemed to be staring off at the dimming eastern sky.

"What are you looking at?" he asked. "The sunset is behind you."

She started and looked up in surprise. "Oh, I—I was just thinking."

"About what?" Hod came close enough to lean against the same tree.

"About Mathu. I miss him. Even though we had been separated a few weeks, I always expected to be with him again. But now? Where is he? I mean, where is his spirit?"

Hod did not answer right away. How could he? He didn't know the answer, but he thought maybe his uncle would.

"Let's go ask Enoch," he suggested, and when he stood up straight, she took his hand and let him lead her away.

They found Enoch baking bread in his stone oven. He was bent forward, reaching with a long wooden paddle deep into the oven that consisted of a stone dome —hollow inside—with room under it to build a fire. When the fire burned down to hot coals, Enoch baked small, flat rounds of bread.

He had piled at least twelve finished loaves beside him, and Hod knew his uncle was preparing this as provisions for their trip. He knew Enoch had been gathering figs and avocados already for his visitors to take with them. When the old man sensed the young people behind him, he turned with a gentle smile.

"I can tell by looking at you two that you have

another question for me. What is it?"

He set the two fresh loaves on a clean stone to cool and came over to them, dusting his hands on his linen tunic all the while.

"Uncle Enoch, Mehri wants to know if her brother is really gone. Has his soul ceased to exist?"

Enoch's face became thoughtful, his brow showing rows of furrows and his eyes widening. "I have learned of this, but only a little. It is a mystery that will not be understood for many millennia. There is more than only this life. That I know."

"Do we really die?" Mehri asked in a whisper.

"Yes. It is the punishment for sin—and we all sin. But He is gracious. He has a plan. I do not know what it is, but I trust Him. He will rescue the righteous."

◁18▷

Three Rivers

THEY ROSE IN THE DARKNESS BEFORE DAWN, FIVE YOUNG warriors and the maiden they were protecting. Each one, even Pazel, was well fed and rested and ready for what lay ahead.

All of the men were armed—Hod with his nephil dagger, Pazel and Chay with the sickle-swords they had acquired from fallen Lamechites, and the Cainite brothers with wooden daggers they had carved from wood while at Enoch's garden.

When they departed, each man carried a waterskin filled from Enoch's spring and a backpack containing food provided by Enoch. Also, each man had a long coil of Pazel's rope looped over his shoulder.

Hod knew that Pazel carried a second somewhat smaller waterskin filled with healing water he had gotten on his trip back from Havilah, but he did not mention this before the others.

Needing to avoid tripping over their clothes while climbing down, they drew the back hem of their garments between their legs and into their belts.

"Uncle Enoch, will you pray for us?" Hod asked, and they all knelt while the old man intoned a blessing over them.

After he had finished, they stood and let him lead them to the far northeastern end of his home. "All of you are welcome to visit me again. Pazel, your home is so close that I expect to see you often."

"I will visit after I return to my mountains. I plan to spend time with my relatives first."

The area they now reached was a nest of sharp, jagged rocks. Beyond these rocks were sheer drop-offs and steep inclines that seemed impossible to negotiate, particularly for Mehri.

"Do you have a recommendation for the best place to start?" Hod asked.

"No, I've never gone down this way," Enoch said. "You'll have to decide, but the sun will peek over the horizon in a half hour. You better get started before the haraanis are out. They will think you are still here, so try to stay out of their sight."

So they took their final farewells from Enoch. Mehri hugged him long before taking Hod's hand and following him to a narrow break in the jagged promontories that Zuph had found.

Zuph and Tagg took the lead with Pazel behind them, followed by Mehri, Hod, and Chay—who insisted on being rear guard. Zuph turned his face to the steep incline and looked for hand and footholds as he worked his way down. After he reached a wide ledge about twenty cubits down, Tagg and Pazel followed.

"I can't do that!" Mehri cried when it was her turn.

"I know," Hod said. "Chay and I will tie a rope around your waist so if you lose your hold, you won't fall.

This method worked so well they were able to make it halfway down the mountainside from one steep drop to the next before the rising sun was bright enough to reveal their presence to any searching enemy.

They had all gathered in a flat area halfway down the mountain and surrounded by more jutting stones when Chay cried out and pointed at the sky.

"Everyone get back! There's a haraani overhead."

Flattened against and in the shadows of the tall rocks, they were all hidden from the bird; however, even though this place provided a safe haven, they knew the next step would leave them totally exposed.

Hod spoke first. "Wait until the haraani is gone, and then we'll have to go over this ledge. There's no other way."

When they were ready to go down, they would have to tie a rope around a secure stone and climb down the rope to a similar flat area forty cubits below. They were safe from their enemies at the moment. The sky was clear of spying birds, and the terrain was too rugged to reach any other way but from above.

"Let me go first," Mehri said.

Hod glanced quickly at her before looking down at their next destination. "Are you sure? You might get hurt. We should test the rope."

"I'm sure. And I trust all of you to make the rope safe. If you lower me down first, the rest of you can probably climb down it."

Pazel grabbed his rope, and then reached for Hod's and Chay's. "She's right. I'm going to tie together three lengths of rope and put knots every arm's length. With all of us helping, we can lower her gently. She'll be fine. Then—with the aid of the knots—the rest of us can climb down."

No one argued with this idea, and soon Mehri was touching her foot down on the next level. The men had no trouble quickly climbing down, but Pazel, who was last, paused and untied the last length of rope.

"Hod," he called. "It's only a few cubits down from here. We might need more rope later on, so I'm going to drop the rest of the way."

"Wait! We'll catch you." As Hod signaled for Chay and the Cainite brothers to gather around him, the length of untied rope dropped at his feet.

"Are you ready?" Pazel called.

After glancing at his comrades, Hod called back. "Yes, let go!"

After the group caught him, Pazel began coiling the rope he had saved. Zuph looked around the flat area they had reached, and then went to one side to investigate a split in the rock floor.

"If we work our way down this crevice, we can stay hidden and cover a lot of distance."

"Lead on since it's your idea," Hod said.

The crevice was an almost vertical cleft—somewhat like a chimney—in the mountain's smooth, steeply sloping face. By turning his face to the rock, Zuph was able to move steadily downward inside the deep but narrow crevice. He worked his way carefully, bracing hands, feet, and back against opposing walls.

When Zuph was down, Hod looked at the girl. "Mehri, you start right after me. If you slip, I'll be close enough to help. We don't have enough rope to let you down this time."

She nodded her agreement, and then one after the other the group worked its way down the crevice. At the bottom they were in an exposed area near the base of the mountain but still high enough to command a breathtaking view of the green fields and forests of these northeastern lands.

"I think we've gotten away without alerting the nephilim," Zuph said.

"There's no sign of haraani, nephil, or Lamechite."

Hod scanned the skies and the land around them. "You're right. They must think we're still with Enoch. By going down that steep side, we fooled them."

The Euphrates River could be seen only a few hundred cubits away, a lazy snake leaving its home at the Garden entrance and curving with few deviations to the north.

"We'll have to cross the river," Zuph said, pointing as he spoke. "I know a shallow spot where we can ford."

"Good. We'd better try to move faster now. This place is very exposed, and we need somewhere safe to stop to eat." Seeing no sign of an enemy, Hod signaled for Zuph to lead the way.

The six comrades trudged on, all a little fatigued by the rigors of the morning but too worried about running into an enemy to stop. When they reached the banks of the Euphrates, Zuph called a halt and the rest dropped their packs and flopped on the grassy ground.

"It's been safe enough," Chay grumbled. "We've fooled the nephilim. Can we eat now? I'm hungry!"

"Me too. My stomach is eating itself," Pazel grinned and punched Chay in the arm while looking at Hod for an answer. But Hod was looking to Zuph for his opinion.

"We should cross the river first," Zuph said.

Although Chay and Pazel groaned, they picked up their packs and obediently waded into the slow-moving river behind Zuph and the others.

"It will get up to our waists in the middle," the Cainite leader said. "And the current is a little faster. No one except Mehri should have trouble."

"I'll hold her hand. Chay, you hold her other hand in case the current is a big problem." Hod glanced at his brother, who instantly obeyed.

The cool, clear water, so refreshing after their day on the mountain, washed away travel dirt and reinvigorated their tired bodies. Once they had safely passed the swifter current in the middle, Pazel and Tagg—the last in the line—began dipping and splashing in the water, all the while laughing like boys.

Hod turned back to frown at them. "Pazel, I thought you were hungry!"

The rest clambered out of the river, up onto the grassy bank, and then sat down to rest in a small clump of trees. Chay and Mehri began pulling loaves of bread out of the bag Enoch had packed. While they ate, they watched Pazel and Tagg playing in the river. Zuph scanned the opposite bank with concerned eyes and then called to the two in the water.

"You two had better come get something to eat. We have to leave soon."

Just as the two water-soaked young men were climbing out of the water, Hod jumped to his feet and pointed across the river.

"Nephilim!"

Two of the giants had just come around a jutting rock close to where the Euphrates bent northward. They saw Hod as soon as he saw them and began running toward the river.

"Run!" Hod shouted. "With their long legs, they'll be across in no time."

Although the four who were eating did not stop to pick up the food Mehri had spread out, Pazel and Tagg paused and grabbed what they could carry before taking off after the others.

The first four had a good lead on the nephilim. With Zuph leading and the two Sethian brothers holding Mehri's hands, the group ran across a meadow dotted with a few trees. As far as they could tell, no cover was available.

"Hey! Hod! They're gaining on us!" Pazel called from far behind.

When Zuph stopped to help the stragglers, Hod looked over at Chay. "You keep going with Mehri. Look for somewhere to hide. I'm going back to help Zuph."

Chay nodded, and then Hod let go of Mehri's hand and ran back to Zuph. By now, the two stragglers had caught up to them, dropped the food, and pulled out their own weapons.

"Tagg and I will double on the first one," Zuph said. "You two take the other."

"No! Pazel and I have better weapons. You and I will take the first one, get rid of him quickly, and help the others."

Zuph grunted his agreement. There was time for nothing else. The nephilim were on them.

Without waiting, Hod ran at the legs of the first giant and, because the nephil was armored to below his hips, slashed at the tendons in the back of his knees. His opponent swept his sword downward toward Hod, who danced quickly away from the blade.

Zuph, as soon as he saw what Hod was doing, also dashed at the nephil and stabbed his olivewood knife into his thighs. Now their foe began to kick and stamp at the small men below him, all the while bellowing out his anger.

The second nephil had caught up with the first and was coming to his aid when Pazel—seeing what the others had done—ran at the second giant's legs and slashed a thigh open with his Lamechite blade. Tagg quickly followed, using his olivewood knife to stab the back of the other leg and keep the nephil from concentrating on Pazel.

Both nephilim by now were angry and seemingly baffled. This was the first time in their experience ordinary humans had dared to fight back.

They swung their heavy iron swords like pendulums, striking downward at these small opponents who moved so quickly, yet never connected with flesh and bone. Hod realized that nephilim no doubt rarely had to fight, that they could usually depend on their reputation to bring any enemy to its knees.

He thought back to the day he had killed Karlef. Elohim had guided his mattock that day, but how easily, with only a few cuts to his legs, they had been able to cause Gradrach to give up and run away.

After what we have done to the nephilim in these last weeks, they will wake up to the fact that we humans are warriors. They will learn how to fight us after this. In the future, they will be much more dangerous, and we must find a better way to bring them down.

The first nephil fell heavily to his knees, evidently no longer able to stand with his severed muscles and tendons. Still, though, he was waving his sword to keep Hod and Zuph at a distance. They left him and ran to help the others.

The second nephil was in a crouching stance, his sword ready to swing when one of the humans was close enough. Just as Hod and Zuph ran up, the giant's sword struck at Tagg and almost severed his arm.

"Tagg!" Zuph ran to his younger brother.

Hod, angered by the fountain of red spurting from the young Cainite's arm, yelled and ran between the giant's legs, slashing wildly with his sword until the nephil's legs ran as red as Tagg's arm. The nephil bellowed his pain, turned, and ran back into the river as if he were chased by a hornet.

"Borklof, come back here!" The fallen nephil called, but his friend did not even look back. Instead, he splashed out into the middle of the Euphrates where he bent and threw water on his wounds.

Hod saw that Pazel had picked up the waterskin filled with healing water he had thrown aside when the fight began and had gone to help Zuph with his brother, so he first turned to face the injured giant, being careful to stay out of reach of his sword.

"Nephil," Hod called out. "We are leaving you here alive with this message for Kron. Tell him the fire-hair has fulfilled the prophecy. I have completed my mission. The destruction of the nephilim will happen because the girl is safe. Tell him he would be wise to stay away from me. He and I are destined to meet, but the time is not yet right. Tell him it is not too late to turn from wickedness and worship Elohim. He may still be able to avoid the catastrophe."

The nephil, now sitting and holding his bleeding wounds, only glared at Hod. But Hod knew he would pass on the message.

When he turned away from the giant and looked at his comrades, Hod was not surprised to see that Tagg's arm was almost healed. He looked quickly back at the giant and saw that he also was noticing the miraculous healing taking place.

I'm afraid the fifth river will not remain a secret long. If this nephil understands the meaning of what he is seeing, he will certainly report it to Kron.

"Come on, men." Hod turned to his companions. "This creature will cause us no more trouble today. Let's catch up with the others."

They walked until Tagg said he felt well and then ran, following Chay and Mehri's tracks. When the tracks ran out, they knew Chay had found a hiding place.

"Chay! Can you hear me? It's safe to come out." Hod looked around as he called and finally saw Chay peeking out from the full leaves high up in a tall tree.

Hod laughed as he walked toward the terebinth. "You, up a tree? What about your fear of heights?"

Chay climbed back down and dropped to the ground before helping Mehri out of the tree. A slight grin threatened to break out on his usually dour face.

"Fear of heights? I don't know what you're talking about!"

For the next six hours, the group walked without hurry over green meadows and through small wooded areas. As dark was approaching and they all were hungry and tired, Zuph signaled them to stop.

"My village is just over this hill. Let Tagg and me go first and tell the people about you. When they learn how you have saved us, they will give you food and a bed for the night."

<⏴19⏵>

The Home of Seth

Aᴛᴇʀ ʀᴇꜱᴛɪɴɢ ᴏᴠᴇʀɴɪɢʜᴛ ɪɴ ᴛʜᴇ ᴄᴀɪɴɪᴛᴇ ᴠɪʟʟᴀɢᴇ ᴀɴᴅ feasting on their generous bounty, Hod, Chay, Pazel, and Mehri prepared to continue their journey early the next morning.

Before they could leave, Zuph and Tagg brought a new bag of provisions to replace what had been lost when the giants attacked them. They also returned the ropes they had carried.

"I still think I should go on with you," Zuph said, continuing a discussion from the night before.

Hod shook his head. "No, your family needs you, and we'll do fine following your directions."

"All right. Remember to keep the Eden Mountains on your right at about the same distance. From what I've heard, the home of Seth is as close to the Garden gateway as my village is to the mountain."

Hod looked up at the steep mountain face, maybe five hundred cubits away. It was stark and foreboding and offered no gentle glades or glens to shelter one from the dangers of life. He supposed it hinted at the full northern side of the Eden Mountains, where nephilim were in control.

"After about three hours walking, you will reach the Tigris," Zuph continued. "Remember to use your ropes to cross it. The water is only chest-high, but the current is dangerously swift. After that you will be in Sethian lands, and I know nothing about them."

ξ

WHEN THEY REACHED THE TIGRIS, PAZEL TIED THE LAST LENGTHS of rope together while the others sat down to rest.

"I wonder if Seth has a husband for me—since I am to be the grandmother of the last righteous man. I'll have to marry first," Mehri said to no one in particular.

Hod felt an unfamiliar emotion grip his heart as he looked at the beautiful girl. During the last week, he had begun to feel a strong attraction to her, yet he had always remained aware that she was meant to marry another. He felt a twinge of envy for that man, whoever he was.

"I don't know." He took Mehri's arm and gave it a gentle squeeze. "You'll find out before long, I expect. After we cross the Tigris, we don't have far to the Gihon, and Seth lives on the other side."

This river crossing was more difficult than the last. It was much narrower than the Euphrates, making the water so rapid it could easily carry off a small person.

"Let me go across first." Chay took the end of the rope from Pazel.

"I'm the heaviest and a good swimmer if I do get swept away, I can make it to the shore. When I get to the other side, I'll tie it down if I can find a place to attach it."

"Good idea," Pazel immediately agreed.

Hod gave his brother a long look. "All right. You are a better swimmer than I am, but I pray you won't have to swim. Zuph said the water was chest deep. Let's hope that's right."

As they watched Chay fight the current, battling to stay even with them, they all felt they were doing this task with him. And when he finally crawled exhausted up on the opposite bank, they all cheered.

No one urged him to hurry, knowing he needed to rest, and no one pointed out to him the one haraani circling high overhead. Soon Chay stood and found a secure root to which he attached the rope. Pazel pulled the line taut before tying it to a tree on their side. After that, first Mehri then Hod pulled themselves across.

Hod stayed close to the girl to ensure that she was safe. When they were all on the other side, Pazel untied his end of the rope and retied it around his waist.

"Now pull me over," he called, and they quickly obeyed.

With all on dry land, Hod signaled for everyone to come near. "You see that haraani way up there? Kron may make one last try to get at us. I know we haven't eaten in a long time. If you're hungry, eat as we walk. Let's go!"

At Pazel's suggestion, they turned and hurried as quickly as they could across the last meadowland between the Tigris and the Gihon. They passed peaceful herds of buffalo, zebras, and deer grazing without disturbance; however, to Hod's surprise, there were no settlements.

"I wonder why no one lives here. It looks like good farming land," Hod said.

Pazel merely shrugged, but Chay thought a moment and then responded. "Maybe the Sethians and Cainites need to keep a buffer between them."

"Very possible," Hod said. "Maybe the Cainites don't want to be too close to the Garden."

"Could be. We know Cain was sent far off. They're probably afraid to get too close. And remember Cain was banned from farming."

Hod took another glance over the landscape. "But that's why his people became herdsmen. This is good grazing land too."

"I think the buffer idea is probably right," Pazel chimed in. "They might fight over who uses it. Look! There are a lot more haraanis up there."

The other three immediately looked up in alarm at the circling birds overhead, at least ten and much closer to the ground.

"I think some of them are carrying Lamechites," Hod said. "Run! The Gihon is just ahead. Seth's people should be near."

Once more, the sons of Elim helped Mehri run while Pazel hurried ahead and reached the river before them. Overhead they heard the birds screeching and the riders called to each other. Up ahead at the river, Pazel was shouting, waving, and jumping up and down. As the three runners got closer, they saw that he was pointing to what looked like a thin rope bridge across the river.

They were only twenty paces from the bridge when three haraanis landed between them and the river. Three armed Lamechites dismounted and stood facing the travelers. Pazel immediately attacked the closest to him, but the other two began moving toward Hod, Chay, and Mehri. A quick glance behind them showed Hod that five more were coming at them from behind.

"Chay, I think this is hopeless. What can we do?"

"Trust Elohim, brother. If I've learned anything these last weeks, it's not to give up. Mehri, you stay between us. Hod, you fight the two ahead. I'll try to discourage those behind us."

Pazel had quickly put an end to the Lamechite he fought and then had taken on one of Hod's opponents.

As they battled, Hod and Chay kept moving ever closer to the bridge.

When Hod and Pazel had successfully dispatched their foes, they pushed Mehri onto the flimsy bridge, a contraption of ropes and logs. Chay, moving backward as quickly as he could, was nearly swallowed up in Lamechites.

"Pazel, get Mehri across. I'm going to help Chay," Hod said before running to his brother's aid.

Hod ran into the swarm of warriors around his brother, sure that by now Chay might be terribly wounded even though he could see his head above his opponents and could see his face still set in determination.

Three Lamechites immediately turned on Hod. He began to slash and parry frantically, expecting each breath to be his last. As he fought, he heard a loud whooshing sound and then noticed that two new fighters had joined the combat on their side. Not having time to look at the fighters, whom he expected were Sethians from across the bridge, Hod shouted his thanks and moved to help Chay handle his foes.

"We've got help, brother. Now let's finish them!"

But before he could swing his sword, Hod realized all the Lamechites, except for three dead ones on the ground, were running back toward the Tigris—running as if they feared for their lives.

Hod turned back to say something to their rescuers and then stopped with his mouth wide open and his sword at his side.

At first sight the new fighters looked human, but they had cloven hoofs and four arms covered by four wings. All this he noticed without quite absorbing it. It was their heads that most amazed him.

They had four faces, one on each side. Depending on which way they walked, you saw a different face. Hod realized that while he had glimpsed the human face turned toward him during the fight, the Lamechites had seen the lion.

Chay took a step toward the creatures and reached out a hand as if to touch one, but before he could do it, the two beings grew to a towering height and then swept away with the same whooshing sound, leaving the brothers in a daze.

Chay and Hod, both wounded, supported each other as they walked slowly to the rope bridge. For a few minutes neither spoke.

Finally, Hod cleared his throat and voiced what both were thinking. "I think those were cherubim."

Chay only nodded at first. Then his voice came out as a croak. "I would say so."

On the other side of the river was a high bluff, not too steep to climb. When they reached the top, both brothers gasped.

Coming toward them—armed with knives, spears, clubs, and farming tools—were over a dozen young men. At first, Hod and Chay jumped back and reached for their swords. But the crowd running toward them had broken into smiles as soon as they realized who the brothers were.

"Cousins!" The first man called out and then threw his arms around Chay.

ξ

WHEN THEY FINALLY ARRIVED AT THE HOME OF SETH, HOD AND Chay found Pazel and Mehri sitting outside a trim little building made of logs and covered over with woven branches. The group of men who had come to their aid stood around them while their leader had gone into the house.

"I'm so thankful you were able to defeat those Lamechites," Mehri said, gently touching Hod's hand before casting her glance to the ground.

"*We* didn't!" he answered and then stood still while Pazel poured healing water over his and Chay's wounds. "Have you met Seth yet?"

Mehri pointed toward the door of the house. "We just told them the sons of Elim were under attack, and they all grabbed weapons and ran to help you."

"These people have been giving me strange looks," Pazel added. "I suppose they are wondering what a Cainite is doing here."

"You're the elder brother." Hod looked at Chay as he spoke. "You should talk to our ancestor first."

Chay clapped a hand on his brother's shoulder. "You're our leader, Hod. You explain it all to Seth."

As they were speaking, the man who had embraced Hod at the riverbank opened the front door and stepped out. "Our ancestor Seth would like to speak with you — with all of you."

They followed the man known as Mahalal into an inner room where Seth sat on a low cushion beside a fire. Hod noticed that the fire was built against a stone wall and that the smoke trickled up the wall and out through the woven branches of the roof.

Of course, Seth was older than any person any of them had ever seen — he was the oldest man alive. Hod thought how young his father looked in comparison. Seth's skin looked like dried leaves wrapped around skull and bones. What hair he had was white and wispy and his lashless eyes were a clear, watery blue rimmed with red eyelids.

"Come closer, young ones, I do not see well these days." Seth spoke in a dry whisper. "Tell me who you are, and why you have come here chased by Lamech-ites."

After Seth invited them all to sit, Hod began to retell their story from the prophecy and the nephilim attack on his home, to his meeting with Pazel, to their encounter with Enoch. Seth, of course, had known of the prophecy since Hod's birth.

Hod then let Chay tell of his adventures in the tower of Kron and encouraged Mehri to tell what had happened to her before he concluded by telling of their descent down the steep side of the mountain and crossing of three rivers on the way.

"So young Enoch sent you to me," the aged patriarch said with a soft chuckle. "I suppose he knew that none of the Dark Watchers dare come so near the cherubim."

Hod felt it his duty to speak for Mehri now. "I think that is true. I only know he said Mehri would live here until she marries. Do you know whom she is to wed?"

"I know nothing about this, but she may stay here. Part of the prophecy is now fulfilled. Because you have saved Mehri, mankind will be saved on the day when the nephilim are destroyed. When the time is right, Elohim will provide her a husband. Where is her family?"

Now Mehri spoke for herself. "We live in Havilah where we are miners. I wish there was some way I could send word to them that I am here and that my brother died on the way."

"I'll do that for you," Pazel said. "I was going to look for relatives in Nod, but I can do that at another time. I would like to go back to Havilah and spend more time with my uncle, so I am glad to take your message."

Seth began to stand, slowly rising to his feet while reaching out his right hand for Hod's help. The young man, who had jumped to his feet as soon as he saw Seth getting up, quickly gave him his arm to hold.

"Come with me, my children. I want to show you the Garden."

Without speaking, they followed Seth and Hod out the front door and around to the back of the house. From there he led them up a small hill with a bench on top of it. Still standing, the old man pointed a trembling forefinger toward a steep mountain face directly before them. The mountain looked like an immense gray rock wall split in the middle by a narrow vee. Through the split they could see green treetops. Halfway down the vee, a gushing flood burst from the mountain and fell several hundred cubits to land on irregular piles of rocks.

"So that is how the four rivers are formed!" Chay exclaimed. "When all that water hits the rocks, it gets diverted in different directions."

"What power must be contained in that water!" Hod whistled as he watched the riveting sight.

"Look up, young ones," Seth cried. "You are missing the most wonderful part!"

They all glanced upward immediately and saw, standing on each side of the cleft in the mountain cherubim holding blazing swords that never stopped moving.

"Those are the two who saved us from the Lamechites," Hod said.

Seth's wrinkles deepened as he smiled. "Then Elohim has guided you here for certain. I have never before seen the cherubim leave the mountain to come to the aid of humans."

ξ

PAZEL RESTED TWO DAYS BEFORE LEAVING FOR HIS HOME IN THE mountains and then on to Havilah. He and Hod spoke alone the night before Pazel left.

"I could never have done all this without you, Pazel. It took supernatural power to prepare us for the mission and then to bring us together."

"I agree. What a great adventure we've had! I'm thankful for the privilege of being part of it all. But I'm also thankful it's over."

Hod chuckled as he thought back over his time with his friend. "Me too. And, although I hope we can all go back to our normal lives, I fear nothing will ever be the same."

"No, it won't. And Kron's eye is on us all now. If he learns of the healing water, he will be after us." Pazel gave Hod a serious look. "Be careful. I won't be nearby to help you out of your next scrape."

"I think I can depend on Chay to be at my side the next time. You know I've never told him or anyone the secret of the fifth river."

"Tell him if you need to but swear him to secrecy. He needs to know why we must keep the river from the enemy. I am leaving my waterskin with you, anyway. You might need it."

Hod squeezed his friend's shoulder. "I'll miss you. You've taught me that Cainites are the same as Sethians. It's the heart that matters."

"That's true. When I met Juban, my grandfather, I learned that the Cainites see themselves very differently then you Sethians see us. It's true our ancestor displeased Elohim, but from our people has come music, metalwork and other arts."

"I didn't know your people were so talented." Hod led his friend to the edge of Seth's home. "Yet I have to say that, except for the Lamechites, I've never met a bad Cainite."

Hod watched Pazel start east toward the head-waters of the Pishon with two young Sethians escorting him that far to help him safely ford the river. After one last wave, Hod turned back toward Seth's house.

The two sons of Elim had talked about staying a month with Seth so that they could spend time at his knee learning as Enoch had done with Adam, but Pazel's warning kept gnawing at Hod.

Later that day, Hod pulled Chay aside. "I am going to tell you something that is a secret. Pazel told me I could share it with you, but you must swear to keep the secret as I have done."

Chay's brow wrinkled with puzzlement. "I'm care-ful about what I swear to. Give me a hint."

"It's about the source of the healing water."

Immediately Chay put his right hand on Hod's right hand. "I swear."

For the next hour, Hod told his brother about Pazel's cave, the crystal river, and the healing water. He also told him about his conversation with Dracon, empha-sizing that he trusted Chay to keep his secret.

As he spoke, Hod remembered how, when he and Chay had been separated from each other only a few weeks ago, his brother had been angry with him.

When they had first been united, he had not been sure he could trust Chay. Even a few days ago, he would not have wanted to tell his brother this news. Now Hod decided the time had come to show Chay he believed in him.

Early the next morning the two brothers set out on what would be a three-day journey to Garth, to the last place they had seen their family.

The two youngest sons of Elim were homesick.

◁Epilogue▷

FOR SIX MONTHS, HOD AND CHAY HAD ONCE MORE RISEN BEFORE dawn, eaten a meager breakfast, grabbed their mattocks, and headed for the fields where they fought the weeds and toiled to raise their food.

But something was different now. They were alone —completely alone.

When, after leaving the home of Seth, the brothers had neared the family compound, their hearts had beaten quicker. Both longed to hug their mother and father and tell them all that had happened to them in the last weeks. When their steps turned onto the last path to the compound, they walked faster and faster.

At sight of the gates, they had begun to call out, ready for the surprise and welcome they would see on so many faces.

But the compound was quiet—and empty. They hurried to the cave where their father and the weaker family members had been hidden only to find that cave open and empty. No sign or hint remained to let them know what had happened.

"I believe they have moved away to hide from the nephilim," Chay had announced stoutly.

Hod had only shrugged, unwilling to infect his brother with his own despair. "I hope you're right."

And so they had stayed at the compound, farming a little while keeping watch for the enemy, yet always in hopes that someone from the family would come back looking for them. Although they had ventured out three times on day-long trips to the south and west in hopes of finding some sign of the family of Elim, they had returned even more discouraged.

ξ

IT WAS AROUND SUNSET OF THE TWO HUNDREDTH DAY OF THEIR solitary existence, and the brothers sat singing around a fire in the middle of the compound. Their melancholy song was filled with loneliness and despair.

"I wonder if Mehri has found a husband yet." Hod spoke from the thoughts that had been evoked by the song.

"It's possible, but she is very young. Seth may wait until she is a few years older. Did you want to be her husband? I saw you holding her hand often."

"I have not yet reached my nineteenth year," Hod said with regret in his voice. "I am too young for marriage. But I would like to find someone like her when the time is right."

Chay was silent a moment before speaking. "I'm sure Elohim will choose a husband for her. Whoever it is will be the right man. Hey, you're getting depressed. Let's sing a more cheerful song!"

The elder brother led off into a lively tune they often sang on their way to the fields and while chopping away at vines. When the last note died away, Hod reached over and gripped Chay's knee.

"Did you hear that?"

"What? I didn't hear anything." Chay looked up and around, out into the darkness.

"Something's moving out there."

Both jumped up, ran into the cave to grab their swords, and came out holding their old weapons ready to face any foe.

"Hod? Is that you?" The voice in the darkness was not immediately recognizable. Chay leaned over to whisper.

"Don't trust him. Kron knows your name."

Hod nodded. "Who is it? Show yourself."

Slowly and with empty palms outspread, two men entered the outermost circle cast by the firelight. The brothers both squinted as they tried to make out the faces.

"Identify yourselves!" Hod barked.

"It's Brosh and Dalit. Don't you recognize us? We've come to look for you."

Hod dropped his sword to his side and then to the ground. "My nephews? Sons of Ahuv?"

Even though they were his nephews, both of these men were several decades older than Hod.

"Yes, our father has sent us here to discover if you have returned." Brosh slowly walked toward the campfire. "I am glad to find Chay with you. We feared the nephilim had killed him."

Chay also dropped his sword and reached out a hand to Brosh before signaling Dalit to join them. "Not killed, just taken captive by Kron. Where is the family?"

The two nephews, glad for warmth and a good meal, sat down with Hod and Chay at the fire and began to tell the story of what happened to the family after the attack of the nephilim.

"Dalit and I were among those who went into the woods to lead the giants away from our home. Many were killed, but those of us who survived waited four days until we were sure the nephilim had left before opening the cave where our grandparents and the women and children were hiding."

"Were they all well?" Hod asked.

"Very well but very worried about the rest of us—especially you, Hod. But our father Ahuv was able to report that you had escaped and were going to find Enoch. This was a great comfort to Grandfather. Once all those injured in the fight were well, Grandfather insisted we find another home."

Chay, who had been listening while staring thoughtfully into the fire, lifted his head at these words.

"Where is this new home? Is it far from here?"

"Yes," Brosh replied. "It is five-day's walk west of where the Pishon turns to the north. No other people have moved that far away from the center of the world."

"Is it good land?" Chay queried.

"Not as rich as Garth, but good enough. I think we should leave tomorrow morning to take you back with us. Are you agreeable to that?" Brosh looked at Hod.

"I am. What do you think, Chay?"

"I think our adventures are behind us and we must return to the family and do our part to help our father build a new home."

They stayed up until late in the night while Hod and Chay filled their nephews' ears with the stories of their travels and battles in the Eden Mountains. They made no effort to leave at dawn since they had not gotten to sleep until four hours before sunrise.

It was midday by the time Hod and Chay had packed up their meager belongings, which included the swords they had taken from their enemies and the waterskin—still half full—given them by Pazel.

When they reached the Pishon, Hod stood a moment looking toward the distant purple mountains where dwelt Pazel and Enoch, but also Dracon and Kron. He was glad his journey today was taking him away from those peaks.

Suddenly Chay threw up his right arm and pointed at the distant sky. "Look! A haraani with a rider and it's flying this way."

"Let's get under cover of the forest and move as quickly as we can," Hod said. "I'm tired of fighting. If he doesn't see us, we'll be safe."

"Aren't you curious about what he wants?" Chay asked.

Hod shook his red hair vigorously. "Not at all! I'm a farmer again. Now, let's get walking!"

About the Author

Q uest for Eden: The Mission, Jeanne Desautel Foster's fourth book, is the first in a three-part series set in pre-flood days. The second book, *The Fifth River,* and the third book, *The Tree of Life* are also available.

Foster, a retired teacher and journalist with degrees in English and education, writes many types of novels including Christian historical and romances. This is her first biblical fantasy novel.

For more information about Foster's books, see her website, www.jeannedesautelfoster.com.

THE MISSION